"You Want Me To What?" Luc Finally Managed To Ask.

"It's no big deal," Peachy responded.

"My taking your virginity is no big deal?"

"I don't think 'taking' is the right word. It's not as though I'm trying to *keep* it."

"True," he acknowledged with a humorless laugh. "You're offering to give it away. To me."

"That's right."

"And this is a no-strings-attached, one-time-only deal?"

"Yes."

"No."

Peachy stiffened. "You mean you don't want to do it?"

Luc fervently wished she'd phrased her statement in a different way. Preferably one that omitted the word *want*. He wasn't oblivious to Peachy's appeal. But there was no way—no way in hell—he was going to do what he'd just been requested to do.

Dear Reader,

Go no further! I want you to read all about what's in store for you this month at Silhouette Desire. First, there's the moment you've all been waiting for, the triumphant return of Joan Hohl's BIG BAD WOLFE series! MAN OF THE MONTH Cameron Wolfe "stars" in the absolutely wonderful *Wolfe Wedding*. This book, Joan's twenty-fifth Silhouette title, is a keeper. So if you plan on giving it to someone to read I suggest you get one for yourself *and* one for a friend—it's that good!

In addition, it's always exciting for me to present a unique new miniseries, and SONS AND LOVERS is just such a series. Lucas, Ridge and Reese are all brothers with a secret past... and a romantic future. The series begins with *Lucas: The Loner* by Cindy Gerard, and continues in February with *Reese: The Untamed* by Susan Connell and in March with *Ridge: The Avenger* by Leanne Banks. Don't miss them!

If you like humor, don't miss *Peachy's Proposal*, the next book in Carole Buck's charming, fun-filled WEDDING BELLES series, or *My House or Yours?* the latest from Lass Small.

If ranches are a place you'd like to visit, you must check out Barbara McMahon's *Cowboy's Bride*. And this month is completed with a dramatic, sensuous love story from Metsy Hingle. The story is called *Surrender*, and I think you'll surrender to the talents of this wonderful new writer.

Sincerely,

Lucia Macro
Senior Editor

Please address questions and book requests to:
Silhouette Reader Service
U.S.: 3010 Walden Ave., P.O. Box 1325, Buffalo, NY 14269
Canadian: P.O. Box 609, Fort Erie, Ont. L2A 5X3

CAROLE BUCK
PEACHY'S PROPOSAL

SILHOUETTE *Desire*®
Published by Silhouette Books
America's Publisher of Contemporary Romance

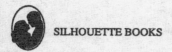

SILHOUETTE BOOKS

ISBN 0-373-05976-0

PEACHY'S PROPOSAL

CAROLE BUCK

is a television news writer and movie reviewer who lives in Atlanta. She is single and her hobbies include cake decorating, ballet and traveling. She collects frogs, but does not kiss them. Carole says she's in love with life; she hopes the books she writes reflect this.

To Melissa Jeglinski:

An editor with the "write" stuff. Thanks for your
personal encouragement and professional excellence.

Prologue

Shortly after 9:00 p.m. on the third Saturday in April, Pamela Gayle Keene—called "Peachy" by just about everybody—caught the bridal bouquet tossed by the newly wed Mrs. Matthew Douglas Powell. According to nuptial lore, this meant that she was destined to be the next female among those present to get married.

Yet less than twenty-four hours after bagging the lace-frilled bundle of blossoms for which so many had so eagerly vied, Peachy found herself clutching the floral omen of her supposedly happily-ever-after fate and contemplating the very real possibility that she was going to die a single woman.

And not just any old sort of single woman, either. Oh, no. Pamela Gayle Keene was a single woman who'd never made love with a man.

She'd come close to doing so once. Very, very close. Unfortunately, while her prospective partner had been extremely willing in spirit, he'd been woefully weak in terms of fleshly follow-through.

Although Peachy was aware that being a virgin at twenty-three years of age would qualify her as something of an oddity in many social circles, she normally did not give much thought to her lack of sexual experience. A public address announcement that the plane she was flying on had suffered an equipment failure and would be attempting a "belly" landing at the New Orleans International Airport changed this state of affairs. All at once the implications of her intact status began to loom extremely large on her emotional radar. Larger than life, one might be tempted to say.

Her first reaction to the news of the emergency—which had been delivered by the plane's pilot in a calm, country-boy drawl—was fear. Her heartbeat accelerated from a slow, steady rhythm to a panicked pounding in a few short seconds. Her stomach knotted. Her mouth went dry. Her palms turned clammy.

"Oh, God," she whispered on a shuddering exhalation of breath. "Oh... Dear God."

She lifted her left hand to the base of her throat, instinctively seeking the familiar contours of the bell-shaped silver locket she'd worn for nearly ten years. The locket was a cherished memento of the first wedding she'd ever attended and the emblem of an experience she'd shared with two very special women. Touching it eased her terror, just a bit.

Although possessed of a certain degree of personal daring, Peachy had always been a nervous flyer. It wasn't that she subscribed to the dictum that if the Lord had intended people to soar into the sky He would have blessed them with wings. She didn't. She simply harbored a gut-level conviction that flying was a decidedly unnatural activity which should be avoided whenever possible. She was also strongly inclined to question the veracity of many aviation safety claims—particularly the ones involving statistics that purportedly showed people were more likely to be killed by bathtub falls than by plane crashes.

A woman across the aisle from her began sobbing as the pilot completed his spiel. A man seated behind her started praying in a language she didn't understand. Up front, the flight attendants launched briskly into a detailed demonstration of the applicable emergency procedures.

"After the aircraft lands..." they said, prefacing each instruction.

After.

Not if.

And not the slightest hint that instead of touching down safely and sliding to a well-positioned stop, the plane might very well end up smashing into the runway and exploding into several thousand fiery pieces.

Peachy appreciated the cabin crew's relentlessly positive attitude. She hoped it would prove an effective counterbalance to the little voice in the back of her skull that kept shrieking, *I always knew flying was dangerous!* She suspected it was the same sort of little voice that had prompted a fabled hypochondriac to have the phrase "See, I told you I was sick" engraved on his headstone.

About the time the flight attendants finished explaining how to exit the plane via its inflatable escape chutes, Peachy's fear gave way to a curious kind of calm. It was not a *que sera, sera* sense of resignation about what was going to happen. Passive acceptance was not—would never be—her style. Rather, this was an empowering feeling of serenity that flowed directly from her participation in the previous evening's wedding.

That wedding had been an incandescently happy event, a celebration of the matrimonial commitment between a man and woman whose lifelong friendship had unexpectedly blossomed into passion. All the people Peachy held nearest and dearest had been there, sharing in the blissful smiles and sentimental tears. If her time was up, if the plane did crash and burn, it was profoundly comforting to her to think that her loved ones would be able to remember her in the context of such a life-affirming occasion.

As for the memories she had to cling to in what might be her final minutes . . .

There was the glow she'd seen in Annie's and Matt's eyes when they'd turned from the altar after exchanging their "I do's" and faced the world as husband and wife.

There was the enduring warmth she'd felt emanating from her parents, who would soon mark their thirty-eighth anniversary, when they'd danced together at the reception.

And above all, there was the breathless joy she'd heard in her older sister's voice when Eden had confided that she and her husband, Rick, were going to have a baby in October, some six months hence.

"Oh, Eden," she'd whispered, perilously close to tears. She knew how desperately her sister and her brother-in-law yearned for a child. She also knew how many fertility experts had declared that their chances of conceiving one were next to nil. "Oh . . . *Eden.*"

"You like the idea of being an auntie?" had been the mother-to-be's bantering response.

"Like it?" she'd echoed, eyeing her sister's still-flat tummy with fierce affection then enveloping her in a hug. "I absolutely *love* it! It's even better than getting to be one of the Wedding Belles when you and Rick—"

"We aren't going to make it," the weeping woman on the other side of the aisle suddenly moaned. "We're all going to die."

Peachy's curious kind of calm slammed against cold, cruel reality and cracked. Regret surged through her in a torrent of could-haves, would-haves and should-haves, of might-have-beens and ought-to-have-dones. Dreams deferred became dreams irrevocably denied. A twenty-three-year life that had seemed rich and rewarding just moments earlier devolved into an unfulfilled existence consisting of little more than missed chances and squandered opportunities.

If only—

Too late.

And then the realization struck. It popped into Peachy's consciousness unbidden, like the evil fairy godmother who'd shown up at Sleeping Beauty's christening to lay a curse on the baby princess rather than to gift her with a special grace.

I'm going to die without ever having done it, she thought, the fingers of her right hand spasming around the ribbon-wrapped stem of the former Hannah Elaine Martin's bridal bouquet.

Funny, how the human psyche reacts in times of great stress. Pamela Gayle Keene had a million marvelous reasons for wanting to live, not the least of which was the desire to discover whether she was to be "Auntie Peachy" to a niece or nephew. Yet she stubbornly fixated on the notion that she had to survive so she could finally have sex. An obsession was born in the space of a single heartbeat.

I don't need to have a *lot* of sex, she assured herself and any straitlaced spirits that might be listening. Just one time with one man will be enough.

Peachy felt her cheeks heat. It was a familiar sensation. Endowed with flame-colored hair and fair, freckle-dusted skin, she'd been blushing since babyhood.

Then again, maybe it won't be, her innate honesty forced her to concede after a few moments. But given the alternative—

The pilot came on the P.A. system again. He provided a terse update on the plane's location then ordered the members of the cabin crew to take their seats and strap in. While the bedrock steadiness of his voice was encouraging, his use of the word "final" when describing their approach to the New Orleans airport seemed a trifle ill-advised.

Inhaling a deep, deliberate breath, Peachy bent forward to assume what had been described as the emergency "posture." She tried not to think about how much doing so seemed an act of compliance with the clichéd admonition about putting one's head between one's knees and kissing one's derriere adieu.

Her long, red-gold hair swung forward, curtaining her face.

Her world was reduced to a fragmented series of sensory details.

The sharp-edged jab of the seat belt's metallic buckle against her midriff.

The sweet fragrance of wedding flowers mixed with the rancid odor of mortal dread.

The frantic thundering of her pulse.

Please, Peachy prayed, the faces of her family and friends flashing through her mind. *Oh, please.*

She brought her hands up, clasping the back of her head as the flight attendants had instructed everyone to do. Drawing another deep breath, she squeezed her eyes shut and waited.

And waited.

Then waited some more.

A split second before the plane bumped down on the runway, Pamela Gayle Keene made a solemn vow about her sexual future.

Sometime later—in the middle of a "How does it feel to have cheated death?" interview conducted by a vaguely familiar male TV reporter with an off-kilter nose and a cemented-in-place hairstyle, to be precise—it occurred to her that the fulfillment of this solemn vow was going to require the cooperation of a second party.

That started Peachy thinking . . .

One

Lucien "Luc" Devereaux, scion of a tradition-rich but financially strapped Louisiana family and veteran of an elite U.S. Army special operations team turned bestselling novelist, had been propositioned by a lot of different women in a lot of different ways for a lot of different reasons since his sexual initiation at age sixteen. Nonetheless, the proposal he received from Pamela Gayle Keene five days after she and all the other people aboard her flight from Atlanta survived an emergency landing at New Orleans International Airport left him temporarily bereft of speech.

"You want me to *what?*" he finally managed to ask, staring at the improbably nicknamed redhead who'd been his tenant and downstairs neighbor in a mansion-cum-apartment building on Prytania Street for about two years.

"It's no big deal," Peachy responded, sustaining his gaze with remarkable steadiness even as she started to flush.

"My taking your virginity is no big deal?" he echoed tightly, wondering whether her dismissive comment had been inspired by her feelings about the sexual act itself, her expectations about his performance of it or a mixture of both. He also wondered why it should matter to him. Because there was no way—no way in hell!— he was going to do what he'd just been requested to do.

Luc watched as Peachy veiled her green-gold eyes with her lush, mascara-darkened lashes. After a few moments, she lifted her left hand and began fiddling with a silver locket at the base of her throat. Her rhythmic fingering of the pendant had an odd effect on his already erratic pulse.

He'd never seen it coming, he thought, trying to rein in emotions that ran the gamut from strangely flattered to furiously stunned and then some. He, the man who'd been accused more than once of having distrust of the opposite sex imprinted on his DNA, had been blindsided by a blush-prone innocent, a decade his junior!

The weird thing was, Peachy had done it by behaving in the same straightforward way she'd behaved since the first day he'd met her. There'd been no deceit involved, no sneakily seductive tricks. Armored against guile, he'd been ambushed by honesty.

It was a perverse state of affairs, to say the least. And Luc Devereaux was a long way from understanding how it had come about.

He and Peachy had had a brief encounter in the foyer of their Garden District apartment building that morning. He'd been heading in after a five-mile run, mulling over the fate of a minor character in his latest book. She'd been heading out to her job as a junior designer with one of the city's finest custom jewelers.

They'd chatted for a minute or two. Right before they'd gone their separate ways, she'd asked him to drop by her apartment after she got home from work.

"I need a favor," she'd said simply, gazing up at him with clear, candid eyes.

"I'll try to oblige, *cher,*" he'd answered, his grin as easy as his unthinking use of the colloquial endearment.

He'd knocked on her door about twelve hours later. She'd invited him in.

They'd talked a bit. She, perched on the edge of a lavishly fringed but slightly moth-eaten hassock. He, sprawled comfortably in a funkily shaped armchair he'd helped her lug home from a flea market the previous spring. Their conversation had been a genial one, spiced with good-natured laughter.

Eventually, he'd gotten around to asking what he could do for her.

She responded promptly and without mincing words.

It had taken him several minutes to accept that she'd actually said what he'd thought she'd said.

"I don't think *taking* is the right word," Peachy suddenly declared, lowering her hand from the locket. She shifted her position on the hassock, crossing her long, slender legs beneath the crinkled, paisley-patterned cotton of the calf-length skirt she was wearing. The toenails of her bare feet were painted a vibrant coral pink. "It's not—I mean, it's so—so—"

"Politically incorrect?" Luc offered sardonically.

She lifted her lashes and gave him a look he couldn't interpret. Something—annoyance? impatience? embarrassment?—flashed in the depths of her eyes.

"It's not as though I'm trying to *keep* it," she retorted.

"True," he acknowledged with a humorless laugh. "You're offering to give it away."

There was a pause. After a few moments Peachy smoothed her curly tumble of red-gold hair back from her face, squared her slim shoulders and calmly replied, "That's right."

"To me."

There was another pause, a little longer than the preceding one. Then, again, a quiet affirmative.

"So that the next time you confront the possibility of dying you don't have to worry about going to your grave wondering what all the fuss was about."

Peachy's eyes flashed a second time. Her delicately made features took on a decidedly determined cast. "More or less."

"And this is a no-strings-attached, one-time-only deal."

"*Yes.*"

Luc inhaled a short, sharp breath, struggling with a sudden surge of temper. He couldn't define the source of his anger, nor determine whether it was directed more at himself or her.

When he thought he could trust his voice he said, "No."

Peachy stiffened. Her chin went up a notch. "No?"

"No," he repeated, underscoring the negative with a shake of his head.

"You mean—" she swallowed "—you don't want to do it."

Luc felt the muscles of his belly clench and fervently wished she'd phrased her statement in a different way. Preferably one that omitted the word *want*.

He wasn't oblivious to Peachy's appeal. Although she was a far cry from his usual type—he was inclined toward experienced blondes and exotic brunettes, not arty, ethereal redheads—he'd felt a powerful tug of attraction the day she'd shown up on his doorstep, seeking to rent the unit one floor down.

He'd refrained from acting on this attraction for a variety of reasons. Peachy's comparative youth had been part of the equation. His firm conviction that getting entangled with *any* female tenant—much less one who'd become the darling of their mutual collection of rather eccentric neighbors within a week of moving in—would be asking for trouble had been a factor, as well.

But the key basis for his decision to clamp down and hold back had been his gut-level feeling that there was a lot more to Ms. Pamela Gayle Keene than immediately met the eye. For all her seemingly free-spirited manner, she'd exuded an aura of potential complications.

Luc grimaced, raking a hand through his hair. "Look, *cher,*" he began, letting his gaze slide away. "My saying no to you—it's nothing personal."

The ludicrousness of his words registered with him even as he was uttering them. *Nothing personal?* Peachy had asked him to be her first lover and he'd rejected her! What in heaven's name could be more personal than that?

He glanced back at his would-be bed partner, expecting an angry reaction. He was startled to find Peachy was no longer looking at him. Instead, she was staring down at her well-pedicured toes. Her mouth was set in a stubborn line, her forehead was furrowed. He had the distinct and rather disturbing impression that she'd dismissed him from her mind and was now contemplating her next option for defloration.

Every instinct for self-preservation Luc Devereaux had—and he had developed a great many of them during his thirty-three years on earth—told him to get up and get out. But he couldn't.

He just . . . *couldn't.*

"Peachy?" he asked after a few seconds, acutely conscious of the thudding of his heart. Even the most automatic of natural functions, breathing, suddenly seemed to require a conscious effort.

She started slightly, then lifted her eyes to meet his.

"I understand, Luc," she said quietly, without bothering to specify exactly what it was that she comprehended. "And...well, I appreciate your being honest with me." She paused for a moment, her lips quirking into a crooked little smile. Then she rose from the hassock in a graceful movement and concluded with a shrug, "I'll just have to find someone else."

From another woman, Luc would have interpreted this last comment as a threat. As an attempt at emotional blackmail. But coming from Peachy...

He got to his feet slowly, keeping his gaze fixed on his tenant's expressive face. She means it, he thought, a chill skittering down his spine and settling in the pit of his stomach. She *really* means it.

"You genuinely intend to go through with this, don't you," he said.

Peachy lifted her brows, plainly surprised. Perhaps even a little affronted. "I *told* you I did."

Yes, she had. But until a couple of seconds ago, he'd been unwilling to believe that she'd been sincere.

"Why?" he asked bluntly.

"I told you that, too."

"Tell me again."

Peachy's green-gold eyes flicked back and forth several times as though she was trying to figure out what sort of game he was playing at. Finally, she expelled a breath in a long sigh.

"You've been in life-or-death situations, haven't you?" she questioned. "When you were in the military?"

"A few," Luc acknowledged after a fractional hesitation, sensing where she was heading and not entirely comfortable with the direction. Although he was intensely proud of the services he'd performed for his country, not all his military memories were pleasant ones. The covert style of war he'd been trained to make had been a dirty, as well as dangerous, business.

"Didn't you find yourself regretting things you hadn't done?"

"While I was in the middle of an operation where I might be killed, you mean?"

Peachy nodded.

Luc felt his lips twist. "If I regretted anything, it was *committed* sins. Not ones I hadn't had a chance to get around to."

"Still—"

"Still," he interrupted, "I take your meaning. Facing down death tends to reorder a person's priorities."

"Exactly."

Luc considered for a moment or two, once again replaying the proposal Peachy had put to him. Did she truly understand the nature of the favor she was asking? he wondered. And more to the point: *Did she truly understand the nature of the man of whom she was asking it?*

No, he told himself. She couldn't. She had no idea of who he was. Of what he was. Of how he'd lived.

"Am I the first man you've approached about this, Peachy?" he abruptly queried.

"You mean, are you the first one I've asked to—?" She then gestured.

"Yes."

Her chin went up again. A blush blossomed on her cheeks. "I don't think that's any of your business at this point, Luc."

"No?"

"You turned me down—remember?"

"I'm considering changing my mind."

Peachy's eyes widened to the point where there was white visible all the way around the irises. "I thought that was a female prerogative."

Luc shrugged with a casualness he was far from feeling. "Consider it a matter of equal opportunity indecisiveness." He waited a beat, then repeated his previous inquiry. "*Am* I the first man you've approached about this?"

Peachy glanced away from him, the color in her cheeks intensifying, the line of her elegantly sculpted jaw going taut. Her reluctance to respond was palpable.

"Yes," she finally replied.

Luc released a breath he hadn't realized he'd been holding, a primitive sense of triumph suffusing him. He closed his mind to thoughts of how he might have reacted had her answer been different. Then, goaded by an emotion he couldn't—or wouldn't—identify he said, "But you have other . . . candidates."

Her gaze swung back to collide with his. The expression in her eyes said he was perilously close to getting his face slapped.

"That's *really* none of your business," Peachy declared through gritted teeth.

It wasn't and he knew it, but he didn't give a damn.

"What about that Tulane University M.B.A. the MayWinnies tried to fix you up with last month?" he pressed.

"The MayWinnies" was Prytania Street shorthand for Mayrielle and Winona-Jolene Barnes, a pair of sprightly seventy-year-old twins who rented the apartment next to Peachy's. Although they cultivated an image of white-gloved propriety, Luc had heard from numerous sources that they'd once been quite free with their favors.

Well, no. Perhaps *free* wasn't the appropriate adjective. Because gossip also maintained that in the course of bestowing themselves on a goodly number of Louisiana's richest and most powerful men, the MayWinnies had amassed a six-figure nest egg, which they had subsequently multiplied many times over in the stock market.

Short of inquiring of the ladies themselves, there was no way for Luc to be certain how many of the stories about the MayWinnies' alleged exploits were true. He was inclined to dismiss a few of them—most notably the one involving a former U.S. senator and a Mardi Gras float—out of hand. He was also prepared to bet a substantial amount of cold, hard cash that many of the tales were dead-on accurate.

As for the rumors about his septuagenarian tenants transforming themselves from good-time girls into gilt-edged investors...

Again, there was no way for Luc to be absolutely sure. However, he and the MayWinnies *did* happen to bank at the same place. He'd long ago noticed that although he and his book royalties were accorded a significant degree of respect, the bank's president practically genuflected at the mention of the Misses Barnes.

"Are you talking about Daniel?" Peachy asked, plainly startled by the specificity of his query.

Luc was a tad surprised by it himself. He hadn't realized he'd registered the individual in question—Daniel, had she said his name was?—quite so strongly.

"Yes," he affirmed after a moment.

Peachy began fingering her locket again. "I only went out with him once."

Luc couldn't tell whether she was being deliberately evasive. He fleetingly considered pointing out that "once" was one more time than she'd been out with him, but discarded the idea.

"So?" he challenged.

"So—he's *nice!*"

Luc lifted a brow, contemplating the possibility that he'd just been insulted. Under normal circumstances there would have been little doubt in his mind that he had, at least by implication. But the inflection Peachy had given the adjective strongly suggested that it was Daniel, not he, whom she'd judged and found wanting.

Nice.

Hmm.

His ready-to-be-bedded tenant had a problem with *nice?*

She wouldn't be unique among her sex if she did, Luc reflected with a touch of cynicism. And heaven knew, such a prejudice would go a long way toward explaining her decision to ask him to take—er, make that "accept"—her virginity. Yet he couldn't quite reconcile that sort of character kink with the woman who'd lived beneath his roof for nearly twenty-four months.

"You're saying that being nice disqualifies a man from inclusion on your list of potential, ah, deflowerers," he clarified.

"I'm saying that Daniel wouldn't understand my situation."

"And you think *I* do?"

"Not anymore." Peachy glared at him. "Look, Luc. This obviously was a mistake. I'm sorry I said anything to you. Just—just *forget* about it, all right?"

And with that, she started to pivot away. Reacting purely on instinct, Luc reached out and grabbed her by the arm, halting her in mid-turn.

It was the first time he'd touched Peachy with anything more intense than the most casual kind of affection. He felt her go rigid in response to the contact. Her gaze slewed back to slam into his, then dropped pointedly to his hand. After a taut moment, he opened his fingers and released her.

God, he thought, sucking in a shaky breath as he lowered a none-too-steady hand to his side. The potency of his emotions shocked him. My... God.

"Why me?" he demanded harshly. He couldn't have stopped the words if he'd wanted to. He had to know.

Peachy blinked and edged back slightly. "Wh-what?"

"Why did you ask *me* to—?" he completed the question with an explicit variation of the gesture she'd made earlier.

There was a long pause. Peachy's eyes moved back and forth, back and forth. Finally, she seemed to reach some kind of decision. After moistening her lower lip with a darting lick of her tongue she countered flatly, "Do you want the truth?"

He nodded.

"All right." She swallowed, then cocked her chin with a hint of defiance. "I asked you because I thought you'd make it easy."

"*Easy?*"

She nodded. "Do you remember me saying that I only wanted you to do it with me once?"

"Vividly."

"Well, it seemed to me—I mean, you've never made any secret of the fact that you're not inclined toward making emotional commitments. That you don't want to be tied down. So I decided, uh, uh—''

"That a one-night stand would be right up my alley?"

"Not in a bad way," Peachy quickly insisted.

"Oh, of course not."

But even as he voiced the retort, Luc had to acknowledge the fundamental validity of his tenant's assessment. He had no desire for a permanent relationship with a woman. He never had. He seriously doubted he ever would. In point of fact, he was supremely skeptical about his ability to sustain one. He'd never hidden that.

Yet for all its accuracy, Luc found Peachy's reading of his character disturbing. The idea that she perceived him as some kind of...of...disposable stud unnerved him in a way he couldn't fully explain.

"You're not the only man I considered," Peachy said earnestly. "I've spent a lot of time thinking about this. My first impulse was to go to the bar at a good hotel, maybe Le Meridien or the Windsor Court, and pick up a nice-looking stranger and let nature take its course."

"*What?*"

"You don't think I could have?"

"For God's sake, Peachy." He could barely speak. The scenario she'd sketched was appallingly plausible. "Do you have any concept how dangerous—"

"I'm inexperienced, Luc," she interrupted, nailing him with a fulminating look. "I'm not an idiot. The hotel bar idea occurred to me while I was still pretty shaken up from the emergency landing. As soon as I got my brains unscrambled, I realized I could never go through with it. So I sat down and wrote out a list of all the eligible men I know. Then I started to eliminate. It was pretty much the same thing, over and over. 'If I do it with him and it's awful, he'll probably be upset and that could get complicated.' Or, 'If I do it with him and it's terrific, he'll probably want to do it again and that could get complicated, too.'" She paused, her cheeks flushing. "I ended up with you."

Luc took a few moments to absorb this remarkable explanation then asked, "What about you?"

"Me?"

"Wouldn't *you* be upset if you 'did it' and it was awful?"

For the first time, a hint of shyness entered her expression. "Actually...that was the second reason I decided to ask you first."

Luc frowned, genuinely flummoxed. "What was?"

"I've been hearing stories about your love life from the moment I moved into the building. Even the MayWinnies—oh, they tut-tut about your behavior, of course. Which is sort of funny, considering the outrageous things they supposedly did when they were younger. Still, as prim as they pretend to be now, I can tell they get a kick out of having a lady-killer for a landlord. In any case, when I was thinking about who I should ask, I realized that if even a *quarter* of what's said about you and women is true, you'd know how to make my first time, uh, well, *un*awful."

There was a pause.

"Supposing it isn't?" Luc finally asked.

"Supposing what isn't . . . what?"

"Supposing not even a quarter of what's said about me and women is true? Supposing it's all lies?"

Peachy regarded him with disconcerting directness. "If that were the case," she said slowly, "I think you'd tell me."

Luc stiffened. No, he thought. She can't be *that* naive! She can't believe—

But she did. He could see it in her lovely, wide-set eyes. For reasons he couldn't begin to fathom, this woman trusted him to be truthful about a subject that was notorious for inspiring lies.

"Men don't usually go around puncturing the myths about their sexual prowess, *cher*," he said, conscious of an unfamiliar stirring of protectiveness.

"Not if they're the ones who've been spreading them," Peachy agreed. "But everything I've heard about *your* prowess comes from other people, Luc. Where they heard it, I don't know. Except I'm certain it wasn't from you. Because as far as I can tell, you don't brag about what you do, how you do it, or whom you do it with. And I . . . well, I admire that."

Luc glanced away, his throat tightening. Peachy's summation of his behavior was very much on target. But if she ascribed his discretion to gallantry, she was sadly mistaken. His first inkling of the true nature of his parents' marriage had been gleaned from a conversation he'd overheard when he was just six years old. It was the memory of the angry, anguished confusion he'd felt when he'd listened to two supposed friends of his father crudely comparing notes about liaisons with his mother that kept him silent about his sexual affairs. The possibility that some careless comment of his might hurt someone as he'd been hurt was untenable to him.

His thoughts shifted without warning to *his* first sexual experience. He'd been seduced during his sophomore year of high school by the wife of one of the many men with whom his mother had broken her wedding vows. While the experience had been physically pleasurable, it had left him with more than a few psychological scars.

"Luc?"

Drawing a long, deep breath, he turned his gaze back to Peachy. She's bound and determined to do it, he reflected. If not with me, then with someone else. And if she does it with someone else—

No! He didn't even want to *think* about that scenario!

Luc exhaled in a rush, his mind suddenly latching on to an astonishing idea.

What if...what if he *agreed* to do what Peachy had asked, then stalled consummation until she came to her senses and called the deal off?

She would come to her senses, he assured himself. Eventually.

He'd meant what he'd said earlier, about facing down death tending to reorder a person's priorities. What he hadn't said—but what he knew from personal experience to be true—was that such reorderings were seldom permanent.

Of course, he conceded, there was always a minuscule possibility that the passage of time would not erode Peachy's single-minded desire to get rid of her virginity. And if that were the case . . .

Thirteen years ago, Luc Devereaux had found himself standing in the door of a military plane, preparing to make his first parachute jump. Half of his brain had been urging him to make the leap. The other half had been screaming that there was still time to turn back from what probably was the stupidest stunt he'd ever contemplated.

He'd glanced at his instructor, a Special Forces captain named Flynn. Flynn had grinned, his teeth flashing a predatory white against his deeply tanned skin. Then he'd leaned in, put his mouth close to Luc's ear and counseled, *"Go with your gut, kid."*

"All right," he said abruptly.

Peachy blinked. "All . . . right?"

"I accept your proposal."

"Oh, Luc—"

"But not tonight."

Two

"This is *not* a date," Peachy stated to her reflection approximately twenty-four hours later.

Leaning into the mirror over her bathroom sink, she painstakingly brushed another coat of black brown mascara on to her lush but virtually colorless lashes. Other types of cosmetics she could basically take or leave. In fact, aside from what she now drolly classified as her "Vampira" period—a mercifully brief interlude during her first semester of design school in which she'd affected a from-the-crypt pallor, dramatically shadowed eyes and blood-red lips—she'd always applied her makeup with a very light hand.

Except for mascara, of course.

She'd gotten hooked on the stuff more than a decade ago and had experimented with everything from bargain basement brands that smelled like petrochemicals to outrageously expensive ones that supposedly contained miscroscopic fibers of cashmere. Without mascara—well, frankly, she thought she appeared rather rabbitty.

Her lashes finally darkened to a satisfactory degree, Peachy stepped back from the sink and scrutinized her mirrored image with a critical eye. There'd been a time when she'd absolutely loathed the way she looked. A time when she would have given anything to trade her gaminely irregular features, sprite-thin body and uncontrollable mop of red-gold curls for her older sister's classically pretty face, shapely figure and straight, chestnut-colored hair. Fortunately that time had passed.

Although she still considered Eden an extremely attractive woman, Peachy had learned to appreciate and enhance her own quirky looks. The three years she'd spent in New York—the first two as a design student, the third as an apprentice with a jewelry firm—had been extremely important ones in this regard.

Where her mass of pre-Raphaelite ringlets and rather avant-garde wardrobe choices, basic black everything accessorized with purchases from army-navy surplus stores, thrift shops and garage sales, generally had been regarded as just a wee bit weird in her hometown in Ohio, they'd turned out to be very much "with it" in the Big Apple. This had done wonders for her shaky self-esteem.

Oh, sure, she'd succumbed to a few in-your-face fashion trends during her first few months in Manhattan. But she'd eventually realized that shocking people in the street really wasn't her thing. She'd abandoned stylistic extremes, let all but two of the holes in her earlobes heal up and begun developing her own personal look. This look wasn't middle-of-the-road by any means. But it wasn't so far out on the edge that it scared innocent little children, either.

Interestingly, her artwork had improved as her vision of who she was and how she wanted to present herself to the world had become clearer. By the time she'd won the design contest that had led to the job offer that had brought her to New Orleans, she'd had more confidence in herself—both personally and professionally—than she'd ever had in her life.

As for the impact the last two years in New Orleans had had on her...

Perhaps it was a response to the ambrosial food or the profusion of flowers or the remarkable diversity of cultures. Or maybe it had something to do with the local credo of letting *les bon temps rouler*. But within weeks of her arrival in the Crescent City—shortly after moving into her Prytania Street apartment, to be precise—Peachy had realized that she felt totally at home. No matter that she'd still needed a map to find her way around, mistakenly believed Burgundy Street was pronounced like the wine and thought chicory coffee tasted like something that should be used to clean paintbrushes. Somehow, someway, she'd found a place where she fit in.

Which was not to say that everything was absolutely perfect. The weather, for example, was a tad problematic. Peachy had heard natives claim that New Orleans, which had been carved from a swamp, only had two seasons—summer and February. She'd come to the conclusion that this was code for muggy and about-to-be muggy. She'd also discovered that the local climate played havoc with what Bible scholars would call her "crowning glory."

Grimacing wryly at her reflection, Peachy plucked a brush from amid the clutter on the counter to the left of the sink. Maybe she should wear her hair up after all, she mused. She'd styled it into a chignon earlier then unpinned it after deciding the coiffure was too fussy and self-conscious. While making herself attractive to Luc seemed a sensible thing to do given the request she'd made of him, she was wary of creating the impression that she'd expended a lot of time and effort preparing for this evening's, uh, uh—

"*Whatever,*" she said, yanking the brush through her incorrigible curls.

It was unsettling, Peachy admitted silently. She knew Luc intended to make love to her, because he'd promised her he would. Yet she had no idea when or where he planned to perform the deed.

Assuming he'd even decided those details, which she was strongly inclined not to do.

How had it happened? she demanded of herself. How had Lucien Devereaux shifted from accepting *her* proposal, to imposing *his* terms in the space of a few seconds? More importantly, why had she acquiesced in a situation where she had every right to be in charge? It was *her* virginity, dammit!

Her mind flashed back to the previous evening.

"What do you mean…'but not tonight'?" she'd asked once the implications of Luc's unexpected declaration had begun to sink in.

"I think we should wait," he'd answered calmly.

"I *have* waited!" she'd exclaimed, swatting a stray lock of hair out of her face. "That's why I found myself on a malfunctioning airplane thinking I was going to die a virgin. The waiting's over, Luc. I want to do it and be done with it and get on with my life!"

It had not been the most felicitous way of describing the consummation for which she so devoutly wished. Peachy had recognized this the moment the words had come tumbling out of her mouth. A sudden lifting of her partner-to-be's dark brows had suggested that he, too, found her phrasing a trifle cold-blooded.

"'Wham, bam, thank you, ma'am?'" he'd quoted after a fractional pause.

She'd felt herself start to blush for what seemed like the millionth time but she hadn't dared back off. "That's one way of putting it."

Luc's deep brown eyes had narrowed very slightly at this point. The corners of his sensually shaped lips had quirked upward. The shift in both instances had been a matter of no more than a few millimeters. Yet the effect on his overall expression had been devastatingly seductive.

"But that's not my style, *cher*," he'd replied, his voice dropping into a velvet-lined register she'd never heard before. Even the offhand endearment he'd been using since the first time they'd met had suddenly sounded foreign to her ears.

She'd opened her mouth to say something. He'd forestalled her before she'd uttered a peep.

"The first time between a man and woman is always awkward, Peachy," he'd observed. "No matter how much experience one—or both—of them has. There's uncertainty about what the other person wants and there's insecurity about whether you can provide it. It's not . . . easy."

There'd been no doubt in her mind that his choice of the final adjective had been deliberate. *Easy* had been the word she'd used earlier in explaining why she'd chosen him as the first recipient of her unorthodox proposal.

"So?" The breathlessness of her voice had appalled her.

"So, I think it would reduce the inevitable awkwardness if we got to know each before we head to bed for the first and only time."

"Got to know—?" she'd echoed incredulously. "We've been living under the same roof for nearly two years!"

"Which means we know each other as neighbors," he'd replied without missing a beat. "I'm talking about becoming acquainted as man and woman. About becoming . . . aware . . . of each other."

Peachy had hesitated. She'd sensed that there was something crucial he wasn't saying and searched his dark, deep-set eyes to try to discover what it might be.

Yet even as she'd sought for answers to questions she wouldn't have been able to articulate if she'd tried, she'd had to concede that Luc's arguments for "waiting" sounded reasonable.

"Well," she'd finally begun. "I suppose . . ."

Luc had smiled. There'd been a brief hint of teeth, reminding her that the human race was innately carnivorous.

"There's also the matter of my masculine pride," he'd said. "I'd like to be sure your first time is something better than—what was your word? Oh, yes. *Unawful*."

And then he'd touched her. Lifting his right hand to her face, he'd brushed his fingertips slowly down the curve of her left cheek. After that he'd stroked them, very lightly, along the line of her jaw.

The contact had affected her like a jolt of electricity. It had gone surging through her nervous system, throwing her already accelerated pulse rate into overdrive and causing her breathing pattern to unravel into short, shallow pants.

For one insane instant she'd honestly thought she might swoon. And in that same insane instant she'd decided that asking Lucien Devereaux to relieve her of her virginity was either the smartest thing she'd ever done or a mistake of such monumental proportions that she'd spend the rest of her life—

The sound of her hairbrush clattering against the tiled floor of the bathroom yanked Peachy back into the present. She blinked several times, conscious of a wild fluttering deep in her stomach. Her hands were trembling. She could feel the nipples of her small breasts straining against the lacy cups of her bra.

A glimpse of her reflection did nothing to restore her composure. Her cheeks were flushed, almost feverish looking. And there was a glazed expression in her eyes that reminded her of the zombie lore she'd heard from Laila Martigny, the fiftyish psychologist who lived in the apartment directly below hers.

Rumor had it that the regal-looking Dr. Martigny was a descendant of New Orleans's famed witch queen, Marie Laveau. But while she would admit to being the seventh daughter of a seventh daughter and to having occasional flashes of what some others might call ESP, Laila simply smiled away questions about her possible connection to the legendary "Madame L."

"Get a grip," Peachy ordered herself through clenched teeth as she bent to retrieve the brush. Her hair cascaded forward in an unruly tumble. She shoveled it back over her shoulders as she straightened up.

A glance at the small alarm clock that sat on the back of the commode informed her that her ill-advised stroll down memory lane had put her behind schedule. It was nearly half past seven. She was supposed to meet Luc for dinner at eight. Although the restaurant he'd chosen was within walking distance, she'd have to hustle to arrive there by the appointed hour.

She stalked out of the bathroom and into her bedroom, muttering as she went. Her resentment at having had her agenda rewrit-
ten flared anew. She didn't need to be wined and dined as a prelude
to sex, she told herself as she started dressing. No. More than that.
She didn't *want* it. And she'd tried to make that crystal clear to
Luc. Only he'd gone right ahead and overridden her wishes.

Well, no, she amended as she smoothed down the skirt of the
jade green silk dress she'd settled on after reviewing the contents
of her closet four times. That wasn't entirely fair. Luc hadn't so
much overridden her wishes as she'd succumbed to his.

But no more. Never again. The instant she sat down with him she
was going to make certain he understood that this evening out was
not—absolutely, positively *not*—a date. What's more, she was
going to tell him that she intended to pick up the check. And if he
had a problem with that . . .

She'd deal with it, she promised herself. She'd deal with it just
fine, thank you very much.

But first she had to find the shoes she planned to wear. And se-
lect a substitute for the demure pearl drop earrings she'd picked
out. What she'd been thinking when she'd chosen them, she didn't
know. The last time she'd had them on had been when she'd attended Easter services with the MayWinnies!

Peachy was frantically rummaging through her drawers when she
heard a knock at her apartment door. "Who is it?" she called,
flinging aside a pair of hammered gold hoops that had briefly
captured her fancy.

"It's me," a distinctively husky voice called back.

She froze. Oh, no, she thought. Not *Terry*. Not now!

The Terry in question rented the apartment next to Laila Martigny. He'd been born Terrence Bellehurst in Syracuse, New York,
and had had a spectacular career as a professional football player
until a quarterback sack in the waning moments of his first Super
Bowl had pretty well pulverized his right knee.

Benched for life by the injury, Terry had forged a successful
second career as a play-by-play commentator. But shortly after
he'd won his third Emmy for sports coverage, he'd undergone a
mind-blowing transformation.

"I got in touch with my feminine self," he'd told Peachy with
characteristic candor shortly after they'd gotten acquainted. "And
honey, it felt *wonderful!*"

Terrence Bellehurst had been reborn as Terree, emphasis on the
second syllable, LaBelle. And for the last four years, Terree had

served as mistress of ceremonies for the classiest drag show in the French Quarter. So classy, in fact, that the MayWinnies had attended several performances and subsequently commented to Peachy—with what had seemed to her to be complete sincerity—that it had been a pleasure to see such perfect ladies on the stage.

Having spent three years in New York City, Peachy had arrived in New Orleans believing herself essentially inured to the vagaries of human behavior. Nonetheless, her first encounter with Terrence/Terree had been a bit unsettling. However, she'd soon been won over by her downstairs neighbor's friendliness. Terrence Bellehurst was one of the frankest, funniest people she'd ever met. As for Terree LaBelle . . . well, "she" would donate the frock off "her" back to anyone in need.

"Hold on, Terry," Peachy shouted, thrusting her feet into a pair of strappy, high-heeled sandals. "I'll be there in a second."

Actually, it was closer to a minute before she unlocked her door and opened it to reveal a six-foot-two-inch male who was covered from throat to ankles by a royal blue kimono-style bathrobe embroidered with silver and cerise chrysanthemums. His head was turbaned with a royal blue terry cloth towel.

Terry gave her a fast up-down-up assessment then inquired knowingly, "Hot date?"

It was the wrong question at the wrong time.

"No!"

Terry arched his brows and shifted into his sympathetic mode. "Cramps?"

Peachy grimaced, realizing she had no right to vent her emotional upset on an innocent bystander. "No, nothing like that, Terry," she replied, moderating her tone and summoning up a quick smile. "I'm sorry I snapped at you. I'm just a little frazzled right now. Would you like to come in?"

"Only for a sec." Terry stepped across the threshold. He gave her another considering look. "You *are* going out, I take it?"

"Yes." Peachy willed herself not to blush. "To dinner."

"With—?"

"A...friend." Mentioning Luc's name would prompt too many questions, she rationalized. Better to let Terry think she was off to some mysterious rendezvous.

"Oh, *really?*" Her neighbor seemed thrilled.

"Yes, really." Peachy produced another smile to take the edge off what she had to say next. "Look, Terry, I hate to be rude—"

"I need an egg."

"I beg your pardon?"

"I came up here to see if I could borrow an egg from you. Or two."

"You feel the urge for a facial?" Peachy guessed. Convinced that his years on the gridiron had had a deleterious effect on his skin, Terry spent a significant amount of time pampering his complexion. The first time they'd met, his face had been slathered with a cornmeal cleansing masque of his own concoction.

"Breakfast, actually."

"It's nearly 8:00 p.m., Terry."

"What can I say? I had an *extremely* late evening. It ended sometime around noon over beignets and café au lait at Café du Monde."

Peachy didn't want to know the details. "My eggs are your eggs," she said. "And I think I have some fresh-squeezed orange juice, too, if you want it."

Terry beamed. "*Bless* you." Then he cocked his head and frowned. "Sweetie, I hate to play fashion police, but aren't you the *teensiest* bit underaccessorized for dinner with a 'friend'?"

"Actually, I was trying to find some earrings when you knocked."

"Oh?" He was instantly engaged. "And what look are we going for, might I inquire? 'Don't touch' or 'Take me, I'm yours'?"

Peachy had to smile. "Somewhere in between."

"Keep the guy guessing, hmm? That's *so* wise of you. But let me cogitate for a moment. Earrings. Mmm. Well, what about those gold and jade ones you lent me during Mardi Gras?"

Peachy knew exactly the pair he meant and exactly where she had them stashed away. She also knew they were exactly what she'd been seeking.

"Terry, you're a genius!" she exclaimed, giving him a quick hug. It was a bit like embracing a side of beef.

"I try," he replied modestly. "But if you wear the gold and jade, you'll have to take off your silver bell locket...."

"I'm sorry I'm late," Peachy said, slipping into the seat opposite Luc. Glancing over her shoulder, she nodded her thanks at the black-jacketed maître d'hôtel who'd held her chair. He nodded back, murmured something about hoping she'd enjoy her meal, then moved away.

Luc had risen to his feet as she'd approached the table. He was clad in black trousers, an open-collared white silk shirt and a dove gray jacket that bore the subtle hallmarks of a master tailor. He reseated himself saying, "The wait was worth it, *cher.*"

The response—so smooth, so sure—nettled Peachy.

"You don't have to do that, Luc," she declared, opening her napkin and draping it across her lap. She kept her spine very stiff, sitting forward on her chair rather than relaxing back into it. The MayWinnies would have awarded her an A-plus for posture.

"Do what?"

"Give me any of your usual lines."

Luc paused in the act of picking up his own napkin and regarded her with an expression Peachy couldn't interpret. She felt her pulse give a curious hop-skip-jump.

"Is it a line if I mean it?" he asked after a moment, his dark gaze drifting over her. "Because you *do* look lovely tonight."

Peachy took a deep breath, reminding herself that she was a twenty-three-year-old woman not a giggly adolescent idiot. "Thank you," she finally answered, striving for a normal tone of voice and coming fairly close. "I had some expert help."

"Oh?"

She gestured. "Terry suggested the earrings."

There was a long-stemmed goblet of ice water to Luc's right. He picked it up and took a sip. As he put the glass down he asked, "Terry knows we're out together?"

"Uh, no." Peachy shifted slightly. "I told him I was meeting a friend for dinner. It's not that I'm...ashamed...of what you and I are doing. But I'm afraid—I mean, it might be, uh, well, it might be awkward, don't you think? Trying to explain. About...things."

Again, she found herself on the receiving end of a look she couldn't read. Again, her pulse leapt as though it had hit a series of speed bumps.

"My sentiments exactly," Luc concurred.

At that moment the sommelier materialized by their table with a bottle of champagne and two crystal flutes. He conversed with Luc in French for a few moments. Then, still talking, he deftly popped the cork and began to pour the pale, bubbling wine. Peachy listened uncomprehendingly to the two men, unable to reconcile their fast, fluent exchange with any of the stilted phrases she'd memorized in high school language class.

She did manage a *merci* after the man filled her glass. He responded at great length. Finally, after giving Luc what she could only describe as a look of approval, he took his leave.

His place was swiftly taken by a waiter who presented them with a pair of exquisitely calligraphied menus plus a small silver basket of toast points and a crock of what appeared to be truffle-studded pâté.

"*Pour lagniappe,*" he announced with a smile.

Lagniappe, Peachy understood. Slang for "a little something extra," it was one of the words she'd added to her vocabulary since coming to New Orleans.

"Do you eat here often?" she asked Luc after the waiter had bustled away. What she really wanted to determine was whether this restaurant was part of some standard seduction routine.

"I come here a few times a month when I'm in town," he answered. "If the staff seems to be fawning—well, I'm an investor in the place. The owner, Jean-Baptiste, is an acquaintance of mine from high school. He started cooking in grade school and always dreamed of opening a restaurant in the Garden District. He came to me with a business proposition about four years ago, right around the time a Hollywood producer offered to shell out an obscene amount of money for the rights to my first book. I said yes to both. My accountant figured I was setting myself up for a tax write-off. I think you'll understand my real motivation once you taste this."

The "this" to which he referred was a toast point he'd lavishly spread with pâté while he'd been speaking. He extended the morsel toward Peachy, clearly intending her to eat from his fingers.

After a brief hesitation, Peachy leaned forward and took a bite. The word "voluptuous" didn't begin to describe the silken smoothness of the pâté. And the *flavor...*

"Goomph," she said inadequately, trying not to drool.

Luc grinned and popped the remainder of the appetizer into his mouth.

Peachy didn't know whether the move was intended to be suggestive of more intimate kinds of sharing. But if it wasn't, it should have been. A quiver—part anticipation, part apprehension—raced through her. She reached for her flute of champagne.

"As for the question you didn't ask," Luc went on once he'd chewed and swallowed. "I usually eat alone. The last time I brought a woman here—women, actually—was about ten months ago. It was the MayWinnies' birthday and I invited them to dinner.''

Peachy nearly choked on her champagne.

"Oh," she was finally able to say, wondering if her cheeks were as flushed as they felt.

"Are you all right, *cher?*" Luc asked solicitously.

"Just…fine," she said. Control, she told herself firmly. She had to regain control of this situation!

Regain control? a little voice inside her skull mocked. *Who are you trying to kid, Pamela Gayle? Luc's been running this show from the moment he told you, "Not tonight"!*

Well, yes, she conceded irritably. Maybe he had been. But *she'd* been in charge—sort of—before that. She'd been the one who'd seized the sexual initiative. Oh, all right! Not *seized* it, exactly. But she'd definitely been the one who'd broached the subject of giving up her virginity.

Peachy took a cautious sip of the champagne. As untutored as her palate was about such things, it was still capable of discerning that she was imbibing something very special. The taste of the wine was incandescently delicious.

"Did you order this?" she asked, setting down her glass and gazing across the table at her future lover with what she hoped was a no-nonsense expression.

"Would you object if I had?"

"*Luc—*"

He spread his hands in apparent conciliation. "It came compliments of the management."

"Oh." She glanced away, wishing she'd done less doodling in French class.

There was a pause. Then: "My question stands, Peachy," Luc said pointedly.

Her gaze slewed back to his face. "What question?"

"Would you object if I *had* ordered the champagne?"

"Yes." She cocked her chin. "I would."

He remained silent for a moment or two, seeming to weigh her unequivocal answer. Then he asked, "Why?"

Peachy took a deep breath. It was the perfect opening for what she'd told herself she was going to say.

"Because this is not a date, Luc," she declared. "You and I—it just *isn't*, all right? We're not going out together. I mean—yes, we're out. And yes, we're together. But we're not, uh, uh—"

"Dating," he finished, reaching for a second toast point.

"I'm serious!"

"I realize that, *cher*."

"Seriously serious."

"Fine. This is *not* a date."

Although she was uncertain whether he was genuinely conceding the point or simply humoring her, Peachy decided to proceed to the second item on her agenda.

"And another thing," she said.

"Yes?"

"I want—no, I'm *going* to pick up the tab tonight."

"All right."

"This isn't open for discussion. I've thought it through very carefully and I've decided that—" She broke off abruptly. "*What* did you say?"

"I said, all right." While Luc's tone was mild, there was a glint in his dark eyes that was anything but.

"You don't . . . mind?"

"Not unless you're classifying this meal as payment for services you're expecting me to render in the future."

It took Peachy a moment or two to understand what he was saying. Once she did, she was appalled.

"No," she said, shaking her head so vigorously she felt her gold and jade earrings bounce against her cheeks. "Oh, no, Luc. Of course not!"

"Good," her dinner companion responded. "Because while I freely admit to engaging in some less-than-respectable activities in my life, I draw the line at turning gigolo." He raised his pâté-laden toast point to his lips. "Even on a one-time-only basis."

The sight of Luc's even white teeth snapping down on the tidbit he was holding sent a tremor running through Peachy.

"I'm sorry," she said after a pause, aware that her voice was much huskier than normal. "I never meant to suggest—I mean, my paying for dinner tonight isn't—" She grimaced, then opted for bluntness. "Look, Luc. You have a tendency to overwhelm people. Maybe you got used to giving orders in the army. Or maybe you're accustomed to bossing around the characters you create. The point is, you like to take charge of things. And given our—no, given *my* situation—"

"You want to be the one who's in control."

There was something in his tone that caused Peachy's breath to jam at the top of her throat.

She wasn't unaware of the fact that Luc's childhood had been infinitely less idyllic than hers. The MayWinnies' pseudo-clucking over their mutual landlord's rakish behavior was frequently leavened with delicate references to his mother's "popularity" with the opposite sex and his father's "fondness" for fine wine. Laila Martigny—who'd financed her education by doing domestic duty for the Devereauxs and others—was even blunter in her comments.

"When I think about the bad that's been done to that boy," she'd once told Peachy, abandoning her normally flawless diction for a patois phrasing that carried the lilt of her Caribbean heritage. "I'm amazed he grew up any kind of good."

Still.

To hear the empathy in Luc's voice . . .

To sense that he understood—truly understood—her feelings of vulnerability . . .

Peachy hadn't expected it. She hadn't expected it at all.

"Yes," she said. "That's what I want."

An odd smile ghosted around the corners of Luc's mouth then disappeared. Propping his elbows on the table, he steepled his fingers and leaned forward.

"Yesterday," he began slowly, "when you were explaining why you'd decided to come to me first, I wondered whether you were leaving something unsaid."

Peachy's heart performed a queer, cardiac somersault. She suddenly found herself recalling her previous evening's impression that Luc had been holding back from her on some key level—that even as he'd accepted her proposal, he'd been silently amending their verbal agreement with an escape clause.

"Like what?" she asked warily.

"Like—" his gaze slid away from her face "—you trust me."

Peachy's initial response was to wonder why Luc should sound so skeptical. But then she realized that what she'd thought was skepticism was something much deeper. Much darker.

"Is there some reason why I shouldn't?" she countered.

His eyes returned to hers. The expression in them was similar to the one she'd seen the night before when she'd told him that she'd expect him to confess if the stories she'd heard about his sexual exploits were untrue.

"There's always a reason," he commented without inflection. "But even so . . ."

There was a pause.

"Even so?" Peachy prompted.

Luc unsteepled his fingers and extended both hands toward her, palms up. After a moment of internal debate, she reached forward and placed her hands in his.

"Even so," he said quietly, feathering his thumbs against the sensitive skin of her inner wrists, "I can promise you that everything that happens between us from this moment on will be by your choice."

Peachy inhaled an unsteady breath. She dimly registered that the rhythmic pounding of her heart was in sync with the stroke-stroke-stroking of Luc's faintly callused thumbs.

She gave a shuddery sigh.

His eyes compelled her. She'd never realized how the brown of his irises shaded around the edges to a hue that matched the raven-darkness of his hair. Nor had she ever noticed the fine flecks of topaz and carnelian—

Way to go, Pamela Gayle, the small voice that had goaded her earlier piped up snidely. *You're really in control now. What's next on the schedule? Melting into a puddle the way you almost did last night when he chucked you under the chin?*

Peachy blinked several times, feeling the humiliatingly familiar surge of hot blood rushing up her throat and into her cheeks. She searched her response-fogged brain, trying to remember what Luc's last words to her had been. Something about a promise that from this moment on—

Oh, yes. Right.

She withdrew her hands from his and folded them primly in her lap.

"Am I to take it that everything that's happened between us *before* this moment hasn't been?" she inquired, keeping her voice steady through sheer force of will. "By my choice, that is."

The question clearly caught Luc off guard. For a moment it looked as though his surprise might turn into anger. His eyes narrowed. His lips compressed into a thin line. The tanned skin of his cheeks seemed to tighten.

And then, astonishingly, his expression eased and he started to chuckle.

"*Touché,*" he said, miming a fencer's salute.

Although uncertain what Luc found so funny, Peachy succumbed to the lure of his laughter. By the time their shared merriment died away, she felt more relaxed than she had since she'd heard the announcement that the plane she was flying on was going to be forced to make an emergency landing.

"I'm still paying for dinner, Luc," she asserted a bit breathlessly.

"Of course, *cher,*" he responded with a roguish grin. "And this is still *not* a date."

Three

———

Lucien Devereaux was an attractive man.

A *very* attractive man.

This fact had registered on Pamela Gayle Keene in a multitude of ways the instant they'd met. Yet she would have sworn that her response to his compelling good looks had been essentially platonic until . . . oh, about twenty-four hours ago.

Forking up the next-to-last bite of the broiled grouper with tomato-tinged butter sauce she'd ordered for her entrée, Peachy assessed the tall, self-contained man sitting across the table from her through partially lowered lashes and uneasily contemplated the implications of what seemed to be her abrupt change of attitude.

Take Luc's hair, for instance. She'd noted its rich, raven-wing darkness and luxuriant thickness in the past, of course. But had she ever before felt the urge to stroke it that she was experiencing at this very moment?

Not that she remembered.

That she'd been prompted to try to capture her landlord's distinctive, slightly asymmetrical features on a sketch pad many times was something she would readily admit. Why shouldn't she? She was an artist, after all. She'd been trained to react to the visually interesting. And heaven knew, Luc's face was that . . . and more.

The boldly marked brows.

The arrogant nose and sharply angled cheekbones.

The mobile mouth, bracketed by experience-etched grooves.

She'd drawn these features over and over again. Yet never until now had she wondered how they might contort at the instant of sexual release. Never until now had she wondered whether sleep might relax their disciplined maturity sufficiently to reveal a hint of the boy he once had been.

At least, she didn't *think* she'd wondered.

Peachy shifted in her seat, crossing her right leg over her left. The stir of silk skirt over nylon stocking sent a shiver coursing through her.

Was it possible that at some subconscious level—?

She denied the notion before it was fully formed. While she'd be the first to concede that she could be oblivious to certain facets of her nature at certain times, she wasn't completely lacking in self-awareness.

And yet . . .

Peachy's mind flashed back to the potent effect Luc's touch had had on her the evening before. Then it jumped forward to the moony-goony way she'd behaved just a short time ago when she'd been gazing into his eyes.

His eyes.

Oh, Lord. Luc's *eyes!*

The searching intelligence in them had impressed her from the very first. She'd seen them glint with anger and spark with humor more often than she could count during the past two years. And she'd seen them turn brooding, too. But until a short time ago she'd never realized that their expressive brown depths contained so many different—

"You know, *cher*," Luc said suddenly. "There's something I've been curious about."

Peachy started, nearly dropping her fork. She drew a tremulous breath, wondering how much of what she'd been thinking might have shown on her face. If Luc had any idea what was going on inside her head . . .

Not that there was anything wrong with her thoughts, she quickly assured herself. Luc had said that they needed to become "aware" of each other as man and woman, hadn't he? Well, that's what she was doing! And given the circumstances, it was a darned good thing her burgeoning awareness of her partner-to-be was as, uh, uh . . . *positive* as it was.

She just had to be careful that it didn't become *too* positive. She had to keep things in perspective. And above all, she had to remember her pledge to Luc that all she wanted from him was a no-strings-attached, one-time-only encounter.

"You want to know what the National Football League *really* thinks about Terree LaBelle?" she suggested after a moment or two.

Her dinner companion gave her an odd, assessing look, then started to smile. "I wouldn't mind having the inside scoop on that, either," he admitted. "But at the moment I'm more interested in finding out how you came to be 'Peachy' Keene."

"You mean . . . how did I get my nickname?"

Luc nodded.

Peachy lifted her napkin to her lips and patted, trying to hide the rush of relief she felt. Questions about her nickname she could handle. She'd had lots of practice with it. Almost as much as she'd had responding to inquiries about whether her hair color was natural.

"You know my real name is Pamela Gayle, right?" she asked.

Luc nodded, taking a sip of the white wine he'd ordered to accompany her grouper and his shrimp *étouffée*. "I seem to recall reading it on your lease."

"Well, when I was little, my dad used to call me by my initials."

"P.G."

"Mmm-hmm." She smiled fleetingly, remembering. "I loved it. Because people called him—still call him, actually—by his initials. J.R., for John Russell. It was like a special bond between us. Anyway, I insisted on referring to myself as P.G. The problem was, I had a bit of a speech impediment when I was small. Not a lisp, exactly. But I kept saying 'shee' instead of 'gee.'"

"Pee . . . shee," Luc said slowly, seeming to taste the syllables. "Which eventually became Peachy?"

"Exactly."

"Hmm."

"I realize 'Peachy Keene' probably sounds like a joke to some people. Which is why I don't use it for dignified legal documents like leases. But other than that . . ." Letting her voice trail off, Peachy fluffed her hair with her fingers then asked, "I don't really think I'm a 'Pamela,' do you?"

She was flirting, she realized a moment later. Not a lot. And probably not too skillfully, either. Flirting wasn't exactly her modus operandi when it came to dealing with members of the opposite sex. But the impulse to tease Lucien Devereaux—at least a bit—was suddenly irresistible.

No. Wait, she amended. *Teasing* wasn't quite the right word for what she felt impelled to do. It was more a matter of...of...*testing*.

And not just him, either. In some strange way, Peachy felt she was testing herself as well.

Luc's eyelids came down a fraction of an inch. The left corner of his mouth curled upward. What had been an introspective expression suddenly became very, very knowing.

"No," he responded, his voice soft, the quirking of his lips becoming more pronounced. "You're a lot of things, *cher*. But you're definitely *not* a 'Pamela.'"

There was a short pause. Peachy took a drink of wine. Luc did the same.

"I take it you're close to your father," he eventually observed, toying with the stem of his glass as he gazed across the table at her.

"Oh, yes," she affirmed, trying to ignore the evocative movement of his lean fingers. The skin of her inner wrists tingled where he'd caressed her with his thumbs earlier in the meal. "Very. And to my mom, too, of course."

"Of course." The words held a faint edge of bitterness.

There was another pause, more awkward than the previous one. After a few moments, Luc glanced away. A moment after that, he lifted his wineglass and drained it.

What was she supposed to say now? Peachy wondered, picking up her own glass and taking a small sip. Given what she'd been told by the MayWinnies and Laila Martigny, it seemed ill-advised to opt for the obvious conversational ploy of shifting the discussion from her mother and father to his.

And yet, mightn't failing to make *some* comment about Luc's parents create the impression that she'd been prying into his background? Although she was prepared to admit that she hadn't shut her ears to what their mutual neighbors had to say, she didn't want him to get the notion that—

"I gather you know mine was not the happiest of families," Luc remarked, bringing his eyes back to meet hers.

Peachy hesitated, briefly considering whether she should deny knowing any such thing. She decided against it for a variety of reasons, not the least of which being that she was a lousy liar.

"I've heard a few things," she finally admitted, choosing her words with care. "I mean, I know your mother and father weren't—uh—didn't—"

"My father was obsessed with my mother and drank because he understood that marriage didn't mean she was truly his," Luc said with trenchant precision. "My mother was obsessed with herself and did as she damned well pleased."

For a split second Peachy thought the lack of inflection in his voice signaled genuine indifference and felt a strange sort of relief. Then she realized it signified precisely the opposite.

She reached for her wineglass with a hand that was not quite steady. "And you were caught in the middle."

Luc's control cracked for just an instant. His eyes flashed, the look in them so dangerously incendiary that Peachy felt herself flinch away from it. Then they turned opaque as stone.

"I learned to fend for myself at an early age," he replied.

Peachy believed it. And something inside her ached as she did so. But she didn't dare show it. Every instinct she had told her that even the slightest hint of sympathy would be rebuffed.

She cleared her throat. "They're . . . dead now? Your parents, I mean."

There was a pause. Luc's features tightened, suggesting some sort of internal conflict. Finally he said, "They were killed in a car crash. Together."

"Oh." Her response was little more than a shaky exhalation. While she'd known his mother and father were no longer living, she'd not been privy to details about their demise.

Luc's mouth twisted. "My father was driving drunk and smashed through the guardrail on a bridge. The official verdict was that it was an accident."

That he harbored doubts about the validity of this judgment was obvious. But Peachy shied from inquiring why. Instead she asked, "How old were you—?"

"Nineteen. I was in my second semester of college. I dropped out. I enlisted a few months later."

The question of what he'd done during those few months trembled on the tip of Peachy's tongue. But before she could find the nerve to voice it, the sommelier, their waiter and a pair of busboys converged on their table. By the time they'd performed their various duties and bustled away, the option of asking was gone. Luc's mood had changed. Whatever impulse had prompted him to lower his guard to a degree unprecedented in her experience with him clearly had been reined in. His defenses were back up.

Deciding the ball was in his conversational court, Peachy turned her attention to the dessert menu their waiter had presented after he and the busboys had cleared the table. It took her a good minute or two to mentally debate the merits of bread pudding soufflé with bourbon sauce versus a classic *crème caramel* versus a "tasting" of fresh sorbets and fruit. Not only did Luc fail to utter a single word during the entire process, he also remained silent once she'd closed the menu and set it aside.

She gazed across the table at him.

He gazed back. Steadily. Inscrutably.

Although it was not a character trait of which she was particularly proud, Peachy knew she was capable of being extremely stubborn. Pigheaded, she supposed some would say. So if Lucien Devereaux wanted to test her will by refusing to speak, that was just fine and dandy with her. She could wait him out.

Couldn't she?

Well...

Uh, maybe...

"Look, Luc," she suddenly blurted out. "I don't want you to think that I spend a lot of time gossiping about you behind your back because I don't."

"No?" There was just enough spin on the word to make it impossible to determine whether it was meant to communicate skepticism or disappointment or a peculiar blending of both.

"No," Peachy insisted, then grimaced as honesty goaded her to clarify. "I mean—okay. Yes. I've talked about you with the MayWinnies, Laila and Terry. I admitted as much last night when I told you why I'd decided to ask you to, uh, help me out. But you're hardly our number-one topic of discussion!"

"Really." Luc began stroking the stem of his wineglass once again, seeming to mull over the implications of her last statement. "And just what—or should I say whom—*is* these days?"

Peachy looked away. Although she'd spoken the truth a moment ago, it hadn't quite come out as she'd intended.

"Peachy?"

Sighing, she turned her eyes back to his and answered, "It's Mr. Smythe."

Mr. Smythe—Mr. Francis Sebastian Gilmore Smythe, to be precise—had joined the Prytania Street ménage about four months ago. A soft-spoken Englishman of sixty or so, he'd moved into the ground-floor apartment that previously had been occupied by Remy Sinclair, a rotund, bayou-bred pasty chef who hero-worshipped Elvis Presley. Remy had given up his lease after marrying a woman he'd met during one of his periodic pilgrimages to Presley's home, Graceland. The two had recently opened a road-house-cum-restaurant about fifteen miles outside of New Orleans.

Elegant and erudite, Smythe described himself as a semiretired dealer of *objets d'art*. Having joined him on several visits to the antique shops of the French Quarter's Royal Street, Peachy knew he had a connoisseur's eye and expertise. But there was something about him . . .

"Mr. Smythe, hmm?" A hint of amusement flickered across Luc's angular face.

"The MayWinnies say he reminds them of Cary Grant in that movie where he played a cat burglar," Peachy commented, wondering at his expression. "The one with Grace Kelly?"

"*To Catch a Thief.*"

"That's it."

"The Misses Barnes are worried about being robbed in their beds?"

The question caught Peachy off guard. "To tell the truth, I think they might enjoy that."

The rather slanderous implications of this comment sank in a split second later and she began to blush. Luc's reaction was an arched brow and a genuine laugh.

"Assuming it was Mr. Smythe doing the larcenous deed, of course," he amended.

Peachy eyed him uneasily. "You won't tell them what I said, will you?"

"The MayWinnies, you mean?"

"Or Mr. Smythe, either, for that matter."

"I'm nothing if not discreet, *cher*."

The response was silken in tone. It was also punctuated by a smile that started out seeming extremely straightforward then turned extraordinarily complex. The combination sent a quicksilver frisson arrowing up Peachy's spine.

Her pulse scrambled.

So did her thoughts.

It was not until a moment *after* their waiter reappeared to take their dessert order that she realized Luc hadn't actually given her the assurance she'd sought. By then it was too late to pursue the matter.

"*Mademoiselle?*" the server inquired politely.

Peachy blinked several times, trying to recall which dessert she'd settled on. "The, uh, sorbets with fruit, please," she finally managed to request.

"Coffee?"

"Um, no." She shook her head, conscious of the shifting of her long, curly hair. "No, thank you."

The waiter angled his gaze toward Luc. "And for you, Monsieur Devereaux?"

"*Café brûlot, s'il vous plait.*"

"*Très bien. Merci.*"

Maybe now's the time to take another crack at that "regaining control" effort you mentioned earlier? the little voice in the back of Peachy's skull queried, reasserting itself with sardonic force after nearly an hour of silence as the waiter moved away.

Leave me alone, Peachy snapped silently.

It was only a suggestion, Pamela Gayle.

Yes, well, when I want a suggestion, I'll give it to—

The realization that Luc had said something to her put an abrupt period to this mental slinging match.

"Ex-excuse m-me?" she stammered.

"I asked about the wedding you went to last weekend," came the smooth reply.

"Oh . . . well . . ." Peachy took a moment to put her thoughts in order. "The groom was Matthew Powell. His brother, Rick, is married to my older sister, Eden. They—Eden and Rick—came to visit me not too long after I moved in on Prytania Street." She paused, thinking back. "I'm pretty sure you met them."

Luc frowned. "Was this during Terry's Eleanor Roosevelt phase by any chance?"

"Terry's Eleanor—" Peachy started, then broke off as the floodgates of memory opened. A bubble of laughter escaped her. "Oh, Lord. I'd completely forgotten about that! Yes. It was. I introduced them to him. Eden was a little taken aback by his appearance even though she didn't have the faintest idea who Terry Bellehurst was. And Rick—well, he's a huge sports fan and he nearly choked. Still, Terry was so . . . so *Terry* that he put them at ease within a couple of minutes. At which point Remy showed up with a plate of profiteroles."

"A nice, neighborly gesture."

"He was wearing one of his spangled Elvis does Las Vegas jumpsuits, Luc."

"Ah."

"Then the MayWinnies dropped by to do their patented sweet-little-old-ladies routine."

"In stereo."

"Except when they were finishing each other's sentences."

"No Laila?"

Peachy smiled ruefully. Laila Martigny would have lent a much-needed touch of sanity to the proceedings.

"Unfortunately, no," she replied. "She was out of town. But someone mentioned her—and her alleged psychic powers *and* her supposed connection to Marie Laveau."

"You know, you're right," Luc declared, nodding. "I *did* meet your sister and brother-in-law. And I distinctly remember them seeming a bit uncertain about your choice of residence."

"*Uncertain?*" Peachy rolled her eyes. "They were begging me to move back to Atlanta before we ran into you. Luckily, you managed to reassure them that everything wasn't quite as laissez-faire as it appeared."

"Me?" Luc lifted his brows and flashed an ironic smile. "I think not, *cher.*"

"Think what you want," Peachy retorted, the nearly two-year-old memory of a brief hallway encounter between her sister, brother-in-law and the man she would one day ask to do her the most intimate of favors very clear in her mind. "I know what you did."

Their waiter returned. He presented Peachy's dessert with a flourish, then deftly performed the ritualized flaming of a brandy-soaked sugar cube for Luc's *café brûlot.*

"*Merci,*" Luc said when he'd been served.

"*De rien,*" the other man responded, surveying the table. After a moment or two he gave a satisfied nod, then pivoted and walked away.

Luc took a long sip of his liquor-laced coffee. Peachy sampled what turned out to be a scoop of mango sorbet. The taste was subtly sweet and exotically refreshing.

"And what about the bride?" her dinner partner eventually asked, setting down his gold-rimmed china coffee cup. "The one who married your sister's husband's brother."

Peachy paused in the act of spooning up a chunk of fresh pine-apple, oddly annoyed by Luc's decision to allow her to have the final word in their previous exchange. She knew he wasn't doing so because he'd accepted her assessment of what had happened when he'd met Eden and Rick. Quite the contrary.

Why, she asked herself, was he so stubbornly resistant to the idea that he might have a positive impact on someone? That Lucien Devereaux was not a candidate for canonization was beyond dispute. But it was a long fall from less-than-saintly to unredeemable sinner. Yet it was her increasingly strong impression that it was the latter category to which he considered himself inalterably consigned.

"Peachy?" Luc prompted.

She blinked, snapping out of her troubling reverie. "Oh. The bride. Her maiden name was Martin. Hannah Elaine Martin. But everybody calls her Annie. She's a Wedding Belle, like me."

"I . . . beg your pardon?"

"A Wedding Belle," she repeated, instinctively lifting a hand to her throat. She grimaced when she realized the futility of the gesture then looked across the table and asked, "Have you ever noticed the silver locket I wear?"

A peculiar expression flickered through Luc's eyes. "Once or twice."

"I don't take it off very often," Peachy felt compelled to explain. "But Terry said I should if I wore the gold and jade earrings, so . . ." She gestured. "*Anyway.* It's shaped like a bell. My sister Eden gave it to me about ten years ago when I was one of her bridesmaids. There were three of us. The others got lockets, too. And somehow, we ended up nicknaming ourselves the Wedding Belles. That's B-E-L-L-E-S, by the way."

"I see." Luc tapped a finger against the rim of his coffee cup. "Who's the third Belle?"

His curiosity surprised Peachy. "Her name's Zoe. Zoe Armitage. She went to college with Eden and Annie. She grew up all over the world, but now she lives in Washington, D.C. She's a social secretary for—"

"Arietta Martel von Helsing Flynn Ogden." Luc pronounced the name as though it were a royal title.

Something unpleasant twisted to life in Peachy's stomach. "You . . . know her?"

"Mrs. Ogden? Only by reputation. She used to be a relative by marriage of someone I served with in the army."

"No." Peachy shook her head. "Zoe."

"Oh." Luc picked up his coffee cup and took another sip from it. "Yes. I met her at a party in Georgetown about eight months ago. It was when I was up in D.C. doing research for my new book."

A surge of emotion that felt uncomfortably close to her adolescent insecurity about her appearance washed through Peachy. In her mind's eye she saw Luc and Zoe together. They made a striking couple. He, dark and suave, like a hero in one of his bestselling thrillers. She, golden-haired and serene, like the princess in a fairy tale.

"Zoe's very beautiful," Peachy commented. She told herself she was stating fact, not fishing for feedback.

"If one has a taste for touch-me-not blondes," Luc agreed, his tone maddeningly ambiguous on the issue of whether he should be included among those who did. "We only spoke for a few minutes. As I recall, Zoe mentioned knowing you and asked how you were doing." His mouth curved into the same ironic smile he'd flashed earlier. "I was very reassuring."

There was another break in their conversation at this point. Peachy returned her attention to her dessert. Her dinner partner continued drinking his *café brûlot*.

Finally he asked, "So how did this weekend's happy couple get together? Did your sister decide to do some matchmaking on behalf of one of her Wedding Belles?"

Peachy took a second to swallow a spoonful of a sorbet so intensely purple she'd wondered whether it might stain her tongue.

"Heavens, no," she answered. "As a matter of fact, it was Annie who introduced Eden to Matt's brother, Rick. Not that she was trying to pair them up. Annie doesn't think that way. It just . . . happened. As for her and Matt—well, they were born twenty-four hours apart in the same hospital and grew up living next door to each other. They were best buddies from diaper days. Matt fell in love with a girl named Lisa in high school and married her after he graduated from college. She died of cancer a few months before their fifth wedding anniversary. He had a really rough time, but Annie helped him through it. Eventually he decided he should try to ease into the single social swing and he asked her to give him some advice. I'm not clear on all the details, but one thing led to another and Annie ended up saying 'I do' exactly one week ago."

"Quite a story," Luc said.

"But not quite your style?"

"Well . . ."

Peachy smiled, then let her thoughts drift back seven days. Memories—lush, lambent and loving—filled her mind.

"Annie and Matt looked so happy when they faced the congregation after the minister had pronounced them husband and wife," she murmured. "And I remember thinking, these two people have been friends for more than three decades. That's longer than I've been alive! Can you . . . can you *imagine?*"

Caught up in a sweet haze of romantic recollection, she meant the inquiry rhetorically. It wasn't until Luc spoke that she realized he'd taken it to be a serious question.

"No," he answered. "I can't."

For the second time that evening, Peachy's breath seemed to solidify someplace between her lungs and her lips. She stared at the man sitting opposite her for several long moments. He stared back, his eyes stark, his expression challenging. Once again, she had the unnerving sense that he was trying to put his worst face forward.

"Is it long-term friendships in general you can't imagine," she asked slowly. "Or just ones between men and women?"

That he hadn't expected her to press the issue was obvious from a sudden stiffening in his posture. His broad shoulders went rigid beneath his immaculately tailored jacket. The small muscles along his jawline quilted.

Yet he didn't look away. Their eyes remained locked together. But whether her gaze was holding his or his was holding hers, Peachy couldn't tell. The balance of power seemed to shift from second to second.

"The latter," Luc eventually replied.

"You don't trust women," she asserted. He didn't trust himself, either, apparently. But that wasn't a topic she was prepared to broach.

Not yet, at least.

Perhaps she never would be.

Lucien Devereaux didn't move. He didn't even blink.

"Present company excluded, no," he said after a moment, his voice as colorless as a pane of glass. "Not much."

Peachy took a deep breath.

"Do you really?" she challenged, lifting her chin a few degrees. She was conscious that her heart was beating very, very quickly and wondered fleetingly if the jump of her pulse was visible at the base of her throat. The notion that it might be renewed the sense of vulnerability she'd felt earlier in the evening. But she steeled herself to go on. "Exclude present company, I mean."

The man Pamela Gayle Keene had asked to be her first lover remained silent for what seemed to her to be an extraordinarily long time. His response, when it came, was a question she'd already put to him.

"Is there some reason why I shouldn't?"

Four

Peachy and Luc left the restaurant about a half hour later, the issues of who trusted whom—to say nothing of exactly how much and precisely why—no closer to being resolved than when they initially had been raised.

Despite an uneasy sense that he was only delaying the inevitable by doing so, Luc declined to pursue the subject. He was relieved to find that Peachy seemed willing to let the matter drop, as well. At least for the time being.

His would-be bedmate was much less passive when it came to dealing with the question of how they should get back to their Prytania Street apartment building. For a variety of reasons, including a genuine concern about the apparent impracticality of the high-heeled sandals she was wearing, he suggested telephoning for a taxi. Peachy countered that her shoes were a lot sturdier than they looked and declared she'd much prefer to walk home.

"It's such a lovely night," she told him. Then she smiled, the slow curving of her coral-pink lips carrying an uncharacteristic hint of coquettishness. "Besides. You said yesterday that we need to get to know each other better. Don't you think a stroll in the moonlight might further the cause?"

It wasn't a matter of "might." Luc knew, with absolutely certainty, that it would. What he *didn't* know was whether "furthering the cause" was a wise idea in his present state of mind.

That his abiding physical attraction to his redheaded tenant might escalate once they began spending time together was something he'd anticipated and braced himself against. And despite a growing realization that controlling himself might be more difficult than he'd expected, he remained fully confident that his head was capable of cooling off anything his hormones chose to cook up. But when it came to coping with some of the other urges he'd started to feel . . .

No matter that he'd sensed Peachy's potential for disrupting his life the first time they'd met. He'd still been totally unprepared for the contradictory impulses she'd evoked in him during dinner. One moment he'd been filled with an almost overwhelming desire to take her into his arms and hold her close. The next he'd been seized by an equally powerful need to push her as far away from him as fast as he possibly could.

And the things he'd told her! About his parents. About their marriage. About their deaths. Those topics had always been off-limits in his relationships with women. Except for Laila Martigny. But since she knew most of the unpleasant details from firsthand observation—

The sound of his name being spoken with a prompting inflection jerked Luc's attention back to the business at hand. Drawing a steadying breath, he focused on Peachy's face. He saw that her coaxing smile had been replaced by a faintly worried—or was it wary?—expression.

Careful, he warned himself. Be very . . . careful.

"You're sure you want to walk, *cher?*" he asked.

"Absolutely."

"Well, in that case . . ."

It *was* a lovely night, Luc reflected as he and Peachy ambled along in companionable silence. The sky was midnight blue and spangled with stars. The full moon shone against it like a newly minted coin. The breeze-stirred air was sweet with the scent of azaleas and other spring flowers. While the fragrance was less intoxicating than it would be a month or so hence when the Garden District's full complement of sweet olive, jasmine, gardenias, oleanders and bougainvillea were in riotous bloom, it was still capable of hazing the human brain.

"Do you know what I like best about New Orleans?" Peachy asked as they strolled beneath the gnarled, moss-draped branches of a huge old oak tree. Her tone suggested she'd been giving the subject considerable thought.

Luc slanted a glance to his right, his gaze resting briefly on the alluring shape of her small, silk-sheathed breasts then lifting to her finely etched profile.

"There's a lot to like," he responded, sliding his hands into the pockets of his trousers and concentrating on moderating his stride. At five foot five to his six foot one, Peachy's steps were naturally shorter than his—even when she wasn't wearing high-heeled sandals.

"Too much, actually," she acknowledged with a lilting laugh. "But that's what's so wonderful. I mean...just look at the houses in this neighborhood." She gestured airily with her right hand. "Oh, sure. Some play it straight enough to please the strictest architectural purist. But most of them incorporate two or three or even four different styles. You've got Greek Revival married to Queen Anne iced with tons of Italianate ironwork. You've got French Second Empire meets Victorian, garnished with Corinthian columns and fanlight transoms. Anywhere else, these places would probably be condemned as eyesores by the local zoning board. But around here..."

"The concept of tasteful restraint isn't given much credence in our city," he agreed with a grin, trying to recall a description he'd once read. It had been written by William Faulkner and involved something about New Orleans being a place created for and by the unabashed senses.

"Exactly!" Peachy exclaimed. "There's an excess of everything here." She laughed a second time, a thread of mischief embroidering her humor. "Except, maybe, moral outrage."

"And *that's* what you like best?" Luc suddenly remembered that Faulkner had credited part of the Crescent City's unique character to voluptuousness. "The lack of righteous indignation?"

"Mmm-hmm."

"Careful, *cher.*" The tip of his left shoe connected with a pebble and sent it skittering ahead along the sidewalk. "You're starting to sound like a native."

"Merci, monsieur."

Although Luc tried to keep his gaze fixed forward as they strolled on, he found it drifting right again and again. For all that the brightness of her hair suggested Peachy was a child of lam-

bently golden sunshine, the cool silver of moonlight became her as
though she'd been born to it. It lent a shimmer to her fair skin. It
also underscored the spritelike delicacy of her features.

"It makes for a very intriguing combination, you know," he
observed after a block or two.

"What's that?"

"A self-proclaimed admirer of excess who's twenty-three and
never been kissed."

Peachy checked herself in midstride, coming to a halt. Luc
stopped walking, too. They pivoted toward each other.

"I've *been* kissed, Luc." She cocked her chin, seeming to dare
him to dispute her assertion. Although the moon's shadowy lumi-
nosity made discerning colors a tricky proposition, it was obvious
that her cheeks had gone very pink. "A number of different times,
by a number of different men."

Luc came very, very close to asking for specifics. But a split second before the query tumbled off his tongue he realized what he
was on the verge of doing and hauled the words back. It was none
of his damned business what Peachy had done or with whom she'd
done it!

Maybe it was the knowledge that he was not—absolutely, positively not!—going to make love with Peachy that had thrown him
so badly off-balance this evening, he thought suddenly. He wasn't
accustomed to having the sexual option so thoroughly closed off
to him. He *particularly* wasn't accustomed to being the one who'd
preemptively shut the door on it.

This was not to imply that he was in the habit of availing himself of every boudoir opportunity that came his way. Even during
his wildest period, he'd said no almost as often as he'd said yes.
What's more, he'd gotten increasingly discriminating as he'd gotten older. In fact if truth be told, he'd been selective to the point
of celibacy for the better part of the last six months.

He'd also been busy as hell working on his newest novel, but that
was another matter.

Nonetheless, he honestly couldn't remember the last time he'd
gone out with an attractive, available woman without believing that
there was at least a chance they would wind up in each other's
arms. Not necessarily a big chance. And not necessarily a chance
he'd seriously consider acting upon. But a chance nonetheless.

Lucien Devereaux was a man who enjoyed flirtation and foreplay. There were times when he almost preferred the preliminaries
to the ultimate consummation. And while he had no great fond-

ness for physical frustration, he'd never pressed a potential lover once she'd told him to stop. Not even on those not-infrequent occasions when his instincts had assured him that with just a little coaxing, a "stop" could be transformed into an enthusiastic "go-all-the-way."

"I stand corrected," he said quietly, disciplining himself to meet Peachy's challenging gaze without wavering.

She eyed him silently, the tilt of her chin still defiant, the stain on her cheeks still clearly visible. Finally, she gave a brusque little nod.

They resumed their walk.

After about a minute Peachy said, "I suppose you've wondered why."

Luc risked a quick sideward glance but couldn't see much. Her chin was down and her hair had swung forward, hiding most of her face. "Why, what?"

"Why I'm twenty-three and never been . . . you know."

Luc considered his answer for a second or two then carefully conceded, "I've given it some thought."

Peachy lifted her head and turned it in his direction. "Are you worried I might have some strange sexual hang-ups I neglected to mention yesterday?"

The possibility *had* occurred to him, but he'd quickly dismissed it. While he didn't doubt that Pamela Gayle Keene had a personality quirk or two, he sensed her psyche was free of any true darkness. Her aura was warm. Her manner, naturally giving. And whether she recognized it about herself or not, she had an intensely sensual nature. Five seconds of watching her fondle that Wedding Belle locket of hers had been enough to tell him that!

"I have a fairly elastic definition of *strange, cher,*" he said dryly.

Her eyes widened for an instant, then she gave another lilting laugh. "I'll keep that in mind."

"Forewarned is forearmed," he riposted.

She flashed him a saucy look. "*Especially* when it comes to kinky foreplay."

Luc lifted his brows, recognizing that they were veering into dangerously provocative territory but enjoying the give-and-take too much to disengage just yet. Still, he warned himself to watch it. He knew he had a real weakness for words. To put it bluntly, sexy talk turned him on. And unbedded though she might be, it seemed Peachy had a real knack for it.

"I hope you're not anticipating a great deal in that direction when you and I conclude our arrangement," he said after a moment.

An odd expression flickered across Peachy's face. She looked uncomfortable. Embarrassed, almost. Her gaze met his for the space of a single heartbeat then angled away. "No," she replied, a hint of huskiness entering her voice. "Nothing like that."

They continued onward.

Good, Luc told himself firmly, forking a hand through his hair. She's starting to have second thoughts. She's starting to wonder whether she really wants what she said she wanted.

And that was precisely what *he* wanted.

Wasn't...it?

Of course it was!

He didn't believe for an instant that Peachy had remained a virgin by chance. Somewhere along the line she'd made a conscious choice about staying chaste. And it was his gut-level conviction that if she abandoned that choice because of a temporary reaction to some not-quite plane crash, she'd end up regretting it for a long, long time. Perhaps for the rest of her life.

He wasn't going let that happen.

Why?

Good question, he acknowledged with a mental grimace. He'd never been one for the white knight routine. Call it an...aberration. But whatever his motive, he was determined to save Peachy from herself—to say nothing of the clutches of some on-the-make bastard in the bar of the Windsor Court Hotel.

"I think it all goes back to sex education," his companion abruptly volunteered.

"Sex education?" Luc repeated blankly.

"Uh-huh."

"You're saying you're still a virgin because of *sex education?*"

"More or less."

"I...see."

He didn't, of course. And the look Peachy gave him made it obvious that she knew it.

"I realize a lot of people think that sex education encourages kids to, uh, do it," she said earnestly. "That it gives them ideas they never would have had on their own. And maybe it *does* affect some of them that way. But in my case...well, I had this Human Sexuality course in eighth grade. It was the same year my sister Eden got married. I knew the basics before I took the class, of course. Still, I had a very rosy-colored view of what sex actually was."

"All candlelight, silk sheets and flower petals?" Luc intuited.

"Followed by crashing waves, fireworks and throbbing violin music," Peachy concurred with a touch of self-directed mockery.

"But no bad breath, body odor, infectious diseases or unplanned pregnancies."

"Exactly."

"So... this course rubbed your nose in reality?"

"I guess you could say that." The concession came slowly. "It emphasized that sex shouldn't be treated casually. That it shouldn't be a matter of itching a hormonal scratch. That it has *consequences*. I took those lessons, plus the feelings I got from watching my mom and dad and Eden and Rick, and I eventually came to the conclusion that I wanted my first time—and, hopefully, all the times that came after it—to be for love. Not liking. Or... lust. But *love*."

The nape of Luc's neck prickled. "You're saying you intended to save yourself for marriage?"

"Not necessarily." The response sounded totally candid. It was followed by a rueful laugh. "Although I *will* admit that I had a lot of white lace fantasies about the one guy I almost—"

Peachy broke off abruptly, then muttered something under her breath.

"The one guy you almost—what?" As if he really needed to ask.

"You don't want to know."

"Yes," Luc countered sharply. "I do."

They walked a few more steps in silence. Then Peachy sighed and said, "His name was Jake Pearman. He moved to town my senior year of high school and he sat next to me in English Composition. I fell madly in love with him. I wanted to marry him in the worst way."

Luc contemplated this scenario for a moment then dubiously inquired, "You honestly wanted to be Peachy... Pearman?"

"I *told* you I had it bad."

"How did Jake feel?"

"He said he loved me, too."

"And... you believed him."

"With all my seventeen-going-on-eighteen heart."

"What happened?"

"We decided we were going to go all the way the night of our graduation prom."

Luc thought back to his own high school days and hazarded a guess based on observation rather than personal experience. "The guy got drunk?"

"Plastered."

"And passed out before you and he could . . . do it."

"But *after* he'd thrown up on my shoes."

"Oh, Lord."

Peachy heaved another sigh. "We broke up a week or so later. Jake said he'd come to the conclusion that he was still in love with a girl from his old high school."

Luc felt an unexpected flare of anger. Talk about adding insult to injury! "I'm sorry, Peachy," he said softly, meaning it.

She glanced at him, clearly surprised. "Thanks. But after all this time . . . well, it's no big deal."

It was the same phrase she'd used to describe her request that he relieve her of her virginity. Luc hadn't believed it the night before. He didn't believe it now. But he decided not to press. If Peachy wanted to play down the hurt she must have felt, that was her privilege.

"At least tell me this Jake lived miserably ever after."

His request prompted a fleeting smile. "No such luck," came the wry reply. "He married the other girl. Last I heard, everything was hunky-dory with them."

They went on walking.

"An experience like that," Luc eventually said, glancing right yet again. "It didn't change your mind about wanting your first time to be for love?"

Peachy looked at him, her brows delicately raised. "You mean, did I consider doing it just for the sake of doing it? To satisfy my curiosity or something like that?"

No. That was not what he'd meant. Not at all. But the emotions that had prompted his question were so amorphous that he wasn't sure how to explain to her what it was he really wanted to know. If truth be told, he wasn't sure he could explain it to himself.

"Something like that," he reluctantly affirmed.

"Uh-uh." Peachy shook her head. Her hair rippled with the back-forth movement, a few strands iridescent in the moonlight. "In a funny way, what happened with Jake reinforced my feelings. Maybe it will sound crazy to you, but I decided that if he and I had truly been in love with each other, our prom night would have turned out a lot differently than it did."

It *did* sound crazy, Luc thought. Mainly because it seemed to be predicated on a romantic faith that was totally alien to him. Still, there was something strangely compelling...almost seductive...about her reasoning.

"You've gone out with other men," he said, knowing he was fishing but unable to prevent himself from baiting the conversation hook. "Since Jake."

"Oh, sure." Peachy's tone was definite. A little *too* definite for Luc's taste. "Not endless legions or anything. Design school didn't leave a lot of time for socializing. My apprenticeship was pretty demanding, too. And moving to New Orleans—well, even with the MayWinnies trying to fix me up and Terry cheerleading from the sidelines, it's taken me a while to figure out who's who and what's what. Still. I haven't spent the last five years being Sally-Stay-at-Home."

"But there hasn't been anyone..."

"No." She gave an edgy little laugh. "If there had been, I wouldn't be out tonight with—oh. *Oh.*"

Peachy stopped dead in her tracks. Luc halted as well. Once again, they turned to face each other.

"I'm sorry, Luc," she said, a stricken expression in her wide-set eyes. "That didn't come out—I mean, I don't want you to think—"

He silenced her by lifting his right hand and pressing it against her lips. He felt a tremor of response run through her at the instant of contact. A moment later she exhaled in a rush, her warm breath misting his fingertips.

"It's all right, *cher,*" he said, lowering his hand back to his side. His fingers were tingling. He curled them up and inward until the edges of their nails bit against his palm. "I understand. You told me last night. You've reordered your priorities. Now it's your *second* time—and, hopefully, all the times that come after it—you want to be for love."

"You're not—" she swallowed convulsively, her eyes flicking back and forth "—angry?"

"Not at all."

And he wasn't. Because Peachy had spoken the truth and the truth was something that he was beginning to understand he needed to keep very much in mind.

What she was doing with him had nothing to do with loving. Liking, perhaps. And trusting, too, it seemed—although he still found the notion vaguely unsettling. But loving?

No. Never.

As for what *he* was doing with *her*...

What could he say? He was acting out a lie. He'd made a pledge he knew he was going to do his damnedest to avoid keeping but he was pretending just the opposite.

Peachy would hate his guts if she ever found out, he thought grimly. And who would blame her? Certainly not he, and he could honestly argue that he was doing what he was doing for her own good!

"Luc?" his companion asked, sounding very uncertain.

He caught his breath, snapping back to the present. "Come on," he said, flashing a quick, careless smile. "We're almost home."

They reached Prytania Street about a minute later and turned east. Four more blocks, Luc calculated. Just four...more...blocks.

He suddenly wondered whether Peachy was expecting him to make some sort of move on her before they ended their "non-date." After a few moments of uneasy reflection he decided that it was very likely that she did.

He didn't *think* she was anticipating that they'd end up in bed together tonight. Nor did he think she'd try to play the seductress if he failed to come on strong. But he realized he couldn't be sure. Until twenty-four hours ago, he'd never thought Peachy would confess to being a virgin in one breath and ask him to deflower her in the next, either.

One kiss, he decided.

Or maybe...two.

But nothing too intense. Nothing terribly intimate. Just a preview of supposedly pending sexual intentions. Plus a prime opportunity for him to discover whether Peachy's mouth tasted as sweet as it—

No, Luc told himself sharply. *Don't even think about it!*

He kept his gaze locked straight ahead. Three blocks to go. Should he kiss her outside, standing on the sidewalk? he asked himself. Or at the entrance to the building? Or maybe he should wait until he'd walked her to the front door of her apartment before—

"How old were you the first time you made love?"

"What?" Luc asked, coming to an abrupt halt.

Peachy pivoted back to face him then repeated her question.

There was a long pause. Finally, flatly, he said, "I was sixteen the first time I had sex."

She blinked, clearly taken aback. "That's...young."

"Yes, well, my partner was considerably older." Luc averted his eyes. A sense of shame welled up within him. It was an emotion he hadn't experienced in a long time. Or if he had, he hadn't permitted himself to acknowledge the corrosive effect of it. After a moment he added, "Two years older than I am now, in fact."

There was a soft gasp. Almost stifled, but not quite.

The sound drew his gaze back to Peachy's face. She looked shocked. And there was something else in her expression as well. Something he couldn't quite get a fix on.

Tensely, he waited for her to speak. To question. To condemn. But she didn't utter a word. She just stood there, her eyes staring steadily up into his own.

"She was the wife of one of the men my mother slept with," he admitted baldly when the waiting became unendurable. "Or so I found out afterward."

"This woman deliberately seduced you?" Peachy's forehead furrowed like corrugated cardboard. She sounded appalled.

Luc gave a humorless laugh, remembering his sixteen-year-old self. What a mess he'd been! Filled with anger at his parents for their betrayals of each other and himself. Addled by the onset of biological urges he could barely control. And swinging helplessly between the adolescent extremes of soul-shriveling insecurity and mind-boggling arrogance.

God. He'd been a pathetically easy target.

"It didn't take much effort, *cher*," he said.

Peachy shook her head, seeming to deny his assessment. "I'm so sorry, Luc."

It was the last thing in the world he expected to hear her say. And compassion—or was it pity?—was the last thing he'd expected to see in her long-lashed eyes. But he heard and saw both and it shook him down to the very marrow of his bones.

"Why?" he challenged. "Celeste was very adept. Whatever her motives for doing what she did and however much she lied about them, she was extremely good to me in bed."

"What she did was *wrong!*"

"What she did—" he drew a short, sharp breath "—was no big deal."

He used the last three words deliberately, and he could tell from the sudden tightening of her features that Peachy recognized he was quoting her.

"She hurt you," she asserted after several seconds of coiled-spring silence.

He flinched. For all that he tried to control it, he actually flinched. "Maybe," he conceded. "But it was a long time ago. And unlike you, *cher,* I stopped aspiring to do things for love when I was a child."

Another blush unfurled across Peachy's cheeks. Her darkness-enlarged pupils expanded a few millimeters more. She looked away for a split second then looked back as though she couldn't help herself. She swallowed several times.

"Still . . ." she finally began, her voice like distressed velvet.

"Still . . ." he echoed, conscious that his center of gravity seemed to be shifting.

His mind flashed back to an exchange they'd had during dinner. He'd held out his hands across the table. After a tiny increment of hesitation, Peachy had taken them. He'd clasped her fingers with his own, then explored the exquisitely smooth skin of her inner wrists with the pads of his thumbs.

Would the rest of her be as intensely pleasurable to touch? Luc wondered, feeling the pressure of hot, heavy blood pooling in the flesh between his thighs. Would her breasts, for example, have the same sleek, satiny feel? Or her hips? Or her long, graceful legs?

Peachy invoked his name on a shaky whisper.

"Shhh," he soothed, bringing his hands up and placing them lightly on her shoulders. The jade green dress she had on bared them completely, although the neckline was modest in terms of its decolletage. After a moment he slid his palms inward to the base of her slender throat. He traced the shadowed indentation just above the collarbone then stroked up to cup her jaw.

Luc could feel the throb-jump-throb of Peachy's pulse. But as fast and frantic as her heart was pumping, he suspected it was outpaced by the pounding of his own.

One kiss, he told himself for the second time.

Or maybe . . . two.

But no more. And nothing—nothing!—without her explicit consent.

Peachy said his name again, this time on a rising note of inquiry. But beneath the confusion Luc heard an edge of frustration.

"I told you earlier," he said. "Everything that happens between us will be by your choice."

She blinked, apparently not understanding. Then her eyes grew round and her lips parted. "You mean *you* expect *me* to—?"

Luc shook his head. He tried not to expect anything from anybody.

"Your choice," he repeated simply.

Her choice, when she made it, was to kiss him.

At least that's how it started, Peachy told herself later. With *her* *kissing him*. But within the space of a few electrifying seconds . . .

Luc's mouth moved against hers with erotic expertise. But slowly. Oh, so slowly. He seemed to be willing to take all the time in the world. To stretch each instant of sweet, searching contact into a sensual eternity. It was as though nothing else mattered to him but pleasuring her.

Peachy's eyes closed of their own volition. She yielded to his experienced embrace with a greedy, grateful sigh.

Yes, she thought.

Oh . . . *yes*.

She began to angle her head even before she felt Luc's right hand, now curved at the back of her skull, coaxing her to do so. She opened to him like a flower, tasting his unique flavor as well as the lingering richness of the *café brûlot* he'd drunk.

His left hand trailed down her back and settled at the base of her spine, urging her closer with a splayed-finger caress. Peachy arched into the embrace, headily conscious of the hardening thrust of her promised lover's masculinity. With that consciousness came a quivering thrill of untested feminine power.

Their tongues met and mated. Teasing. Intertwining. Languidly evoking the give-and-take of a much more intimate coupling. Luc muttered something unintelligible against her lips, his voice low and urgent.

Peachy hadn't lied. She *had* been kissed before. But never had she been kissed in a way that caused her blood to roar so loudly in her ears she couldn't hear herself think.

Assuming she was, of course. Thinking, that is. Because there seemed to be some serious glitches between her brain and body. Inundated by sensation, the former seemed to have lost the knack of keeping track of what the latter was doing until after it had been done.

She had no memory of having lifted her arms to grasp Luc's shoulders yet she found herself clinging to them, her fingers clutching at the taut-muscled stability beneath his well-tailored jacket. Her head was spinning. Excitement, mostly. But probably a little oxygen deprivation as well, because she seemed to be having trouble breathing.

The kiss deepened. Became more demanding. Desire suffused her like a dark, rich wine. The bones of her legs started to liquify.

And then, without warning, the insidious little voice that had pestered her during dinner spoke up.

You know, Pamela Gayle, it began on a strange note of wonderment. *Maybe your first time will be for—*

The rest of the comment got lost in the shock of her realization that something was very wrong. Luc had broken off the kiss. He'd lifted his mouth from hers and was easing her away from him.

Peachy's eyelids fluttered open. It took her a second or two to focus, another second or two to bring herself to the point of coherent speech.

"Luc?" she finally managed, staring up at his face. His features were taut, his mouth compressed into a thin line, the flesh of his cheeks drawn hard against the strong bones beneath. And he wasn't even looking at her! His gaze seemed riveted on something behind her. "Wh-what's wrong?"

He stiffened slightly, his eyes shifting to meet hers. Peachy caught a split-second glimpse of emotion so starkly powerful that she started to step back.

The emotion vanished. Completely. As though it had never been there in the first place.

"It's all right, *cher,*" Luc said, his voice rumbling up from somewhere deep in his chest. His hands tightened against her waist, keeping her where she was.

All right? Peachy thought dizzily, resenting his restraining grip but dimly conscious that it probably was preventing her from toppling over. Was he *nuts?* Did he have any concept of what had just happened? Of how he'd made her feel? Of what he'd made her want to do with him?

Odds are, he has a pretty good idea, the little voice in the back of her skull snidely opined. *Number one, he's been with a whole lot of women. And number two, you've made it crystal clear to him that you're only out to get—*

Peachy throttled the little voice into silence by sheer force of will.

"Why did you . . . stop?" she asked Luc.

His sensually shaped mouth twisted into an almost-smile. The constraining hold gentled into a caress. "I stopped," he answered softly, "because I think we've done enough getting to know each other for one night."

"But—"

Once again, he stoppered her lips with his fingers. Then he said, "Trust me, Peachy."

Pamela Gayle Keene went to bed alone about forty minutes later, her body pulsing with carnal possibilities. She spent most of the remainder of the night tossing and turning and thrashing her sheets into knots.

Trust me, Peachy.

Luc's words—half command, half entreaty—lingered in her mind the way his kiss seemed to linger on her lips.

Did she trust the man she'd asked to be her first lover? she asked herself, staring into the darkness. *Did she?*

If she listened to her heart, Peachy knew the answer had to be yes. But if she listened to her head . . .

She had never deluded herself that Lucien Devereaux was some sort of saint. In point of fact it was his reputation as a distinctly *un*saintly character that had prompted her to ask him to perform the sexual initiation her brush with death had made her so determined to undergo.

But what if the Prytania Street gossip had it wrong? she wondered, her heart skipping a beat. What if Luc *wasn't* the consummate lover-and-leaver of women he was said to be? What if he were really—?

What? she demanded of herself. What if Luc were really *what?*

Peachy realized she had no idea.

She also realized that she intended to find out.

Which led to another critical question.

For all the extraordinary admissions he'd made to her tonight, did Luc really trust *her?*

Five

The knock on the door of Luc's fourth-floor apartment came shortly before ten the next morning. He wasn't surprised to hear it. He'd been expecting a visitation ever since some instinct had goaded him to open his eyes while he was kissing Peachy and he'd caught sight of Francis Sebastian Gilmore Smythe coming out of the front door of their Prytania Street residence.

"In a minute," he called, yanking the page he'd been working on out of his typewriter. Crumpling the sheet of paper into a ball, he lobbed it toward a wastebasket that was positioned about eight feet from where he was sitting. It bounced off the rim and landed on the scuffed hardwood floor along with a dozen or so similarly discarded pages.

There was another rap-rap-rap on the front door. The sound was polite but persistent.

"All right," he called again, picking up a mug from amid the clutter that covered his desk. He swigged down the mouthful of chicory-infused coffee it contained, grimacing slightly at the luke-warm liquid's bitterness. He replaced the mug on the desk with a *thunk*. "I'm coming."

Smothering a yawn with the back of his hand, Luc padded out of his small office on bare feet. His eyes felt gritty, as though their sockets had been lined with sand. The muscles of his neck and shoulders seemed to have been used for knot-tying practice by a pack of clumsy-fingered Boy Scouts.

A little more than ten hours had passed since he'd escorted Peachy home. Their parting had been an awkward one, full of aborted gestures and unfinished sentences but devoid of physical contact. Half of him had been desperate to get away from her. But the other half...

"I'll see you tomorrow, *cher*," he'd said as Peachy had stepped into her apartment.

His erstwhile one-night stand had turned, her green-gold gaze meeting his dark one with heart-stopping directness for a moment or two, then sliding away. The color in her cheeks had been high. Her hair, illuminated from behind by a light inside the apartment, had gleamed like a cloud of fine-spun copper.

"Tomorrow," she'd echoed throatily, then quietly closed the door.

Luc hadn't bothered with bed once he climbed upstairs to his own place. He'd known he wouldn't be able to sleep. His brain had been thrumming, his body throbbing. He'd debated briefly between two time-honored methods of dealing with sexual stress, then opted for the one that had never been alleged to cause pimples, impotence or hairy palms.

After emerging from a freezing cold shower he'd dried off, donned a well-worn pair of jeans and plunked himself down at his typewriter to work on his latest novel. Tentatively titled *Dark Horse,* it was supposed to be the same type of fast-paced thriller that had landed him on the *New York Times* bestseller list three times in a row. And indeed, he'd kicked the story off in his usual act-now-introspect-later style. But somewhere around the start of chapter three, his seemingly standard-issue protagonist had begun to exhibit some unexpected complexities. Shortly after that, his straightforward good-guys-versus-bad-guys plot had veered off on a morally ambiguous tangent. By the end of chapter four, he'd found himself in wholly unexpected territory.

Short of murdering his key characters and starting anew, Luc hadn't been able to come up with a plan for maneuvering his book back on its anticipated track. So after several weeks of escalating frustration he'd decided to go with the flow—if a lousy three-page-a-day output, one-third his normal rate, could be called a "flow"—and see where it took him.

His agent, who'd read the first half of his first draft, kept telling him that it was the best thing he'd ever written. Ditto, his editor in New York. There were times when Luc believed them. There were others—like the wee hours of this morning, for example—when he strongly suspected that their assessments were more than a few bubbles off literary plumb.

Luc reached his front door. He took a moment to mentally gird himself for the encounter he felt certain was to come then unlocked the dead bolt and swung the door open.

"Mr. Smythe," he said to the dapperly dressed older gentleman standing on his threshold. "I've been waiting for you."

Francis Sebastian Gilmore Smythe stepped inside, apparently unfazed by the tenor of this greeting. "So you *did* see me last night."

"Just a glimpse."

"Hardly surprising, what? You were a trifle . . . preoccupied."

Luc closed the door, knowing the choice of the understated adjective was a deliberate ploy by a skilled interrogator and warning himself not to react to it. He intended to acknowledge nothing about his behavior the night before, including the fact that "a trifle preoccupied" came nowhere near to describing the intensity with which he'd been focused on Peachy.

"That was a very neat about-face you did," he remarked after a moment.

The older man's steel-gray brows lifted a millimeter or two, the nonverbal equivalent of a *touché*. "Yes, well, I thought it better to nip back inside than to risk what might have been a rather awkward encounter."

"Mmm."

"Does Peachy—?"

"No."

Mr. Smythe eyed Luc assessingly for a second or two before observing, "All for the best, I daresay."

The inflection—half commenting, half questioning—was the essence of cunning. But once again, Luc disciplined himself not to rise to the conversational bait. He simply met his tenant's gaze with a steady stare.

"I see." There was a hint of rueful admiration in the older man's voice. "So it's going to be that way, eh? Well, lad, I can't say that I blame you."

Luc let his expression relax, just a little. "Do you want to do this standing up or sitting down?"

"Oh, sitting down, please," came the quick, courteous reply. "By all means."

Luc led the way into the living room and gestured for his visitor to take a seat. He was conscious that he probably was making a tactical error by allowing Mr. Smythe to become ensconced on his turf but decided he didn't really care. The pattern of this encounter had already been firmly established—probe and parry, inquire and evade.

"So?" he prompted once they were both seated.

Mr. Smythe cleared his throat and toyed with the gold signet ring he wore on the little finger of his right hand. "It's a bit difficult to know where to begin, actually," he admitted. "Prying into other people's personal lives is hardly my cup of tea."

"Oh, really?" Luc mentally reviewed the résumé he'd been given when his old Special Forces buddy, Flynn, had come to him with the story of a colleague of a one-time lover of a former relative by marriage who had a hankering to retire to New Orleans after a highly classified career with British Intelligence. "After thirty-plus years with MI5, I'd think you'd have quite a taste for it."

"That was business, dear boy. And I do wish you'd refrain from mentioning my former profession. I'm perfectly comfortable with your knowing the truth about my background, of course. Even without your connection to Gabriel Flynn, it's obvious from your books that you understand the nature of the game. But there are some *others*..."

"You don't want people asking you to dish the inside dirt on the royal family, hmm?"

Mr. Smythe looked pained. "It was unpleasant enough when people associated MI5 with traitors like Philby and Burgess and Blunt. And then there was that idiocy about James Bond and those ridiculous double-O licenses to kill. But lately—I mean, *really!* What in heaven's name is the tabloid press thinking of? British Intelligence, bugging Buckingham Palace?"

"You're telling me it was actually New Scotland Yard?"

"Hardly." The former Intelligence agent paused, studying Luc in the same assessing fashion he had minutes earlier. Then he said, "But I didn't come here to discuss the crumbling foundations of the House of Windsor, as well you realize. Let's cut to the heart of the matter, shall we? Aside from the fact that it's none of my business, what do you have to say about what I saw last night?"

"Nothing."

"I ... beg your pardon?"

"Aside from the fact that it's none of your business, Mr. Smythe, I have nothing to say about about what you saw last night."

"You were kissing that girl in the middle of the sidewalk!"

"'That girl' is a consenting adult," Luc retorted, surprised by how sharply his visitor's disapproval stung. The list of people whose opinions about his actions genuinely mattered to him was very short. He had no memory of having expanded it to include Francis Sebastian Gilmore Smythe.

"Her *age* is not the point."

Goaded, Luc snapped, "What is, then? My lack of discretion?"

An odd expression settled over the older man's distinguished face. He seemed to retreat into himself. Luc could practically hear the hum of what he knew to be an exceptionally clever brain shifting into a higher gear.

God, he thought. If Mr. Smythe should somehow figure out—

"Not . . . entirely," came the even response to his edged inquiry. The abstracted expression was gone. The older man's gaze was focused outward once again. "Although you might have chosen a less public venue for demonstrating your feelings."

Luc shifted, suddenly very uneasy. There was something unnerving about the way Mr. Smythe was looking at him. The expression in his eyes was so intent. *Tell me the truth,* it seemed to urge. *Tell me and I'll understand.*

For one lunatic moment, he seriously contemplated the idea of spilling the beans. Of offering Francis Sebastian Gilmore Smythe the unvarnished facts about what he was doing—or not doing—with Pamela Gayle Keene and why. Lord knew, it would be a relief to be able to confide in a man who—

A man who—*what?* he demanded of himself, shocked by the direction of his thoughts. Who'd been a total stranger to him a little more than four months ago?

And supposing he did tell? What did he expect would happen? That Mr. Smythe would hear him out then promise to support him in his deception? Maybe even provide him with a little fatherly counsel on how to pull it off?

Fatherly?

The muscles of Luc's stomach clenched like a fist at the word. Where the hell had *that* come from? he wondered angrily. He'd done without benefit of paternal advice—without paternal much of anything, in point of fact—for most of his life. The last thing he needed was a surrogate daddy figure!

"Luc?"

Luc stiffened. He stared at Mr. Smythe, hoping the confusion he was experiencing didn't show on his face. It occurred to him that he couldn't recall the last time this particular tenant had addressed him by his given name. He had no idea why he'd chosen to do so now.

"Would it ease your mind if I told you that my intentions toward Peachy are honorable?" he finally asked, his tone as rigid as his spine.

The older man cocked his head. "Define *honorable*."

Luc's hands fisted of their own accord. "I'm not going hurt her."

"But you recognize that you could." It was more assertion than inquiry and it cut like a surgical blade.

"I *won't*."

There was a pause.

"She's not your usual type, lad," Mr. Smythe commented after about fifteen seconds, steepling his fingers.

"What would you know about my 'usual' type?" Luc countered, clamping down on a surge of resentment. The older man was right in his assessment in every way that mattered, of course. And yet . . .

"Flynn had a few things to say on the subject. His notion of balancing the scales, I think. I don't know him all that well, but I got the distinct impression he wouldn't consider it cricket to tell you about me without telling me about you."

"You're right," Luc agreed, his mouth twisting. His former comrade-in-arms had a real fetish about fairness. "He wouldn't."

"I confess to making a few inquiries on my own, as well," the older man continued candidly. "Force of habit, I'm afraid."

"You pumped the other tenants."

"I indicated a vague interest, and several of them gushed information."

Luc thought he detected a faint hint of disappointment in this last remark. "Not as challenging as interrogating members of the former KGB, hmm?"

"Hardly. Although I will concede it was rather more amusing." Mr. Smythe paused, his expression turning reflective. "The odd thing is, I was beginning to wonder whether I'd allowed myself to be bamboozled. About your reputation with the ladies, that is.

Because until last night . . . well, frankly, dear boy, your behavior since my arrival has been positively monkish. Which isn't to imply I've had you under surveillance or anything distasteful like that. But living on the ground floor of this building as I do, I can't help noticing people's goings and comings. Or the lack of them, as the case may be."

Luc squelched an urge to ask what Mr. Smythe had noticed vis-à-vis Peachy's comings and goings, reminding himself as he had the night before that it was none of his damned business. "I've been working on a book," he offered by way of explanation for his recent celibacy.

"And you can't service both your literary muse and your libido?"

Luc rubbed his palms against his denim-clad thighs, feeling his muscles tighten. "Not this time out."

"You mean with your previous novels—?"

"No problem."

Mr. Smythe frowned, seeming to weigh what he wanted to say next very carefully. "I'm not doubting your word," he eventually began. "But what I witnessed last night—"

"I misjudged," Luc interjected. A rush of sensory memories— the sweet taste of Peachy's ripe mouth, the silken texture of her porcelain skin, the sunshine scent of her flame-colored hair—assailed him. He did his best to stem the seductive surge, to deny the potent physical responses it prompted. Exerting all his willpower, he forced himself to look his visitor squarely in the face. "Don't worry. It won't happen again."

There was another long pause.

"You're sure, lad?" Francis Sebastian Gilmore Smythe finally asked, a curiously gentle note entering his voice.

"I don't make the same mistake twice," Luc answered flatly, holding the other man's gaze. He still intended to carry through with his scheme to help Peachy, of course. But he would never again lower his guard around her the way he had the night before.

Never.

Ever.

"Well, in that case . . ." The older man inclined his head like a judge rendering a final verdict, then started to rise from his seat. "There's no need for me to trouble you further, is there? I do hope I haven't offended you. By coming here as I have, uninvited. By making inquiries about something which, as you very rightly emphasized, is absolutely none of my business. But I've grown quite fond of Peachy in the time I've known her, and what I witnessed last night—or thought I witnessed—well . . . I found myself feeling rather protective. Inclined to act in *loco parentis,* you might say."

"I understand." Luc got to his feet in a swift, seamless movement.

"Which isn't to say Peachy needs someone standing guardian over her," Mr. Smythe added wryly. "She's obviously a capable young woman."

"Very."

They walked slowly to the apartment door. As they reached it, Luc came to the startling realization that he didn't want his visitor to leave. While the earlier impulse to confide the truth about his involvement with Peachy had passed, he still felt a powerful urge to continue talking with the older man. "You're welcome to stay," he said abruptly.

"Why, thank you, Luc," Mr. Smythe seemed sincerely gratified by the less-than-gracious invitation. "I'd quite enjoy that. But I have another call to make."

"You're not going to see Peachy, are you?"

"You mean to discuss—? Heavens, no. Of course not. Wouldn't dream of it."

Luc shifted his weight from one foot to the other. "Uh...look," he began awkwardly. "You mentioned something a minute ago about hoping you hadn't offended me. Which was fine. Because you haven't. So I hope I'm not going to offend you either with what I'm about to say. Chances are, I don't really need to say it. But just in case—well, I'd really appreciate it if you'd keep our conversation to yourself."

"Ah." Mr. Smythe grimaced. "Rather difficult, that."

"Why?"

"I'm afraid my visit to you wasn't an entirely independent endeavor."

"You're saying someone else knows about me and Peachy?"

"Well—"

"Who, Mr. Smythe?"

Another grimace. "The Misses Barnes."

"You *told* the MayWinnies?"

"Good Lord, no!" The denial was underscored by a vehement head shake. "Never."

"Then how—?"

"One of them saw you, dear boy."

Luc felt as though he'd been slammed in the solar plexus with a sledgehammer. *"The May Winnies saw me kissing Peachy?"*

"Oh, no. They missed that bit," the older man swiftly assured him. "They went to a concert last night, you see. And shortly after they arrived home one of them—Miss Mayrielle, I believe it was—happened to glance out the front window of their apartment and noticed you escorting Peachy into the building. Which would have been fine. Two people. Walking together on a pleasant spring night. Perfectly innocent, what? Unfortunately, earlier in the evening Peachy rather coyly told Terry she was having dinner with a 'friend.' And Terry, incurable romantic that I gather he is, jumped to the predictable conclusion. He also apparently felt it necessary to share the glad tidings with his dear friends, the Misses Barnes. So when Miss Mayrielle spotted you and Peachy... well, it seems that as sanguine as she and her twin sister are about your amorous activities with *other* women, they're rather shocked by the prospect of you having your way with a young lady they regard as an honorary granddaughter."

"Oh, God," Luc groaned. When he thought of all the indiscreet things he'd done in all the ill-considered locations without once getting caught...

And then a question occurred to him.

"Just how do you know all this?" he demanded.

"From the Misses Barnes, of course. I encountered them downstairs in the lobby this morning. I was coming in from a walk. I usually take a stroll at night but well, it was no-go last evening, what? In any case, they—the Misses Barnes—were toddling out to church and their customary Sunday meal at Galatoire's. I could see they were rather distressed about something, so I inquired if I might be of assistance. One thing led to another and I ended up offering to speak to you. Man-to-man. Old bull to young buck and all that. They seemed most appreciative."

"But you didn't tell them—"

"Not a word." Mr. Smythe paused, his brow furrowing. "I was rather surprised, actually. By Miss Mayrielle and Miss Winona-Jolene confiding their anxieties to me, that is. Because I've always sensed a certain degree of...mmm...wariness in their attitude. Not that they haven't been perfectly charming. If charm were a toxic drug, those two ladies would be lethal. Nonetheless, I've felt they were inclined to hold me at arm's length."

"Yes, well, that's probably because they suspect you of being a gentleman bandit."

"What?"

Luc winced, realizing his slip. He hesitated, then decided he had no choice but to explain his careless comment. Without crediting Peachy as his source of information, he quickly recapped what she'd told him over dinner.

Mr. Smythe's reaction was intriguing, to say the least. He obviously was thunderstruck to learn of the MayWinnies' speculation about him. Yet beneath the astonishment lurked an unmistakable spark of masculine pleasure.

"I remind them of Cary Grant, you say?" he asked when Luc had finished speaking. He ran a smoothing hand down the front of his navy blue blazer. It wasn't exactly an act of preening, but it was close.

"In *To Catch a Thief*," Luc confirmed, amusement tempering his uneasiness about the welter of complications he saw arising from his decision to accept—or, rather, to pretend to accept—Peachy's proposal. If he'd had *any* idea . . .

Oh, but he had! As soon as he'd understood what his all-too-appealing tenant was asking of him Friday night, he'd refused. He'd seen the potential for bollixing up both their lives if he didn't, so he'd said no as kindly but as unequivocally as he could.

Only then Peachy had calmly declared that she guessed she'd just have to find somebody else to do the deed. Suddenly, rejecting her request that he deflower her had seemed like an untenable option.

And it still seemed that way, God help him.

"Do you think I should tell them?" Mr. Smythe asked.

Luc blinked. "Tell who what?"

"The Misses Barnes." The older man began fiddling with his cuffs. "Do you think I should tell them the truth about my background? I daresay the notion that their downstairs neighbor is some sort of notorious criminal is quite unsettling to the dear ladies."

"I think they can handle it," Luc said dryly. "You may not be aware of it, but those 'dear ladies' allegedly ran with a pretty wild crowd when they were younger."

"Well, yes. I *had* heard something to that effect. But even so . . ."

The decision to tell or not to tell was Mr. Smythe's, of course. But before he made it, Luc felt there were a few points that needed to be put on the record.

"Discovering they have a real-life spy skulking around their apartment building certainly would give the MayWinnies something to gossip about," he observed.

"Indeed." A frown. "They are rather fond of tittle-tattle."

"They might even tout your story to their grandnephew."

"Grandnephew?"

"Trench, I think his name is. No. Wait. It's *Trent*. Trent Barnes. He works for one of the local TV stations."

"Are you by any chance talking about the chap who interviewed Peachy after her plane nearly crashed? The one with the peculiar hair?"

Luc nodded, the reference to Peachy's brush with disaster sending a shiver up his spine.

"Good Lord." The older man seemed taken aback. "A journalist. I never made the connection. And the ladies certainly never mentioned—then again, if they think I'm some sort of international scoundrel they probably wouldn't, would they?"

"Probably not," Luc agreed. "You've got to factor Terry into the equation, incidentally. Because even if the MayWinnies *don't* tell their grandnephew about you, it's a sure bet they *will* tell Terry. And that could get sticky. Terry has a real thing for British royalty. Next to Eleanor Roosevelt, he thinks the Queen Mum is—"

"I quite understand," Mr. Smythe cut in, paling slightly. "I think I'll leave well enough alone for the time being." He paused, his expression becoming guarded. "I, ah, don't suppose you'd happen to know how Dr. Martigny comes down in all this? I mean...does she subscribe to any of the Misses Barnes's suspicions about me?"

Luc felt a flash of surprise at the question. Why in heaven's name would Mr. Smythe be interested in whether Laila—

Oh.

Hmm.

A Creole psychologist who'd worked her way through night school scrubbing other people's floors, dishes and dirty laundry and a retired secret agent who'd accepted an upper crust Eton-to-Oxford education as a birthright. Not the most obvious candidates for coupling he could think of. But not the least likely, either.

In fact...the more he contemplated the idea, the more he liked it. Hell. Once he resolved the situation with Peachy, he might even try to promote it!

"Laila Martigny doesn't subscribe to anything but magazines," he stated. "She makes her own judgments about people. Always has. Always will." He smiled crookedly, sifting through the few childhood memories he had that it didn't hurt to recall. "And the only reference to royalty I've ever heard her make involved the voodoo queen, Marie Laveau."

That the older man wanted to pursue the subject was plain. And for a moment or two, it seemed as though he might. But then he simply dipped his head and said, "Thank you, lad."

There was a long silence. Finally Luc asked, "So what are you going to tell the MayWinnies, Mr. Smythe?"

"Francis."

"Excuse me?"

"I'd very much like it if you called me Francis."

Luc hesitated, feeling strangely honored by the unexpected request. It was as though he'd been awarded a stamp of approval he hadn't known he was seeking. "All right," he agreed after a few seconds, not entirely certain what he might be letting himself in for by doing so, but oddly willing to take the risk.

"Good."

"My question still stands, Francis."

"As to what I'm going to tell the Misses Barnes about your intentions toward Peachy?"

"Yes."

Francis Sebastian Gilmore Smythe's mouth curved upward in a way that could only be described as conspiratorial. "I'm going to tell them exactly what you told me, Luc. What else?"

Peachy glared at the drawing on her sketch pad and decided it was about time to throw in her pencil.

She'd spent hours struggling to come up with a design for a very special brooch. The one-of-a-kind piece had been commissioned by an ardent admirer of Terree LaBelle. It was supposed to look like a Mardi Gras mask. Unfortunately, the rendering she'd just finished bore an unpleasant resemblance to the white plastic face protector worn by the homicidal maniac featured in a series of cheesy horror movies.

It's pretty awful, the obnoxious little voice inside her skull critiqued. *But it's better than the first couple you did. They were the spitting image of—*

There was a knock on Peachy's front door.

"Luc," she whispered. Her heart seemed to skip a beat. Maybe two. Her breath snagged at the top of her throat. There was a heated fluttering deep within her body.

He'd said he'd see her tomorrow. And since tomorrow was now today...

Too bad you didn't put on a little makeup, the ubiquitous voice sniped. *And maybe something* slightly *more attractive than baggy, four-year-old jeans and a ratty old sweatshirt. Or were you figuring Luc would just take you as you—*

Knock. Knock.

"Peachy?"

Knock. Knock.

"Honey?"

Peachy closed her sketch pad with a less than steady hand and set it aside. Just as it had been impossible not to recognize Terry Bellehurst's husky tones the night before, there was no doubting that the dulcet voices emanating from the other side of the door belonged to Miss Mayrielle Barnes and her younger-by-eight-minutes twin sister, Miss Winona-Jolene Barnes.

Knock. Knock. Knock. Knock.

"Are you home, dear?" Where the first two queries had been uttered solo, this one was performed in soft, sweet unison.

"Coming," Peachy called as she rose from the drafting table she had set up in the corner of her living room. She crossed to the front door, fluffing her hair and fussing with her sweatshirt as she went. The MayWinnies fervently believed that good grooming was crucial to female empowerment. Although she knew they'd never overtly criticize her appearance, she was certain they'd sigh inwardly about her failure to live up to her womanly potential.

How do you think they'd react if they found out about your propositioning your mutual landlord? the little voice inquired as she reached for the chain lock.

Peachy froze, her fingers spasming. Oh, God. She didn't even want to imagine that! The MayWinnies must never—*ever*—know about her and Luc.

"Peachy?"

"Just...just a second." She fumbled with the lock and finally managed to undo it. Then, after sucking in a steadying breath and squaring her shoulders, she opened the door.

"Good afternoon, dear," her silver-haired callers chorused, their sky blue eyes twinkling. Standing just slightly over five feet tall and weighing no more than one hundred pounds apiece, they were dressed in identical, raspberry-colored suits and matching raspberry straw hats. The lace-trimmed collars and cuffs of their identical white blouses frothed at their throats and wrists like whipped

cream. Their complexions were like crushed rose petals—wrinkled, yet retaining a subtle vibrance.

"Good afternoon, Miss May...Miss Winnie." Peachy hoped she was nodding at the correct woman as she spoke. She was too unsettled to search for the tiny visual clues she normally keyed on to tell the sisters apart.

"Are we catching you at an inconvenient time?" the twin she'd addressed as Winnie asked anxiously.

"We certainly don't want to intrude," the other twin added, equally worried.

"Oh, no." Peachy shook her head. "I was just, uh, working. On a commission."

"How wonderful!" the women exclaimed in delighted stereo.

"I just know you'll create somethin' beautiful," May—or was it Winnie?—gushed.

"Like those sweet flower pins you made us for Christmas," Winnie—or was it May?—added. "I can't begin to tell you—"

"—how many compliments we've had about them."

"They're just *darlin'!*" Both women beamed.

"Thank you," Peachy said, returning their smiles.

It was impossible not to be warmed by the older women's approval. They were, without a doubt, the most admiring people Peachy had ever met. Indeed, she was of the opinion that the MayWinnies' penchant for praising was a key reason for their reputed success with men. Forget psychotherapy and mood-altering drugs. Five minutes of basking in the Misses Barnes' relentlessly complimentary attention would persuade the wimpiest of ninety-pound weaklings that he was the stud muffin of the century.

"May we come in, darlin'?" Winnie—yes, it definitely was Winnie, the coy tilt of the head made that clear—asked.

"Just for a minute or two?" May coaxed with the downward dip of the chin that was one of her most appealing little mannerisms.

Peachy swatted a lock of hair away from her face, realizing that there was no polite way to refuse her next-door neighbors' request for admission. And even if there were, she wasn't sure she wanted to turn them away. She genuinely enjoyed visiting with the Misses Barnes. As long as she could keep them off the subject of Lucien Devereaux, she'd be okay.

"Of course." She gestured a welcome. "Please do."

The twins advanced into her apartment, murmuring flattering variations on their usual observations about the "original" decor. They eventually seated themselves on a chintz-covered settee

Peachy had scavenged from the streets during her student days in New York City then painstakingly reupholstered with fabric she'd purchased at a flea market.

"Would you like something to drink?" she asked, trying to remember what she had on hand. "Herbal tea? Fruit juice? Mineral water?"

"No, thank you," the sisters said, refusing simultaneously.

"We just had the most scrumptious luncheon at Galatoire's," Winnie noted.

"Fresh lump crab with mayonnaise," May explained. She pronounced the last word *my-nez.* "And shrimp remoulade to follow."

"I ate too much," the younger sister moaned.

"We *both* did," her older sibling amended. "And we *do* have to be careful."

"Because if we don't watch our girlish figures—"

"—no one else will!"

The twins exchanged glances at this point, then broke into merry giggles. Although she'd heard the joke more than a few times before, Peachy joined in the laughter as she sank into the overstuffed chair Luc had occupied Friday night. The MayWinnies' artless appreciation of their own humor was irresistible.

Eventually the laughter tailed off into silence. Peachy saw her guests trade looks again. Unlike the droll glances that had triggered the cascade of giggles, these looks looked very... well... *significant.*

"Uh—" Peachy began, scooting forward in her seat.

"We've been thinking about you, Peachy dear," May announced, folding her hands and crossing her ankles.

"About you and Daniel," Winnie specified, crossing her ankles and folding her hands.

"Daniel?" Peachy repeated blankly, then stiffened as her brain slotted the name into place. A series of internal alarms went off. "Oh. No. I mean, uh, he and I only went out once, Miss Winnie. And I, uh, I don't think that I, uh, we—I appreciate your having introduced us, of course. Because Daniel's, uh, well—" Lord. She couldn't even remember what the guy looked like! "He's very, uh, *nice—*"

The MayWinnies sighed, their eyes pools of profound regret. *"Exactly."*

"Excuse... me?"

Winnie gave her a just-between-us-girls smile. "Nice is nice, dear."

"But it's not really enough," May concurred with a knowing nod.

"We should have realized that. A young woman like you."

"So artistic."

"Bohemian, even."

"Why, you've lived in New York City!"

"You need—"

"—*want*—"

"—someone older than Daniel."

"Someone more experienced."

"Not *unnice*, of course."

"But less of a boy."

"More of a man."

They know, Peachy thought, feeling her entire face flood with hot, humiliated blood. Somehow. Someway. The MayWinnies know!

Was it possible Luc had said—?

No. Never.

Then who?

Terry.

Oh, God. Yes. Of course. It had to be!

Luc isn't going to be happy about this, you know, the little voice observed, quite unnecessarily. *You promised him no complications.*

And what about what she'd promised herself? Peachy wondered, digging her fingernails into the arms of the chair. She was still determined to be rid of her virginity. But she didn't want the circumstances of her defloration to be common knowledge!

"We have the perfect person for you," May said.

"We really should have thought of this long ago," Winnie confided.

"And the wonderful thing is—"

"—you've already met him."

"Miss May," Peachy began, desperate to prevent her guests from saying the name she knew they were on the verge of saying. "Miss Winnie—"

"It's our grandnephew. Trenton."

Peachy gaped, feeling as though every synapse in her brain had fused. "Wh—who?" she finally managed to stammer.

"You know him as Trent, dear," Winnie said.

"Trent . . . Barnes?" The name *was* vaguely familiar. But she couldn't think of why it should be.

"That's right," May affirmed with obvious pride. "He does the TV news."

"He interviewed you at the airport, darlin'. After your dreadful experience with that awful emergency landin'. He asked how it felt, knowin' you'd cheated death."

Peachy remembered. Abruptly. Explosively. The image of a newsman with crooked features and strangely immobile hair materialized in her mind's eye.

"Are you talking about the reporter with the broken nose and the weird, stuck-in-place ha—" she broke off, mortified by her tactlessness. "I—I'm sorry. I didn't mean—"

"Trenton doesn't fix his hair like that in real life," May interrupted soothingly, seeming unoffended by the less-than-flattering description of her relative. "It's just when he's doin' those stand-up things."

"Although it *does* look awful unnatural," Winnie remarked. "We've been considerin' askin' Terry what he uses when he's Terree."

"Terree's always so perfectly groomed."

"But without seemin' . . . *shellacked.*"

"And as for Trenton's nose—"

"Didn't some congressman punch him?" Peachy blurted out, a fragment of a conversation she'd overheard during the reception for Annie's wedding coming back to her. "Late last year? Around Christmas?"

"For the woman he loved," the MayWinnies chorused with great emotion.

"Huh?"

"The congressman," the younger sister hastened to explain.

"Not Trenton," her older sibling added. "He was trailin' after this Congressman Talcott Emerson III, thinkin' he was up to some hanky-panky with this divorced, beauty queen blonde. Only it turned out the congressman had truly lost his heart. Which is why he clobbered Trenton, 'cuz he felt Trenton was impugnin' his darlin's honor. They're engaged now. The congressman and the blonde, I mean."

"Trenton got fired from his station in Atlanta because of the incident," Winnie concluded. "Which is how he comes to be reportin' here in N'Awlins. May and I agree, he probably got what was comin' to him. Houndin' those two people was just plain tacky.

It's not as though the congressman was married. Or that he was doin' the deed and billin' the taxpayers. Why I can remember quite a few politicians—''

"*Winona-Jolene*," May interrupted in a shocked voice.

Peachy watched the two sisters do a little eyeball-to-eyeball communicating. After several silent seconds, Winnie turned back to her and limpidly declared, "I can remember 'em, dear, but I'm too much of a lady to name 'em."

"I completely understand, Miss Winnie," she assured the older woman, struggling not to laugh.

There was a pause.

"Well?" May finally nudged, her expression expectant.

"What do you think?" Winnie asked, going beyond expectant to eager.

"About me and, uh, Trenton?"

Two elegantly hatted heads nodded.

Peachy summoned up a bright smile and formulated a response she hoped committed her to nothing. "Have him call me."

The second visitor to Luc's apartment arrived roughly eight hours after Francis Sebastian Gilmore Smythe departed. He had not expected her. Afterward, he realized he probably should have.

"So," his caller began, sweeping across his threshold with her head held imperiously high. "First I hear from Terry that Peachy had a romantic rendezvous last night with some mysterious male 'friend' who has her so enthralled she's lost the ability to accessorize. Then I hear from the MayWinnies that this mysterious male 'friend' is you and that they plan to match Peachy up with their grandnephew—the television reporter with the environmentally offensive hair—to prevent you from seducing her as you've seduced so many others. And finally I hear from Francis Smythe that he's a retired spy, not an antiques dealer, and that I shouldn't worry about your intentions toward Peachy because the two of you have already settled the issue, man-to-man."

Luc closed the door. His hand had clenched on the knob at the reference to Trent Barnes. Peachy was *his*, dammit! he thought.

He caught his breath, shocked by the possessiveness of this last assertion. Peachy? His?

No. Not at all. Never.

Well . . .

All right. Perhaps Peachy was his. In a sense. But only temporarily. Only until she abandoned the notion of giving away her
virginity. Or until he succumbed to the—

No! Absolutely not!

Exhaling sharply, Luc forced himself to let go of the doorknob.
Then he turned to face the woman he considered the very antith-
esis of the female who had give birth to him. "You've heard a lot,"
he said quietly.

"Yes, I have," Dr. Laila Martigny, the mocha-skinned seventh
daughter of a seventh daughter, serenely agreed. She regarded him
with wise, topaz-colored eyes for several moments then said, "But
now, at last, I would like to hear the truth."

"Luc!" Peachy exclaimed about three hours later. She'd been
heading in to take a shower when she'd heard an imperative knock
on her door. "I—I didn't expect—"

But you hoped, didn't you? the little voice gibed.

"So I gather," Luc returned, his dark gaze flicking over her. "I
apologize for bothering you so late."

Peachy shifted her weight, her right hand creeping up to fiddle
with the bell-shaped locket that once again dangled at the base of
her throat. No matter that the bathrobe she had on covered her
from neck to ankle. There was something in Luc's eyes that made
her acutely aware that she was naked beneath the bulky garment.

"That's all right," she said, rubbing the silver pendant between
thumb and forefinger, trying to ignore the nubby tease of the terry
cloth against her strangely sensitized flesh. "And it's barely nine
o'clock. That's not late."

"Still..."

"Well, you *did* say you'd see me tomorrow," she reminded him,
her gaze drifting downward from Luc's compelling face to the triangle of hair-whorled chest revealed by the partially unbuttoned
shirt he had on. Her mouth went dry. She felt herself start to flush.
She glanced away and went on, babbling, "Which is now. Today,
that is. Only it was tomorrow yesterday. Last night, I mean. When
you, uh, said you'd...uh...see me."

Would you care to rephrase that, Pamela Gayle? the relentless
inner voice queried sarcastically. *With just a little more effort, you
could probably sound* totally *incoherent!*

"And here I am," Luc replied with a touch of irony. "Seeing
you."

Peachy forced herself to look up into his face again. "Do you—" she swallowed "—want to come in?"

Luc's eyes narrowed. The right corner of his mouth indented. After a moment he shook his head and softly said, "Not tonight."

Her heart lurched.

"Oh," she finally forced out. She had no idea what she was feeling. Maybe nothing. Maybe something so intense her emotional circuits refused to register it.

"I wondered if you'd like to go dancing."

"N-now?"

Luc put his hands in the back pockets of the well-worn jeans he was wearing. The movement pulled the denim taut against his flat belly and the masculine bulge below. "Tomorrow," he clarified. "We could go to Remy's place. Good food. Good music. *Fais do-do.*"

Fais do-do—like *pour lagniappe*—was a phrase Peachy had picked up shortly after her arrival in New Orleans. She knew its literal translation was "make sleep." In reality, however, it was the term of choice for an Acadian dance party.

"Well . . . I, uh . . ."

"Second thoughts?"

She was unnerved enough by Luc's proximity—to say nothing of the faint edge of challenge she thought she heard in his voice—to answer without fully considering the consequences. "After what happened last night? Try fifth or sixth."

Her landlord lifted his brows.

"What about you?" she asked sharply, lowering her hand from her locket.

A shrug. "More like seventh or eighth."

There was a pause. Peachy spent most of it trying to decide whether she'd just been complimented or insulted.

"The MayWinnies think I should go out with their grandnephew," she finally announced. She had no idea why she felt compelled to share this bit of information. She only knew it suddenly seemed vital that she do so.

"Do they?"

"Trent Barnes. The TV reporter."

"The one with the concrete coiffure."

"He doesn't spray his hair in real life," Peachy retorted, bristling for reasons she couldn't explain. "Only when he's on camera."

There was another pause, not quite as long as the previous one but no less fraught with tension.

"Are you?" Luc asked at last, removing his hands from his pockets.

"Am I what?"

"Going to go out with the MayWinnies' grandnephew?"

For several seconds Peachy seriously considered the possibility of lying. Of telling Luc that yes, she was. Of telling him that she and Trent Barnes had already arranged a date. A date which she thoroughly expected to enjoy, thank you very much.

Then her mind flashed back to a snippet of the conversation they'd had the previous night.

"You don't trust women," she'd asserted after he'd admitted that the idea of a long-term friendship with a member of the opposite sex was something he found virtually impossible to envision.

"Present company excluded, no," he'd responded flatly. "Not much."

"Do you really?" she'd countered. "Exclude present company, I mean."

"Is there some reason why I shouldn't?"

No, she thought with fierce conviction. There isn't. And there never will be.

"Peachy?" Luc prompted.

She lifted her eyes to meet his. "I told them he could call."

His expression was impossible to read. "And what about tomorrow night?"

"You, me and *fais do-do?*"

"Mmm." Luc raised his right hand. For a tremulous instant Peachy thought he intended to caress her face as he had Friday night. Instead, he stroked the tip of his index finger against the front of her locket. "A woman can get to know a lot about a man by the way he moves to music, *cher.*"

The little voice in her skull muttered something about the main difference between dancing upright and doing "whatever" lying down being ninety degrees.

Peachy cocked her chin, not caring that her cheeks felt as though they were the color of freshly boiled crawfish. A spirit of daring filled her. And with it came a heady rush of the same feminine power she'd experienced when Luc had kissed her.

"It works both ways, Monsieur Devereaux," she replied. "Keep that in mind tomorrow night."

Six

A woman could get to know a lot about a man by riding with him in his car, too. Or so Peachy decided the following evening.

Luc had suggested that he pick her up at her workplace and that they head to Remy's directly from there. Her desire to keep her personal life private stronger than ever in the wake of the May-Winnies' Sunday afternoon visit, she'd been quick to agree with this agenda.

Although the jewelers who employed Peachy granted her and other members of their design staff a certain degree of artistic leeway when it came to appearances, she still felt a need to duck into the ladies' room at the close of business and do a little sartorial loosening up before she met Luc. The voice in the back of her skull offered minimal commentary as she traded her workaday skirt, blouse and pumps for a flirty, floral print dress and a funky pair of flats, added dangling silver earrings to go with her locket and released her hair from the confinement of its usual on-the-job braid.

Only as she was doing a final check in the mirror did the voice revert to its normal form and insidiously inquire, *Do you think you'll look any different after you've finally done it, Pamela Gayle?*

Peachy didn't know. But as she stared at her reflection, she was tinglingly aware that there was a chance she might find out by morning.

Walking outside, she found her lover-to-be engaged in what looked like a chummy conversation with a balding, burly cop. The topic under discussion appeared to be the car—a classic Corvette convertible—against which Luc was leaning. The vehicle was in a No Parking zone.

"Yeah, boy, you right. She's worth it," she heard the officer concede with a rumbling laugh as she approached. "Even so, don' let me be catchin' you again, hear?" Grinning broadly, he began to walk away with a stride that was half stroll, half swagger. "Hey, dawlin'," he greeted her as he passed by. "Where y'at?"

"Buddy of yours?" Peachy asked Luc when she reached him.

Even teeth showed white against tanned skin. "He is now."

"Oh?"

Luc pushed himself away from the Corvette with lazy, muscle-rippling grace. He was dressed in black formfitting denims and a black T-shirt. His dark hair was brushed back from his brow. He looked ready for a walk on the wild side. Indeed, Peachy would have been tempted to describe him as the epitome of every good girl's secret fantasy except for one thing. She knew from personal experience that good girls' secret fantasies revolved around bad *boys*. And while he might be a lot of things, Lucien Devereaux definitely was not an adolescent.

"It makes sense to get friendly with people who can give you a ticket or toss you in jail," he said.

"Your car *is* in a tow-away zone," she felt impelled to point out.

Another flash of teeth. "That's because there is one thing, besides moral indignation, the Big Easy is short on."

"And what might that be?"

"Legal parking spaces."

Peachy had to smile. If she'd heard this complaint once, she'd heard it a hundred times since coming to the Crescent City. She'd also heard endless tales of woe about vehicles that had been hauled off to the auto pound on Claiborne Avenue.

"So how did you persuade your new friend not to write you up?" she asked curiously. "A little bribery, perhaps?"

"I prefer to think of it as achievin' an accommodation," Luc replied with a casual shrug, his usually crisp diction sliding into a drawl.

"Luc." The question about the bribery had been a joke. "You *didn't*—"

"Actually, I told Officer Kerrigan I was waiting for a young lady who was well worth the risk of a fine or a few days in a cell. He said he'd stick around and judge for himself. Once you came sashaying out of the building . . ."

"'Sashaying?'" Peachy repeated as Luc opened the car door for her, uncertain whether she should feel flattered or offended by his choice of words.

"Absolutely, *cher.*"

The husky affirmation was accompanied by a brief but blatant assessment of her legs. Flushing slightly, she bent her knees and lowered herself into the car's passenger seat. She tugged surreptitiously on the hem of her dress as she did so, wondering whether the garment wasn't just a wee bit too short.

Luc shut the door, walked around to the driver's side of the car and got in. "Almost but not quite," he said as he fastened his seat belt.

"What?" Peachy asked, reaching for her own safety harness.

"Your skirt. It's almost too short, but not quite."

She fumbled with the seat belt buckle, feeling the color in her cheeks intensify. "Oh," she said as Luc started the Corvette and eased it away from the curb.

They traveled in silence for quite some time, making stop-start progress in the rush-hour traffic. Peachy found herself admiring Luc's driving skill—particularly his knack for avoiding the potholes that seemed to pockmark so many of New Orleans's streets. She also noted that he honked his car horn far less frequently than most of the other drivers on the road did.

"There's something in the glove compartment for you," he announced as they reached the Mississippi-spanning Crescent City Connection Bridge.

"Something for me?" she echoed, surprised. Leaning forward, she opened the dashboard. She hesitated, not wanting to rummage around when she had no idea for what she was supposed to be searching.

"There in front. The letter-sized manila envelope."

Peachy pulled out the specified item and closed the glove compartment. The envelope was unmarked, its pristine exterior giving no clue as to the nature of the papers it obviously contained. Again she hesitated.

"Go ahead," Luc instructed. "Open it."

The envelope was partially sealed. Although she was by nature the type of person who ripped the wrapping paper off presents, Peachy cautiously slipped a finger beneath the flap and carefully pulled it free. A moment later she took out what seemed to be some sort of document. She unfolded the stapled-together pages.

It took her several seconds to comprehend that what she was looking at was the results of a medical checkup performed on Lucien Devereaux. A very *thorough* medical checkup, including a series of blood tests for sexually transmitted diseases.

"Oh," she breathed, genuinely stunned. The envelope that had contained the papers slipped from her hand.

"Just in case you had any anxieties about my health."

She hadn't, she realized with a jolt. And given his history...

Peachy flipped through the pages of the reports then risked a quick look to her left. "I, uh, appreciate this, Luc," she began. "I never—I mean, uh, I wouldn't have—"

Dark eyes slewed in her direction for just an instant. Peachy felt a tremor of response run through her. She crossed her right leg over her left and pressed her thighs together. The leather of the car seat felt slick against her skin.

"It's not a very romantic gesture," Luc observed neutrally.

Peachy's heart gave a queer hop-skip-jump. She stiffened. "What we're doing isn't *supposed* to be romantic," she replied, her voice as tight as her spine. Whether she was reminding him or herself she wasn't sure.

"Indeed," her companion said after a few moments.

Peachy returned her attention to the papers she'd been given, buffeted by a welter of contradictory emotions. Discussing infectious diseases as a prelude to physical intimacy was definitely *not* on a par with candlelight, rosebuds and violins, she decided with a grimace. Yet there was something compellingly responsible— something unexpectedly caring—about Luc's having raised the issue with her. She couldn't help wondering whether any of the other men on her list of potential first-time lovers would have done the same. Her inclination was to think not.

Then again...

She uncrossed her legs. Maybe she was being mushy-minded. Maybe handing out his health records was part of Lucien Devereaux's standard pre-sex operating procedure. The pages she was holding were photocopies, after all. And rather cheap-looking photocopies, at that. Who knew how many duplicates he'd made? And who knew how many women he'd given them to? The document was dated November 20, so he would have had plenty of time to—

November 20?

"This report is six months old!" Peachy exclaimed.

"It's still valid," he replied calmly.

Her temper flared. Inexperienced though she might be, Pamela Gayle Keene was not ignorant of the less pleasant facts of contemporary sexual life. It galled her that her companion apparently thought she was. "The only way it can be valid, Luc," she said tartly, "is if you haven't been with anyone since you had the blood tests done."

"Exactly."

Indignation turned to incredulity as the meaning of this one-word answer sank in. No, she told herself. It can't be. He can't actually be—*no!* There's just no way.

"You . . . you expect me to b-believe . . ." she stammered.

"I try to expect very little," Luc responded trenchantly, changing lanes. "It helps cut down on disappointment. But whether you choose to believe it or not, those negative results are as valid tonight as they were when I first received them."

Peachy gnawed on her lower lip, trying to reconcile this categorical statement with what she thought she knew about the man who'd promised to relieve her of her virginity. There'd been a time when it had seemed she couldn't open a newspaper or magazine without finding a photograph of "bestselling author, Lucien Devereaux" and some "lovely associate." Yet now that she thought about it, she realized it had been months since she'd seen such a picture. She also realized that the Prytania Street gossip about Luc's social life had been rather, well, nonspecific for quite a while. During the first year or so after she'd moved in, the MayWinnies and Terry had dished all sorts of provocative details about the various and sundry women in their mutual landlord's very active social life. But lately . . .

Men don't lie about *not* having sex, Peachy mused with a tinge of cynicism. Unless they're married and trying to deceive their wives. Given the circumstances, it wouldn't make sense for Luc to claim that he hadn't been with a woman for six months unless— unless—

Unless he really hadn't.

"Why?" The question came geysering up from deep within her. "I—I mean—"

"I know what you mean," Luc replied without inflection. "What I don't know is the answer to what you're asking."

She stared at him, struggling to get a fix on his expression. It was like trying to find a finger hold on a polished pane of glass. "If you've been celibate for six months, there must be a *reason.*"

Luc's mouth twisted. "Well, I think we can rule out the one that's kept you a virgin for twenty-three years, *cher,*" he returned. "I certainly haven't been abstaining in the hope that my next sex partner will turn out to be the love of my life."

For a moment Peachy thought he was mocking her and the confidences she'd shared with him as they'd walked home Saturday night. The notion of such ridicule cut like a knife. But then she realized that the derision she heard in his voice—if derision was the right word—was self-directed. Her pain was transmuted into an odd sort of compassion.

"Luc—" she began.

"I'm sorry, Peachy," he said, the words harsh and hurried. "That was a vile thing to say. I apologize."

She swallowed hard. "It's . . . all right."

Luc shook his head, rejecting her words. She saw his long, strong fingers tighten on the Corvette's steering wheel until their knuckles turned white. His chiseled nostrils flared as he exhaled in a frustrated-sounding rush of air.

"I hadn't really thought about it until recently," he confessed after several extremely awkward seconds. "About that fact that it's been six months since I . . . had sex." He paused, obviously having difficulty deciding what he wanted to say and how he wanted to say it. "I've been so wrapped up in working on my new book that I honestly didn't notice. Or if I did, I didn't give a damn." He shook his head again, more vehemently than the first time. "God. I don't know how to explain—"

"It's *all right,* Luc," Peachy repeated firmly. She wanted to reach out and underscore her sincerity with a touch, but something inside her warned against the gesture. "You don't owe me any explanations."

There was a pause. Not a terribly long one, but sufficient in length to allow Luc to regain control of himself—and the situation.

"Some people might argue otherwise, given our agreement," he finally remarked, glancing right. His voice was smooth again, his dark eyes steady.

Peachy shifted involuntarily, but managed to sustain his gaze. "I'm not 'some people,' thank you very much." She lifted her chin. "I'm *me*."

"There is that." Luc looked back at the road. A few seconds passed. "Still . . ."

Don't, she told herself quickly, fighting the lure of the last word. Just let it pass.

But she couldn't. She had to know.

"Still—what?" she asked.

Luc said nothing—did nothing—for at least ten seconds. Then, without so much as a sideward flick of his eyes, he transferred his right hand from the steering wheel to her left knee and stroked upward two or three inches with faintly callused fingertips. He traced a spiral against her skin with the edge of his nails. Although the contact was light, it was infused with erotic intention.

Peachy exhaled on a shuddery sigh as Luc slid his fingers inward, finessing tender flesh, finding nerves she hadn't known existed and rousing them to life with exquisite care. A spasm of pleasure shook her. She bit her lower lip, trying not to moan. Fine ribbons of heat uncoiled within her belly. She could feel herself melting, growing moist, at the apex of her thighs. The urge to arch into the caress—to squeeze her legs together and trap her companion's oh-so-expert hand between them—was almost overwhelming.

And then, suddenly, it was over. Luc's right hand was back on the wheel. His gaze was still locked straight ahead. "The fact that I'm six months out of practice doesn't give you pause?" he casually queried.

Peachy sucked in a tremulous breath, her senses reeling. She forced herself to focus on Luc's profile. Something about the set of his angular jaw suggested to her that he was not as unmoved by what had just happened as he apparently wanted her to believe. Ditto, the stark pulsing of a vein in his left temple. And yet . . .

Her memory flashed back to the previous evening.

"Second thoughts?" Luc had asked her.

There'd been an edge of challenge to the question, she recalled. At the time she'd thought that it had been meant to goad her into accepting his invitation—an adult variation on the childhood charge of "Chicken," as it were. But now she found herself wondering if the inquiry's real purpose hadn't been to stir up doubts about whether she genuinely wanted to go through with the arrangement they'd made.

Maybe that had been the real purpose of the kiss Luc had provoked her into initiating Saturday night as well. And of the very
calculated caress he'd just given her.

Could it be that he was trying to warn her off her intended
course? she wondered. To demonstrate just how powerfully her
sexual initiation might impact her?

*Did you ever consider the possibility that the man's changed his
mind and doesn't want to do it with you?* the little voice in the back
of her skull abruptly demanded. *He turned you down at first, remember?*

Peachy clenched her hands, crumpling Luc's photocopied medical records.

*Maybe he's started to worry whether you're going to be able to
keep your end of the deal,* the voice went on sardonically. *You've
nearly swooned on him twice. And you would've been hot to trot
a minute ago if he'd put his hand much farther up your dress. Lord
knows how you'll react once you get around to the main event! You
might turn into a bunny-boiling crazy woman like what's-her-name
played in that movie—*

The sound of Luc's voice saying her name yanked Peachy off this
extremely disturbing train of thought. Glancing around, she realized that they'd arrived at their destination—a ramshackle clap-
board roadhouse on the edge of a swamp. There was a modest neon
sign winking out the name Remy & Lorraine's above the building's main entrance.

"Peachy?" Luc repeated, catching her chin between thumb and
forefinger, forcing her to face him. His brow was furrowed. His
eyes bored deeply into hers.

She wanted him to make love to her, she realized.

Really.

Truly.

With every fiber of her being.

She wanted Lucien Devereaux.

And he wanted her. Oh, he could pretend otherwise. But she
knew he did. Sexually inexperienced though she might be, she was
not oblivious to the meaning of certain fundamental changes in
certain fundamental portions of a man's anatomy. And she'd felt
those changes Saturday night when they'd kissed.

Maybe Luc's desire wasn't as intense as hers seemed to be. And
maybe it stemmed primarily from the fact that he'd been a long
time without a woman. Nonetheless, the desire existed and it was
directed at her.

As for his possible concern that she might espouse one thing before and expect something entirely different after...

She understood Luc's wariness. He'd been betrayed at the profoundest of levels by several members of the female gender—including his own mother. Was it any wonder he was reluctant to trust?

There was no way she could force him to believe that she'd meant every single word she'd said to him Friday night. The best she could do was to be as honest as she knew how and to hope that he found her worthy of his faith. And once he'd done for her what he'd promised he'd do—

"Peachy?" Luc said for a third time.

No regrets, she told herself firmly.

No recriminations.

And no requests for a return engagement, no matter what.

"Sorry," she apologized. "I was thinking about your question."

Luc released her chin and lowered his hand. "My...question?"

"About whether knowing that you've been celibate for six months gives me pause."

Luc undid his seat belt, his expression unreadable. "And does it?"

A breeze stirred Peachy's hair. She combed it back from her face with her fingers as she contemplated her response. "Actually," she said slowly, borrowing the coy tilt of the head Miss Winona-Jolene Barnes had perfected decades before. "I think I like the idea of being your comeback performance."

There was a short, stunned pause. Then the look on Luc's face changed.

Uh-oh, the little voice muttered as a frisson of uniquely feminine alarm skittered through Peachy's body.

"You only... *think?*" he countered, his voice insinuating.

While Peachy's nerve didn't exactly break at that point, it definitely bent a bit. She went from emboldened flirt to self-conscious virgin in the space of a few seconds. "Well, uh—" she began.

"Lucien, mon vieux!" an ebullient male voice suddenly bellowed from the front door of the roadhouse. *"Peachy, m'petit!* Dis ain' no drive-in, you know! So leave off whatever it is you're up to in dat car and come taste what Remy's got cookin'!"

It was an invitation Pamela Gayle Keene couldn't refuse.

Nor, it seemed, could Lucien Devereaux.

* * *

"No more," Peachy gasped as Luc finished twirling her expertly through the final measures of a pulsating zydeco tune. She felt absolutely exhausted on the one hand, utterly exhilarated on the other. "Please."

"Had enough, hmm?" her partner said, forking his fingers back through his thick, sweat-sheened hair.

"Temporarily," she conceded, plucking the front of her cotton dress away from her body. She was glad to see that Luc was perspiring as heavily as she was. It helped make up for the fact that while she was gulping for oxygen, he was breathing in a slow, steady, stroll-in-the-park pattern. "Give me a few minutes and I'll be ready to *laissez les bon temps rouler* again."

Grinning his approval, Luc slipped a supportive arm around her waist and led her back to their table as the band segued into a traditional Cajun two-step. Within a few seconds of their arrival, a short-skirted, big-haired waitress materialized with two glasses of iced tea. Peachy's, she simply plunked down. Luc's, she placed directly in front of him while simultaneously batting her eyelids and displaying her not-inconsiderable cleavage.

"Anythin' else?" she asked, lashes fluttering, bosom bouncing.

"No, thanks," Luc said with a cordial smile.

"Awright." The woman pouted her disappointment, then pivoted and walked away.

"Now *that's* sashaying," Peachy observed with a touch of acid, watching the back-forth action of the waitress's voluptuous hips. She reached for her glass.

"No, *cher,*" Luc contradicted with a chuckle. The sound was as deep and rich as the chocolate mousse Remy had practically force-fed them earlier in the evening. The mousse had been preceded by a multicourse dinner. "That's tryin' way too hard."

Peachy sipped her iced tea, recalling the wallflower misery of her thin-as-a-rail adolescence. "I thought that's what men liked."

"Some men." Luc picked up his own glass and drank. "Some time."

"Meaning?"

"Meaning, there's a lot to be said for having it served up on a platter. But there are occasions when having to work for it can be much more fun."

Peachy fanned her face. Given what had happened—or not happened—in the car, she'd half expected this evening to turn into a disaster. But something had changed once she and Luc had stepped over the threshold of their former neighbor's establishment. The dangerous emotional undercurrents that had been building between them had eased. Silence-spiked sexual tension had given way to flirtatious banter. She'd soon found herself having more fun than she'd had in a long, long time.

Which was not to say she wasn't being careful. She knew it wouldn't do to get too comfortable with Luc or too accustomed to his company. Theirs was a temporary relationship. And once it was consummated...

We can still be friends, Peachy told herself.

Oh, puh-leeze, the little voice editorialized, stirring to acerbic life after several hours of benign silence. *Gag me with a greeting card.*

"Have you ever had to work for it, Luc?" she asked, setting her glass down.

He lifted a brow. "Present company excluded?"

It was a curious response, all things considered. "I...suppose."

"Then no. Not really." Luc's gaze drifted from her eyes to her lips to her locket and back up again. "It's too bad. It probably would have done me some good."

Remy Sinclair and his bride of four-and-a-half months, the former Lorraine DeBasio of Brooklyn, New York, arrived at their table a few moments later for a friendly conversation. Well, no. The word *conversation* implied a certain degree of give-and-take. What occurred once the couple had seated themselves was more in the nature of a monologue delivered by the size-four Lorraine and punctuated by occasional comments from her adoring, three-hundred-pound-plus husband. About all Peachy and Luc were required to do was to listen and laugh. Since Lorraine had the wit and timing of a stand-up comic, this wasn't much of a strain.

"They're so great together," Peachy said when the Sinclairs finally moved on.

"Unmatched, but quite a pair," Luc agreed.

"Have you ever wondered how they, er—" she paused, brows delicately arched.

Dark eyes sparked provocatively. "More than once, *cher.*"

They danced again after that. The music was mostly upbeat, but mellowed occasionally into a sweetly fiddled love song. It was at the end of one of these waltz-style tunes that Peachy asked Luc what time it was. It look a moment for the answer he gave to penetrate the sense of contentment that had settled over her.

"Eleven o'clock?" She blinked in disbelief. "I had no idea."

"Time flies when you're having fun," Luc observed, thrusting his hands into the pockets of his jeans and rocking back on his heels.

Peachy fluffed her hair. "You . . . you could say that."

"But all good things must come to an end."

"You could say that, too."

He eyed her assessingly for several moments then asked, "Do you want to go home now, *cher?*"

Peachy hesitated, wondering whether he meant "home" to separate beds on different floors of the same building or "home" to. . .

"It *is* late," she said after a few seconds, feeling a tinge of heat enter her cheeks.

"And you do have to get up and go to work tomorrow."

That means 'Not tonight,' Pamela Gayle, the little voice declared.

"You're right, Luc," she agreed, summoning up a smile. "We should be heading back. Just let me pay a visit to the ladies' room first, okay?"

"I'll meet you at the table."

The powder room was very crowded. It took Peachy a good five minutes to gain access to one of the two stalls, and by that time, her need to relieve herself was acute.

Maneuvering her way to a sink so she could wash her hands ate up another minute or so. A glance into the mirror above the basin sent her scrambling for a comb. She also spent a few moments trying to desmudge her eye makeup.

She was just about to make her exit when she heard a shrill scream followed by several loud thuds and the sound of shattering glass. An instant later the powder room door swung open and Lorraine Sinclair stepped in.

"Nothing to be alarmed about, ladies," she said, gesturing for calm. "Just boys being boys and a couple of men trying to straighten them out."

"Somebody say somethin' insultin' about somebody else's mama?" one of the women standing behind Peachy inquired in a knowing tone.

"If my Bobby Ray's fightin' again, I'll split his skull with a skillet," a platinum-haired young woman to her right vowed.

"Good luck, Noreen," someone else quipped. "That boy's got a concrete head. You couldn't crack it with a pickax."

There were several more thuds followed by some inarticulate shouting and more shattering glass. Peachy flinched from the violence the noise implied. What in heaven's name was going on out there? she wondered. And more to the point, was Luc involved in it?

There was a loud crash on the other side of the wall. The floor seemed to shake. A moment later a fist with the word *love* tattooed across the knuckles slammed through the door of the ladies' room. Several women shrieked. The fist was quickly withdrawn. Peachy thought she heard a hollered apology for the intrusion but she couldn't be certain.

"Dammit!" Lorraine exclaimed, her eyes flashing with temper as she stamped her foot. "That's the third door in four months!"

More thuds. More shouts. More crashes.

And then, suddenly, there was silence.

"My God, they've all gone and killed each other," the bottle-blonde who'd been addressed as Noreen said in a hushed voice. She did not sound entirely displeased by the idea.

A moment later there was a polite knock on the damaged door.

"Peachy?" an instantly identifiable male voice calmly inquired. "I don't want to rush you, *cher.* But if we don't leave now, it's going to be way past tomorrow before I get you home."

Luc couldn't remember the last time he'd used the elevator in his Prytania Street residence. It was a cranky piece of machinery that seldom stopped on the correct floor on the first try and frequently refused to open its doors more than halfway on those rare occasions when it did. And *slow?* Molasses in January traveled at the speed of light by comparison!

Nonetheless, when Peachy suggested he take the elevator rather than the stairs up to his apartment upon their return from Remy's, he was quick to agree. It wasn't that he doubted his ability to haul himself up four flights if he had to. He didn't. But since an alternative to ascending to his apartment under his own power was readily available...

"Are you *sure* you don't want to go to an emergency room?" Peachy asked as she pressed the button for the fourth floor.

"No need," Luc answered, shaking his head. He'd sustained enough physical damage in his life to know when professional attention was required and when he could get by with ice packs and aspirin. "I look much worse than I feel."

"I certainly hope so." She studied him, frowning. "Charity Hospital isn't that far away, Luc. I could drive you there—"

"Drive me, hmm?" He grinned crookedly, enjoying her concern even as he sought to ameliorate it. "Admit it, *cher.* You don't really care about my condition. You're just dying to get another shot at my 'Vette."

"Oh, right," she retorted. "One time behind the wheel and I've become automotively obsessed." Turning away, she jabbed the fourth-floor button again. After a moment she began tapping her foot against the floor and muttering under her breath.

Luc leaned back, watching the huffy little show of temper with amusement. Peachy had driven the Corvette home from Remy's at his request. It hadn't been an easy thing for him to ask her to do. He had a strongly proprietorial attitude when it came to his car. But given that his vision was compromised by a badly swollen right eyelid and his left hand seemed temporarily incapable of gripping a steering wheel, he'd decided his sense of vehicular possessiveness had better take a back seat to safety considerations.

Aside from the fact that Peachy had rattled his molars by hitting a couple of potholes, she'd handled the 'Vette very well. A lot better than he'd expected, frankly. It probably was reflective of prejudice on his part, but he hadn't figured that someone with her refined artistic sensibilities would respond to a classic American muscle car.

"Come on, come on," she urged as the elevator doors finally began to close.

"Wake me when we get to the fourth floor," he requested, closing his left eye. The right was pretty well puffed shut.

"Drowsiness can be a symptom of a head injury, you know."

Luc lifted his left lid just in time to see Peachy smother a yawn. "It can also be a symptom of wanting to go to sleep because it's half past midnight."

"Yes, well, if you turn out to be concussed or something . . ."

Her voice trailed off as the elevator creaked to life and began its ascent. Forget molasses in January, Luc thought when the car finally reached the second floor. A crippled snail could move faster than this!

He glanced over at Peachy. She was staring at the control panel and fingering her locket. Not for the first time, he found himself envying the tactile attention she lavished on the bell-shaped memento.

His gaze drifted downward to the soft swell of her gently rounded breasts. He could see the subtle budding of her nipples against the bodice of her dress. Exactly how much she had on beneath the simple cotton garment he wasn't certain, but their bodies had brushed together enough on the dance floor for him to strongly suspect that it wasn't a whole heck of a lot.

He'd had a good time with her tonight, he reflected, conscious of a tightening in his groin. As good a time as he'd had in—Lord, he couldn't think how long. He'd gone further than he'd intended to during the drive out to Remy's, of course. But if his behavior made Peachy stop and think, really think, about the course she'd set for herself, then it had served an honorable purpose.

As for his getting involved in the free-for-all at the end of the evening . . .

The other guy had swung first and unprovoked, Luc reminded himself. And even though he'd swung back and connected, he'd pulled the punch. After that, well, as his old military buddy Flynn had observed on more than one occasion, might didn't necessarily make right but there were times when it was quicker than mediation.

The elevator lurched to a halt with a discordant grinding of gears. After a moment the door groaned open. A quick check of the control panel told Luc they were on the building's third floor. The ominous stillness of the car made it clear they weren't likely to go any higher anytime soon.

"Why don't we go to my place," Peachy suddenly suggested.

Luc stared at her, too stunned to speak. Dear God, he thought, his heart starting to hammer. Was she actually proposing that the two of them—that he and she—*now?*

His shock obviously showed. For a moment Peachy seemed bewildered by his reaction. Then a look of exasperated comprehension appeared on her face.

"Oh, for heaven's sake!" she snapped, glaring at him. "I didn't mean it *that* way. I've got a first aid kit in my apartment. I thought you might be able to use it. I wasn't planning to lure you into my virginal boudoir and jump your bones."

Luc winced inwardly, sensing injury beneath the indignation. He felt a pang of shame. "I'm sorry," he said after a few seconds, searching for a way to explain his mistake. "I'm not accustomed to having people offer to . . . salve my wounds."

"Gee," came the sarcastic response. "I wonder why that could be."

There was a long pause. Finally Luc drew a long, steadying breath and said mildly, "This kit of yours, *cher*. Does it have an 'ouchless' Band-Aid?"

Peachy's chin, which she'd had cocked at a distinctly defiant angle, came down a notch or two. "Maybe," she replied, still a bit miffed. Then the corners of her soft lips twitched into the beginning of a smile. "But even if it doesn't, I'm pretty sure the antiseptic I've got is guaranteed not to sting."

The antiseptic did, of course.

Sting, that is.

Luc didn't mind the faint medicinal bite. He'd experienced far worse during his military days. Besides, the pain was a welcome distraction. It helped keep him from fixating on how intensely he was enjoying having Peachy fuss over him.

He'd known there was a risk in accepting her offer of aid. But when he'd balanced that risk against the hurt he'd heard in her voice plus his sudden desire to prolong their time together . . .

No contest.

Once they'd gotten inside her apartment, Peachy had dispatched him to the bathroom while she went into the kitchen for some ice cubes.

The air in the bathroom carried her scent. The soft, sweet fragrance hazed his brain for a few seconds but he managed to shake it off. Less easy to ignore were the two pairs of bikini-style panties and the lace-trimmed bra hanging from the shower curtain rod. Tempted beyond caution, he was reaching up to touch one of the dainty garments when Peachy appeared in the doorway carrying a tray of ice cubes and several large towels. He snatched his hand back, feeling like a pervert.

"Oh, *no*," she groaned as the tray slipped out of her grasp and crashed to the floor. "I completely forgot—"

Dumping the towels, she brushed by him and yanked the underwear off the rod. She glanced around for a second, clearly trying to decide what to do. She finally stuffed the lingerie in a small hamper in the corner of the bathroom. Then she turned to face him, the color in her cheeks very high.

"I'm sorry, Luc," she said. If she'd noticed anything peculiar about his behavior, she gave no sign of it. She glanced down, grimacing at the overturned tray and scattered ice cubes. "God, I am *such* a slob sometimes."

"Don't worry about it, *cher*," he quickly responded. "Let me help you get this picked up."

"Um . . . why don't you sit down?" she invited once they'd retrieved the ice cubes and put them in the sink. She gestured toward the toilet. "It'll make it easier for me to, uh, salve your wounds."

She had a very soothing touch, Luc soon discovered. She also seemed inordinately sensitive to his physical responses. If he winced, she flinched. If he caught his breath, she bit her lip so convulsively he feared she might draw blood.

"Peachy," he finally said, circling her slender wrists with his fingers. Her pulse was very rapid. "This is obviously hurting you more than it's hurting me. Let me do the rest."

She looked at him with wide, green-gold eyes. A hint of weariness shadowed the delicate flesh below them, underscoring the gamine fragility of her features. Her upper lids were smudged with mascara, lending a sultry aspect to her expression.

"No." She shook her head, her hair shimmering about her shoulders. She eased her hands free of his and took a step back. "That's all right. I'm almost finished."

"You're sure?"

"Very."

She bent forward from the waist. Her silver locket swung free, drawing Luc's gaze the way a magnet draws iron. She leaned in a bit, lifting her right hand to dab something on his left temple. The movement caused the bodice of her dress to gap, offering him a tantalizing view of the upper curves of her breasts.

His breath rasped in his throat. A surge of heat threatened his self-restraint. A host of erotic images cartwheeled through his mind. He clenched his hands at his sides.

"You never answered my question, you know," Peachy observed.

"Which question . . . was that?" Luc managed to say.

"About whether what happened tonight has happened before."

He closed his eyes. It did nothing to lessen his awareness of her. He could feel her through his pores. "You mean, do I make a practice of wading into other people's bar fights and getting beaten up?"

She clicked her tongue at his description. "Remy said it would have been much worse if you hadn't been there. That it would have gotten completely out of hand."

"Remy is prone to exaggeration." He opened his eyes.

Peachy straightened, gazing down at him with an odd solemnity. "I saw the way some of the men looked at you when we were leaving."

"They were probably wondering why I was getting to go home with the prettiest woman in the place."

She dismissed the compliment with a shake of her head, her expression intent. "You held back, didn't you," she said. "You helped break up the fight just like Remy said, but you held back. You could have done a lot more damage, and those men knew it."

Luc exhaled on a harsh sigh. He'd seen the looks, too. He knew, far better than she, what they meant. "Probably," he tersely conceded.

"Have you?"

"What? Done a lot more damage than I did tonight?"

Peachy nodded.

It was not something he wanted to get into, but he realized he had no real choice. "Yes."

"In the military?"

"Yes." He stared up at her, suddenly uncertain what the reason for this interrogation was. After a moment he asked flatly, "Do you want details?"

"No!" It was practically a gasp. "Of course not."

"Some women do, *cher.*"

"Why?" Her eyes were wide.

He shrugged, deciding not to soften the truth. "It's a turn-on."

Peachy's hand move up to her locket. Luc watched her gifted, giving fingers close around the pendant as though it were a talisman against all that was wrong with the world. For the second time since they'd arrived home, he felt ashamed.

She's so damned innocent, he thought. *And I'm so damned—*

"I can't imagine that," Peachy said softly. "I mean—whatever you've done, you've done. But that isn't *you,* Luc."

"Maybe it is."

"No."

He lifted his hands and clasped her waist. She swayed slightly. He was assailed by the same antithetical urges he'd experienced Saturday during dinner. Half of him wanted to enfold her in an embrace. The other half wanted to shove her away.

"You don't know me," he said, the words bitter on his tongue.

Peachy said nothing for what seemed like a very long time. Then her mouth curved into a smile that hinted at a womanly wisdom which transcended sexual experience—or lack of it. "Actually, I think I do."

"Peachy—" he began, tightening his hold on her.

"Peachy?"

The second invocation of the nickname came a split second after the first and stunned both of them into stillness. The subsequent appearance of a robe-clad Laila Martigny in the threshold of the bathroom was like a shock of electricity. It jolted Luc to his feet and sent Peachy backing away from him.

"I heard a loud crash and then a lot of strange sounds," the psychologist said with perfect aplomb, her jewel-bright eyes moving back and forth between them. "I became concerned, so I came upstairs." She brought her left arm up in an elegant sweep, a set of keys dangling from her fingertips. "I found these in the front door."

Seven

You know, Pamela Gayle, Peachy's relentless mental kibitzer mused the following Saturday morning as she finished cleaning her bathroom. *It's a good thing you aren't paranoid. Because if you were . . .*

"Yeah, yeah," she muttered, balling up a bunch of dirty towels and stuffing them into the hamper. "If I were, I'd be convinced there's a plot to keep me and Luc apart. But I'm not and there isn't. This sort of thing takes time, that's all."

But it's been nearly two weeks since you made your vow about losing your virginity, the voice persisted as she stalked out of the bathroom and into her bedroom. *And eight whole days since Luc promised to help you do it. Just how much time are you talking about? You could get run over by a truck this very afternoon, you know. And then where would you be? Dead and undeflowered, that's where! Maybe you should consider leaving instructions that you want to be buried in white.*

Shaking her head at this morbid scenario, Peachy began yanking the sheets off her bed. Soon, she told herself, conscious of an increasingly familiar ache low in her body. It's going to happen very soon. And once it does, I can get on with my life.

She sighed, thinking back over the events of the last few days. Things *had* been a little weird recently, she acknowledged. Even by Prytania Street standards. Not that she could point to any single episode and label it as overwhelming peculiar. But when she put one vaguely odd moment together with several others, then factored in a series of slightly off-kilter encounters with a number of her neighbors...

Well, suffice it to say that she could have developed one heck of a conspiracy theory had she been so inclined. Fortunately she wasn't.

Peachy heaved a second sigh, wishing there was someone she could talk to about her situation but knowing there was not. Her mother was off-limits for a variety of reasons, not the least of which being that she was away on a second honeymoon cruise. Eden was a definite no-go, too. Lord, she could just imagine how her older sister would react if she told her the truth about what she was attempting to do!

Confiding in the other two Wedding Belles was impossible as well. As much as she liked Annie and Zoe, she wasn't intimately enough acquainted with either one of them to call up and say something like, "Hi, I've decided to get rid of my virginity and I'd like your advice on speeding up the process." She also understood that anything she told them inevitably would get repeated to her pregnant sibling. Eden, Annie and Zoe had been roommates in college and they'd remained close during the ten-plus years since their graduation. They did not keep secrets from each other.

As for unburdening herself to one of her neighbors...

Peachy sank down on the edge of her linen-denuded bed, shaking her head in emphatic rejection. No way, she told herself. No how.

Under different circumstances, she might have considered engaging Laila Martigny in a discreet discussion about what she wanted to do and with whom she wanted to do it. She trusted the older woman implicitly and had found her to be an excellent source of advice in the past. But given Laila's almost maternal attitude toward Luc, confiding in her seemed extremely unwise.

She'd certainly been operating in a mother hen mode in the wee hours of Tuesday morning, Peachy reflected with a wry smile, remembering how the older woman had alternated between tending to Luc's injuries and taking him to task for fighting. Luc had accepted both the older woman's care and criticism with equanimity. In point of fact, once he'd recovered from his obvious shock at her sudden intrusion, he'd seemed rather relieved to have her there.

Her own reaction to Laila's unheralded arrival had been decidedly ambivalent. Something had been on the verge of happening between her and Luc and her downstairs neighbor had ruined it. Not on purpose, of course. But the result had been the same as if it had been done deliberately.

To put it bluntly, an opportunity had been lost. An opportunity for exactly what, Peachy wasn't sure. She certainly wasn't foolish enough to think that Luc and she would have ended up making love if Laila hadn't appeared. The man had been bruised and bleeding, for heaven's sake! And she'd been tired. Very, very tired. Even so, had the interruption come just a few minutes later...

Would Luc have kissed her for the second time if Laila hadn't walked in? she wondered. Would she have kissed him in return? And afterward, would they have reached an understanding about when and where and how they would consummate their arrangement?

Peachy flopped back on the bed and stared at the ceiling, trying to ignore a sudden tightening in the tips of her breasts. A fat lot of good an "understanding" would have done them the last four nights, she thought sourly. She and Luc had spent what? Maybe ten whole minutes together during that time?

She'd come home Tuesday evening to find him trying to fix a power failure that affected the entire apartment building. He'd been so preoccupied with his landlord duties, he'd scarcely said hello to her. And by the time he'd gotten the electricity restored, she'd been too weary to do more than bid him a terse good-night.

The prospects for a rendezvous had seemed better on Wednesday. Luc and she had encountered each other in the lobby as he'd been coming in from his usual morning run and she'd been going off to work. After ascertaining that he was much recovered from the injuries he'd sustained in Monday night's brawl, she'd suggested he stop by to see her that evening.

"To talk," she'd said. "And . . . whatever."

He'd smiled, his gaze dipping briefly to the silver bell locket at the base of her throat. Then he'd agreed.

He'd knocked on her door shortly after 7:00 p.m. She'd let him in. They'd scarcely gotten beyond the "And how was your day?" preliminaries when the MayWinnies had shown up, laden with a box of homemade pralines and several thousand photographs they'd taken during a trip to Tokyo the previous year.

Although she'd already seen the pictures twice before—and had no great fondness for the Misses Barnes's ultrasweet version of New Orleans's most famous confection—Peachy hadn't had the heart to request that her next door neighbors come back another time. She'd asked them in. They'd eagerly accepted, then flutteringly professed embarrassment at discovering that she already had company. They'd also revealed a disconcerting awareness of many of the events of Monday night.

"Remy's darlin' wife, Lorraine, called us," Miss Winnie had demurely explained.

Wary of the interpretation the two older ladies might put on Luc's presence in her apartment, Peachy had stammered out an excuse about his having come by to check that everything was back to normal after the previous day's electrical failure. Luc had supported her story without hesitation, deftly fielded a few concerned questions about his various cuts and bruises, then smoothly excused himself.

The MayWinnies had stayed, of course. And stayed. And stayed. And Peachy had been coaxed into consuming so many pralines that she'd been surprised she didn't go into sugar shock.

Thursday had turned out to be a variation on the same theme.

Another meeting in the lobby.

Another suggestion that they get together to talk . . . and whatever.

"Only this time," Luc had qualified, "let's try my place."

She'd gone up to his apartment about the same time he'd come down to hers the previous night. Within minutes of her arrival, Francis Smythe had materialized at the door bearing muffulettas sandwiches and a six-pack of Dixie Beer from Central Grocery.

There was a documentary on public television he was longing to see, he'd urbanely explained, but something seemed to be wrong with his set. Might he use Luc's to view the program? Unless, of course, Luc and Peachy had other plans . . .

Oh, no, Francis, Luc had replied. No other plans.

None at all, Peachy had mendaciously affirmed, plastering a cheerful smile on her face. She'd gone on to declare that she'd simply come by for a chat. And now that she'd had it, it was time for her to run along.

It wasn't until she'd gotten back to her apartment that she'd started wondering about Luc's use of the older man's given name. She couldn't recall having heard him call Mr. Smythe "Francis" before.

She couldn't recall having told Terry that she'd go to see him perform Friday night, either. Yet he'd stood in her apartment the following evening, adamantly insisting that she had and warning that he—to say nothing of his alter ego, Terree—would be crushed, simply crushed, if she reneged on her pledge at the last minute.

Faced with the possibility of an emotional meltdown, Peachy had done what she'd had to do. She'd abandoned her intention of going upstairs to Luc's place once again and kept her alleged promise to her downstairs neighbor.

All in all, the night out with Terry and some of his friends had been a great deal of fun. It had also netted her several potentially valuable makeup tips plus some remarkably jaundiced assessments about what members of the opposite sex *really* wanted.

Peachy sighed a third time and levered herself into a sitting position. "I know what *I* really want," she grumbled, swatting a lock of hair out of her face.

So why don't you do something about it? came the acidic challenge.

The question stopped her cold.

Why didn't she—?

For heaven's sake! She'd gone to Luc. She'd told him the truth and asked him to help her. She'd received his pledge that he would. Short of divesting herself of her clothes and painting a bull's-eye between her—

Oh, Peachy thought, biting her lower lip.

Oh, indeed, the little voice said cuttingly. *Hasn't it occurred to you that you're being awfully passive in all this? Yes, you took the initiative in approaching Luc eight days ago. And yes, it required a certain amount of nerve to explain what you wanted from him and why. But what have you been up to since then, huh? Not much. What happened to all that talk about needing to be in control of this situation?*

"I kissed Luc last Saturday night," Peachy argued, uncertain why she felt it necessary to make the point aloud.

Only because he maneuvered you into it.

"But—"

How badly do you want to get rid of your virginity, Pamela Gayle?

"I—"

More to the point. How important is it to you that Lucien Devereaux be your first lover?

A quiver ran through Peachy, teasing her nerve endings like a heated feather. She caught her breath, remembering with marrow-melting exactitude the realization she'd come to Monday night while sitting in the parking lot of Remy's roadhouse.

"Luc," she whispered. "Oh, Luc."

And then her mind shifted to something he'd told her twice during their first evening out together.

"Everything that happens between us will be by your choice," he'd said.

Everything.

By her choice.

Peachy lifted her chin. It wasn't enough for her to tell Luc what she'd chosen, she thought. She had to *show* him that she'd meant what she'd said.

She had to entice him.

She had to incite him.

No. More than that.

She had to flat out seduce him.

The man's been celibate for six months, the little voice in the back of her skull noted helpfully. *How hard can it be?*

Lucien Devereaux knew he was in trouble as soon as he picked up the delicately perfumed invitation that was slipped under his door shortly before 4:00 p.m. What he couldn't gauge until three and a half hours later when he presented himself at Peachy's apartment as requested was exactly how much.

A lot of trouble, was his first estimate.

A *whole* lot, was his second.

"I'm glad you could come, Luc," Peachy said as she ushered him in.

"I'm glad you asked me," he responded, watching her shut and lock the door. He thrust his hands deep into the pockets of the unstructured black linen jacket he was wearing. He gave fleeting thanks for the easy fit of the matching slacks.

Peachy was clad in an embroidered, cream-colored gauze dress that he was certain he'd seen several times before. Only he couldn't recall it clinging to her hips and thighs on any of those previous occasions the way it seemed to be clinging now. Nor could he remember the bodice ever having been unbuttoned to the point where the shadowed cleft between her small breasts became tantalizingly visible every time she took a deep breath.

There was something different about her face and hair, too. Her long-lashed, green-gold eyes held a mysterious new allure. Her mouth seemed riper and fuller. And her lush, red-gold curls—styled into an artless upsweep rather than allowed to tumble free—tempted his fingers as they'd never done before.

While Luc was sophisticated enough to understand the part cosmetic artifice played in Peachy's altered appearance, his gut told him that the real transformation was an internal one. His erstwhile one-night stand had undergone some sort of fundamental change since he'd last seen her. She seemed surer of herself. She was also infinitely more aware of her sensuality. It was almost as though—

The idea detonated inside his brain with devastating force.

She's done it, he thought, his entire body clenching like a fist. *Dear God in Heaven. She's gone out and done it with somebody else!*

There was no way to describe the intensity of the anger that ripped through him in response to this possibility. It assailed him with primal power, undermining every assumption he had about himself. The shocking surge of possessiveness he'd experienced six nights before when Laila had mentioned the MayWinnies' intention to match Peachy with their nephew had been benign in comparison.

"Luc?" The invocation of his name reached him across a great distance. It was accompanied by a gentle touch to his sleeve. As light as the contact was, it seemed to burn through the fabric of his clothes and brand the flesh beneath.

He struggled, exerting every bit of willpower he had to control the tumult raging within him. He stared at the woman standing next to him, desperately searching for evidence to refute his assumption.

That his reaction was irrational, Luc understood. If Peachy had given her virginity to someone else, he was off the hook. And off the hook was what he'd been telling himself he wanted to be ever since he'd agreed to her lunatic proposal.

Only he hadn't wanted it to be like this! If the price of his being able to wriggle out of a promise he'd never intended to keep was an innocent young woman squandering something he knew she'd one day regret not having saved for the right man and the right moment, it was far too high.

"Luc?" Peachy repeated. "Is something wrong?"

He exhaled a shuddery breath and shook his head. "No."

"You're not having a delayed reaction from Monday night, are you?"

It took him a moment to register what she was asking. Except for a few yellowish bruises on his knuckles, a slight tenderness around his right eye, he'd pretty much put the free-for-all at Remy's behind him.

"No," he repeated, shaking his head a second time. "I'm fine."

"Then what—?"

"It's you," he said bluntly. "You seem...different...tonight."

Color blossomed in Peachy's cheeks. Her lashes swept down for a provocative instant then lifted so she could meet his gaze once more. "Do you really think so?"

The question wasn't coy. And because it wasn't—because it lacked the taunting, "I have a secret" quality Lucien Devereaux tended to associate with male-female relations—the storm within him began to abate.

"Yes, I really think so," he told her, surprised by the steadiness of his voice.

"Good."

"Has something—" he weighed varying degrees of directness then opted to be oblique "—happened?"

"In a way." Peachy linked her arm through his and steered him away from the door. "I realized I was being unfair to you."

"Unfair...to *me?*" Whatever answer he'd been expecting, this was not it.

"It's not enough for me to tell you I want to lose my virginity, Luc," she explained with dulcet calm. "I have to show you."

There was a pause. Luc used it to calculate the viability of various escape routes. Eventually he cleared his throat and asked, "Is that what you intend to do this evening? To...show me?"

Peachy smiled. Her lips appeared to have been glossed with a mixture of honey and red wine. He clamped down on a sudden wayward urge to bend his head and discover whether they tasted as sweetly intoxicating as they looked.

"I've been so concerned about *your* making things easy for *me*," she replied, "that I never thought about *my* making things easy for *you.*"

Luc inhaled sharply, beginning to understand the nature of the change his bed partner had undergone. And with this nascent understanding came the recognition that his chances for swaying her from the course she'd chosen nearly two weeks ago were dwindling rapidly—if they hadn't already disappeared.

Pamela Gayle Keene had sloughed off the effects of her aviation trauma and come to her senses as he'd hoped she would. But she still obviously wanted to be rid of her virginity. And there wasn't a doubt in his mind that if he demonstrated too much reluctance about fulfilling his promise to initiate her into the pleasures of the flesh, she'd find someone else to do it.

Hell. With her new appreciation of what she had to offer a man, she'd have volunteers lining up, begging to be of service!

The image was intolerable to Luc in ways he couldn't begin to articulate.

All right, he decided abruptly. He'd do as she'd asked. He'd give her what she'd determined that she wanted. One time, with no strings attached.

And after that one time was over...

"It's *not* 'no big deal,' Peachy," he quietly asserted.

Something flickered through her eyes. "I know that," she responded. "I also know I'm sure about what I'm doing."

Luc had to give Peachy credit. Despite her extremely limited experience, she had a real flair for staging a seduction scene.

Her living room had been decorated with about a dozen bouquets of flowers and enough candles to illuminate the St. Louis Cathedral on Jackson Square. They were the clichéd accoutrements of romance, to be sure. They were also damned effective.

The Frank Sinatra tape crooning from the stereo was a hackneyed ploy, too, but the lyric potency of the music got to Luc, as well. He just hoped he'd never mentioned his weakness for the ballads of Tony Bennett.

The invitation that had been slipped under his door had specified that a "light supper" would be served. A buffet of purported aphrodisiacs would have been a more accurate description. The meal began with oysters and ended with strawberries triple-dipped in chocolate. They dined at a linen-draped table set with crystal and silver he recognized as belonging to the MayWinnies.

That Peachy would offer champagne went without saying. The beverage was perfectly chilled, its tiny bubbles bursting in effervescent celebration on his tongue.

Luc had a moment—sometime between his acceptance of a third glass of the sparkling wine and his refusal of a fourth—when he considered the possibility of getting drunk to the point where he couldn't perform. He rejected the idea for two reasons. The first was his long-standing contempt for the way his father had abused alcohol. The second was his memory of Peachy's story about her senior prom.

"It's very quiet tonight," he remarked about an hour after his arrival, watching Peachy bite slowly through three thin layers of chocolate then sink her teeth into the ruby flesh of a succulently ripe berry. His heart was beating like a drum. His breathing was fairly even, but only because he was concentrating on keeping it so.

His hostess ran her tongue over her juice-sheened lower lip before answering. "That's because we're the only ones home."

"Oh?" Luc shifted his position slightly, stretching his legs beneath the table.

"Terry's at work." A nibble at the berry. "The MayWinnies went to Baton Rouge for the weekend." Another nibble. "And Mr. Smythe and Laila are out."

There was an odd little spin to the third component of this reply. Flashing back on the conversation he'd had with his newest tenant one week ago, Luc asked what seemed to be the obvious question. "Together?"

Fiery curls shimmered in the candlelight. Creamy pale skin took on a lambent glow. "Mmm-hmm. I saw them walking out of the building, arm in arm, about ninety minutes ago."

"Interesting."

"Very."

Finishing her berry, Peachy discarded the ruffle-leaved stem then proceeded to lick the tips of her fingers. Her expression turned dreamy and distant as she did so, leaving Luc to speculate restively about the nature of her thoughts. He shifted his body again, then removed his napkin from his lap and deposited it on the table in a careless heap. His flexed his hands, taking a steadying breath of restraint.

The heady perfume of fresh flowers blended with the subtle scent of melting beeswax and wafted through the air.

Candle flames flickered, their wicks burning down with a softly hissing sizzle.

Frank Sinatra stopped singing. After several moments, Tony Bennett began.

The invitation was inevitable. Irresistible.

"Dance with me, *cher?*" Luc asked.

Green-gold eyes focused on his face, the look in them sending a profligate degree of anticipation flaring through his body.

"Yes, please," Peachy said, her voice as husky as his own.

He rose in a smooth fusion of flesh, sinew and bone and walked around to the opposite side of the table. He held out his hand. Peachy took it. He drew her to her feet and into his arms.

The fit of their bodies was effortless, instinctive. So was the way they moved to the lushly romantic song issuing from the stereo on the other side of the room.

Luc closed his eyes, breathing in Peachy's fragrance. He stroked his right hand down the supple line of her spine, savoring the tremor of response beneath his palm.

"Please," she whispered on a heated sigh, her hips moving in languorous insinuation.

"Shhh," he soothed, knowing she must feel the urgency of his need but determined to make this one-time-only encounter last. Opening his eyes again, he dipped his head and pressed a kiss to the side of her throat. He heard her breath catch at the caress and felt the sudden acceleration of her pulse against his questing lips.

"I want . . ."

"I know," he assured her, seeking and finding the tender warmth behind her right ear. "But there's no reason for us to rush."

They went on dancing.

Teasing. Tantalizing. Tempting.

The music became slower.

Their movements moderated to a swaying, sensuous embrace.

"Luc," Peachy murmured, gazing up a him. Her cheeks were flushed. Her lips were moist and trembling.

Whispering her name, he feathered his mouth across hers. She opened to him like a flower. Her tongue stole out and touched the tip of his own, triggering an involuntary groan deep in his throat.

"Now," she urged, echoing the pulsating demands he was receiving from his lower body. "Please."

He broke the kiss and eased back slightly, bracing himself against the goad of his libido. He looked down into her hazy, half-closed eyes. "Are you sure, Peachy?"

"Yes, Luc." She slid her hands up his chest, her fingers splayed. "Oh, yes."

Shifting his stance, Luc swung Peachy up into his arms and pivoted toward her bedroom. She curled into his embrace, tucking her head against his shoulder. He felt her warm breath fan against his skin. Tightening his hold, he found himself tenderly murmuring protective promises he'd never before uttered. His heart was hammering . . . hammering . . . hammering . . .

He'd gone five or six steps before it finally dawned on him that the sound he was hearing had nothing to do with his cardiovascular system. Someone was pounding on the door of Peachy's apartment.

"Wha—?" He heard his would-be lover gasp, an awareness that something was wrong apparently registering with her. She brought her head up a split second later, slamming the top of her skull against the edge of his jaw.

Luc staggered, but somehow managed to set Peachy down on her feet rather than unceremoniously dropping her on her rear end. He blinked several times, trying to clear his head. He actually seemed to be seeing stars.

"This is the N'awlins Police Department," a male voice yelled. "Y'all open up in there!"

Peachy didn't know whether to cry, scream or kick something. She settled for whirling away from the door she'd just slammed on a team of thoroughly chagrined members of the NOPD and stomping into her living room.

"Dammit," she swore through gritted teeth, flinging herself down on her chintz-covered settee. Her vision blurred for a second. She clenched her hands until her nails dug into her palms. "Dammit all to hell."

"I'm sorry," Luc said softly, coming to sit beside her.

"Why?" She shifted left as his thigh brushed hers. "It wasn't your fault."

"I *am* the one who supposedly looks like this alleged serial killer someone saw on—what was the name of that syndicated TV show again? 'Help Catch America's Most Heinous Criminals'?"

His wry tone sent an involuntary giggle fighting its way up out of Peachy's anger-tightened chest. She swallowed the sound before it could escape, then edgily acknowledged, "Something like that."

"So I do bear a certain degree of responsibility for what happened."

Another impulse toward laughter tickled the back of her throat. This one she decided not to fight. Releasing it actually made her feel a little better. "If you insist."

"And I probably deserve some credit for defusing the situation as well."

She slanted a glance to her right, wondering at his mood. "Because your buddy from the No Parking zone was one of tonight's would-be arresting officers?"

"Exactly."

"He didn't seem to recognize you at first."

"It's difficult to identify a suspect when you're busy ogling someone who might be his accomplice. Or his intended victim."

It took her a few moments to unravel this assertion. "Are you saying what's-his-name, Officer Kerrigan, was ogling *me?*"

"That's how it looked," Luc affirmed with a crooked grin. "Of course, given that I was spread-eagled against the wall with one cop screaming I had the right to remain silent and another frisking me for hidden weapons, I could have mistaken the reason his eyes seemed to be bugging out of their sockets."

Peachy shuddered suddenly, remembering the unmitigated craziness that had reigned in her apartment foyer during the first few minutes after the police had come bursting in. Most of what had happened was a blur. But there was one image that was etched into her mind's eye with crystalline clarity. It was the image of Luc deliberately interposing himself between her and the uniformed intruders. His movements had been swift and sure, his intention clearly to shield her from harm.

"They didn't hurt you, did they?" she asked after a moment or two.

He shook his head. "Compared to that clout on the jaw you gave me, *cher,* they handled me like I was a piece of their grandmama's fine china."

She winced, conscious of a residual ache in the crown of her skull. "I'm really sorry about that."

"Well, as long as you didn't do it on purpose . . ."

His voice trailed off into silence. They sat without speaking for nearly a minute. Peachy sighed and closed her eyes.

"Do you think the police do this sort of thing very often?" she finally asked.

"What? Interrupt two consenting adults on the verge of making whoopie because they got an anonymous phone tip about a possible mass murderer?"

Peachy opened her eyes. She didn't want to be reminded of how close she'd come to fulfilling the vow she'd made nearly two weeks ago. "Who would *do* such a thing?"

"Call in the tip, you mean?"

She frowned, trying to make sense of what had happened. "Could it have been somebody's idea of a joke?"

"I have some friends who have pretty weird notions about what's funny," Luc dryly conceded, running a hand through his hair. "But even they'd draw the line at siccing the police on me."

"What about—" she hesitated for a fraction of a second "— enemies?"

"I've got a few of those who have pretty weird notions about what's funny, too. But these days they seem to get their kicks writing nasty reviews of my books."

"Then you think it was an honest mistake?"

"I'm a little iffy about the 'honest' part. But I'd definitely vote for it being a mistake."

Peachy sighed heavily then muttered, "Maybe I should just chalk it up to the plot to prevent me from losing my virginity."

"I beg your pardon?"

She felt herself flush. She hadn't realized she'd spoken aloud. "Nothing."

"You think there's some sort of conspiracy to keep you chaste, *cher?*"

"No." She manufactured a laugh. "Of course not."

"Then why—"

Unnerved by his interest, she snapped, "Because I'm *frustrated!*"

Luc gazed at her thoughtfully for several moments. Then, "Do you want to make love now?"

The inquiry caught Peachy completely unprepared. She opened and shut her mouth two or three times while her heart performed strange flip-flops within her breast. "Do y-you?" she finally stammered, her voice about a half octave higher than normal.

The corners of Luc's flexible lips curled upward. "Ladies first."

She swallowed, riven by a host of contradictory impulses. She wanted, she acknowledged painfully. She wanted in ways she'd never imagined possible. But not like this. Not as though their coming together was a chore on some checklist!

Finally, awkwardly, she answered, "I'm . . . not exactly in the mood anymore, Luc."

"A police raid isn't your idea of a prelude to passion, hmm?"

Her stomach fluttered at the word *passion.* "It's only temporary," she maintained. "I mean, I still want to . . . do it. I haven't changed my mind about that. I just don't want to do it tonight. Not after what happened."

"I understand."

There was a long silence. The insecurities that had been nibbling around the edges of Peachy's consciousness began to gnaw in earnest. Eventually she was driven to ask, "Have you?"

Luc lifted his brows. "Have I what?"

"Changed your mind."

"No."

The answer was quick and unequivocal. It should have been reassuring. Yet Peachy found it anything but. She felt compelled to press the issue. "Do you want to?"

"What? Change my mind?"

"No." She shook her head, wondering whether he was being deliberately obtuse. "Do you... *want* to make love with me?"

Luc regarded her steadily for what seemed like a very long time. Finally he said, "I promised you I would."

"Because I asked."

"Peachy—"

"You turned me down at first, Luc," she said, the words tumbling out in a rush. "Remember? And then you changed your mind. Only you never explained why. You just said you'd do what I wanted. But when I think back about the way I approached you—when I think about the reasons I gave for believing you'd be willing to—" She gestured, her mind replaying the scene. "God. I must have sounded as though I thought you'd sleep with... with *anybody!*"

"It wasn't quite that bad," Luc returned with disconcerting mildness. "I had the feeling you granted me a few standards."

Peachy eyed him uncertainly, her awareness of the vast difference between their levels of sexual experience acute. "Most men would have been insulted by the things I said."

"Perhaps. But just as you told me the other night on the drive out to Remy's that you're *you*, not 'some people'... I'm *me*, not 'most men.'"

She mulled this statement over, cognizant that he was still sidestepping the question of why he'd reversed his initial rejection of her proposal. After a time she ventured, "I'm not really your type, am I."

An expression she couldn't decipher streaked through the depths of his dark eyes. "And what do you think you know about my type, *cher?*"

She mentally reviewed the media photographs she'd seen and the gossip she'd heard. "Enough."

There was another silence. Finally Luc expelled a breath in a long, drawn-out sigh. Instinct told Peachy he'd come to some sort of decision.

"I'm going out of town tomorrow morning," he told her quietly. "Book business, in New York. I'll be back Wednesday afternoon. There's a small hotel I know in the Vieux Carre." He mentioned a name that was vaguely familiar. "It's quiet and discreet and it's never been raided by the police. We can meet there after you're done with work."

She swallowed. "And then we'll—?"

Luc lifted his right hand and stroked the tip of his index finger against her mouth. Peachy felt her pulse spike. "If you're back in the mood, *cher,*" he responded. "Absolutely."

Eight

The message was hand delivered to Peachy's work cubicle approximately ninety minutes before the close of business on Wednesday. She'd been "back in the mood," and then some, about seventy-two hours by then.

"P. G. Keene?" the young courier who materialized in her doorway asked in an adenoidal voice. His hair was shaved down to a platinum stubble, the lobe of his left ear was pierced with a trio of brass studs, and his wiry body was encased in an eye-assaulting ensemble of bright yellow and bile green spandex. He held a small padded envelope in one hand. A battered knapsack dangled from the other.

"Yes," Peachy affirmed a bit breathlessly, getting to her feet. The courier's arrival had jerked her out of a bordering-on-the-erotic reverie about Luc. A spillover, she supposed, from the explicitly sexual dreams she'd had about him the night before. And the night before that. And the night before the night before that. She wondered fleetingly whether her face betrayed the direction of her thoughts, then decided it probably didn't matter. There was a glassy expression in her visitor's eyes which suggested that he was attuned to his own private vision of reality.

"Cool." The courier handed over the envelope then reached into the knapsack and extracted a clipboard and a pen. "Sign after the *X*, 'kay? At, like, uh, line sixteen."

Peachy did as she was instructed. Her heart skipped a beat when she saw that the name scrawled to the left of the *X* on line sixteen was L. Devereaux. The boldness of the penmanship was unmistakable.

"Cool," the courier repeated when she'd finished, stuffing the clipboard and pen back into his knapsack. After favoring her with an amiable but unfocused grin, he pivoted toward the door and ambled out.

The thickness of the envelope made it impossible for Peachy to deduce its contents by touch. Returning to her worktable, she slit it open and reached inside.

The first item she brought out was an unmarked key, provocative in its anonymity. The second was a terse but tantalizing note written in the same hand as the signature on the courier's form.

"Room 408," it read. "I'll be waiting."

Two hours later, Pamela Gayle Keene stood in front of a cream-painted wooden door on the fourth floor of the small hotel about which Luc had spoken Saturday night. Her cheeks were flushed. Her hands were trembling. There was an anticipatory throb between her thighs.

She opened her purse.

She took out the unmarked key.

The shock she'd experienced in the immediate aftermath of reading the note that had accompanied the key had faded. She'd been offended at first by what had seemed to her to be the arrogance of the brief communique. Then she'd realized that the words could be taken another way. Implicit in them was a renewal of Luc's promise that the final decision about what was or wasn't going to happen between them would be hers.

Her would-be lover would be waiting.

If she chose to go to him.

And if she did not . . .

Peachy inserted the key in the lock and turned it. Although common sense told her that the *click* of release was barely audible, there was a part of her that would have sworn it was loud enough to echo through the empty hotel hallway.

She opened the door.

She stepped inside.

"Luc?" she asked, closing the door behind her.

"Here, *cher.*"

The quiet response came from her right. Peachy turned in that direction as Luc appeared from between a pair of fluttering gauze curtains. The black filigree of a wrought iron balustrade was visible through the sheer, breeze-stirred fabric. The scent of jasmine drifted into the room.

Separated by a distance of about eight or nine feet, they stood without speaking for nearly a minute. He gazing at her. She gazing at him. Although she'd checked her appearance in the ladies' room mirror at work before leaving then sneaked another self-conscious peek in a gold-framed looking glass in the hotel's antique-furnished foyer when she'd entered, Peachy had no idea how she looked to Luc.

As for how he looked to her...

He was dressed in black jeans and a black long-sleeved shirt. The severity of the garments underscored the coiled-spring muscularity of his lean body and the chiseled attractiveness of his features. Although motionless as a statue, he radiated a potent, pulsating vitality.

Peachy swallowed hard, her awareness of the sensual immediacy of Luc's presence threatening to undermine her already shaky poise. She saw his eyes narrow, the directness of his scrutiny becoming flagrant in its intensity.

"Did you think I wouldn't come?" she blurted out, unable to stop the words.

His brows quirked for an instant then relaxed. "I tried not to."

The response—like the change of expression—could be interpreted several different ways. But after a brief hesitation, Peachy decided not to press for a clarification. Instead, she began to take stock of her surroundings. She knew the hotel had been fashioned out of a pair of Creole town houses dating from the early 1800s. The room in which she was standing reflected the elegance of that period in both its architecture and furnishings.

"This is beautiful, Luc," she eventually observed, her appreciation of the setting genuine. Her initial reaction to the notion of surrendering her virginity in a hotel had been ambivalence. Making love in a rented room had seemed so...illicit. Yet now that she was here, she realized the idea had a great deal of merit. Not only was the setting undeniably lovely, it was also neutral, no-strings territory.

"I'm glad you approve."

"Have you—" green-gold eyes met brown ones "—been here before?"

It was a question Peachy knew she had no right to ask and her companion had even less reason to answer. Yet after a few moments Luc offered her the reassurance she wanted. "No," he said simply. "But it comes highly recommended."

"By whom?"

A smile ghosted around the corners of his flexible mouth. He moved across the room toward her, coming to a halt just within touching range. "That would be telling, *cher*."

She lifted her chin. "And telling is something you don't do?"

"Not if I can avoid it." Luc paused as though contemplating an addendum to this statement, then apparently changed his mind. After a few seconds he asked, "Would you like to see the rest of the suite?"

Peachy caught her breath, a thrill darting up her spine.

The rest of the suite.

Meaning . . . the bedroom.

"All right," she assented.

Luc reached out and took her hand. Their palms met and mated. Their fingers intertwined. "This way," he said softly.

"I'm afraid I'm not going to be very good at this," Peachy confessed in a shaky voice about twenty minutes later as her lover-to-be eased her down on a canopied bed that was roughly the size of the first apartment she'd rented in New York City. A desire to please trembled through her senses, fusing with an already complex aggregate of emotions.

"You will be," came the calm reply.

"How—" her breath snagged at the top of her throat as what had started as a soothing caress turned overtly sexual "—can you be so certain?"

"Experience, *cher*."

Then he kissed her.

It was a long, slow kiss that seemed intended to arouse as much as reassure. Peachy knew she was not the only one trembling when Luc finally lifted his mouth from hers.

"Tell me what you like," he urged in a deep, dark, velvet tone.

"I don't know," she answered a little dizzily, aware of the touch of his fingers as he began to undo the row of buttons that ran down the front of her dress. "I've never . . ."

"Then tell me what you *want*," he amended, a hint of the imperative entering his voice.

She tilted her head back. Luc had freed her hair from its workaday braid some minutes ago. The untrammeled curls bounced against her shoulders.

Lifting her right hand, she lightly caressed the side of Luc's face. A hint of new beard growth abraded her fingertips as she traced a line from cheekbone to chin. After a few moments she offered him the truth. "You," she said in a throaty whisper. "I want you."

His hand stilled for a breathless instant. His jaw clenched beneath her touch.

"Just this once," she added swiftly, remembering the terms of their arrangement and repeating them as much for herself as for him. She stroked downward to his suavely muscled chest. "Just for right now."

She heard him exhale with a groan that could have included an invocation of her name. His fingers resumed their business on the front of her dress. His touch was a tad less deft than it had been previously, but infinitely more determined.

A few seconds later the garment was undone to the waist.

Luc slid his hands outward over the verge of her shoulders, easing the fabric of her dress off and partway down her arms. Peachy shivered as soft, sultry air played over her newly bared flesh. She breathed in sharply, the musk-male odor of his skin and hair teasing her nostrils. She caught a whiff of something else—something not quite right—then lost it in an inundation of more compelling sensations.

"Beautiful," he declared huskily, charting the delicate upper swell of her breasts then cupping beneath. "So . . . beautiful."

She arched into his caressing, claiming palms, shifting in an untutored effort to increase the intimacy of the contact. His hands tightened against her flesh. Something deep inside her spasmed in response. Her blood seemed to thrum and thicken. She felt as though she were being infused with sun-warmed honey.

They kissed again. Deeply. Deliberately. Deliciously. Peachy tasted the flavor of her name on Luc's lips. He absorbed the soft, startled cry of pleasure she gave when his fingers stole beneath the fragile material of her bra to toy with the eager, aching tips of her breasts.

The anxiety she'd experienced earlier was gone. The fear she'd thought she might feel at this turning point in her life had never materialized. She yearned, uninhibitedly. Wanted, without reservation.

Yes, she thought. Oh, yes.

Luc's shirt came off. Peachy kissed along the hard edge of his collarbone then licked, very daintily, against the hollow at the base of his corded throat. The salty tang of his skin lingered on her tongue. His pulse, when she found it, was avid in its rapidity.

"Cher," he murmured, his voice roughened by the same forces that had accelerated the beating of his heart. "Oh, sweet...*cher."*

He eased her from sitting to supine so skillfully Peachy was hardly aware of the transition taking place. Any impulse toward objection was swept away by the gliding upward stroke of his left hand between her legs. She twisted, lifting her hips an inch or two off the mattress.

"Please." The word was heated and half-suffocated. *"Please."*

Luc stretched out beside her on the bed. Somehow, someway, her bra had come undone. He brushed the flimsy, lace-trimmed cups aside with his free hand. His fingers slid over one breast in leisurely appraisal, assessing its responsiveness with an expertly erotic touch. He buffed the nipple with the pad of his thumb, causing it to stir and swell. Peachy caught her lower lip between her teeth as an arrow of heat streaked downward to pierce the core of her femininity.

Luc transferred his attentions to her other breast. Molding. Massaging. But this time it was the lap of his supple tongue that coaxed her nipple from a plush-velvet bud to a thorn-hard point.

And then he drew the aching crest into his warm, wet mouth, suckling once—twice—with exquisitely calibrated demand.

Peachy found herself clutching at his broad shoulders in much the same way she'd done the night he'd kissed her for the first time. She gasped, engulfed by a shockingly volatile surge of response. She tingled clear down to the tips of her pedicured toes. Pressure began building within her, clamoring for a release she'd imagined but never experienced firsthand.

More kisses.

More caresses.

And then Peachy caught the scent again. Only this time it was stronger. Strong enough for her mind, as fevered with sensory expectation as it was, to shift the odor out of the not-quite-right category.

Something was definitely wrong.

"Luc," she managed, evading his lips for an instant.

"I know, *cher*." He nuzzled against her cheek then nipped at the lobe of her ear. His hands seemed to be everywhere. Testing. Teaching. Gleaning the secrets of her body and giving them back to her with ardent generosity.

Peachy shook her head, her hair shifting around her face and over her neck and shoulders. She struggled to focus, her grip on rationality growing more tenuous with each passing second. "N-no," she disputed. "You...d-don't."

Luc froze a split second after she stammered out the negative. His body stiffened. His hands stopped moving. After a moment he lifted his head and looked down at her. There was a stunned expression in his heavy-lidded eyes. The rest of his features were stark with stress.

"*No?*" he repeated on a rasping exhalation, his face darkening.

Peachy blinked, the change in his mood and manner too sudden for her to accept all at once. And then she realized the potentially disastrous misunderstanding the change implied.

"Oh, God," she gasped, appalled, levering herself up on her elbows. Her body, primed for something else, protested the abrupt shift of position.

"Peachy—"

She shook her head a second time, fleetingly registering the wanton vulnerability of her position. Her breasts were bare, the roseate nipples engorged. Her thighs were parted. The skirt of her dress was pushed up to the place where sheer hose gave way to only slightly more substantial panty.

"*No,*" she said again, feeling herself succumbing to a full-body blush. "I don't—I mean, I wasn't—"

At that point, a fire alarm started to shrill.

"Do you remember that conspiracy you mentioned Saturday night, *cher?*" Luc questioned wryly several hours later as he thumbed the appropriate buttons on the control panel in the elevator of their Prytania Street residence.

Peachy gave a weary laugh, massaging the nape of her neck with her right hand. There was a nasty throbbing in her temples. Frustration, she supposed. Plus a minor case of smoke inhalation.

"You think I may be on to something?" she asked as the elevator door creaked closed.

"Well . . ."

"Let me guess. Those strange friends of yours you think would probably draw the line at calling in a phony tip to the police wouldn't necessarily cavil at committing arson?"

Luc grinned crookedly, then grew serious. "I'm sorry, Peachy. Again."

She gestured the apology away. "What happened tonight was even less your fault than what happened last time."

"I *did* pick the hotel."

"On somebody else's recommendation."

The elevator's pulley system engaged with a gnashing of metallic teeth. There was an upward jerk as the car began its laborious ascent.

Peachy closed her eyes, vibrations from the floor of the elevator echoing through her body in odd and evocative ways. She shifted her weight from one foot to the other, the fabric of her dress whispering over her thighs.

"Are you all right?" Luc asked.

She opened her eyes after a moment or two, disciplining her expression as well as she could. "Fine," she answered, hoping her voice sounded less husky to him than it did to her. "I was just thinking about those beautiful old buildings going up in flames. To say nothing of all that antique furniture."

"At least everyone got out safely."

"Thanks in part to you."

"All I did was point the way to the fire exit."

"*And* carry an unconscious, two-hundred-pound woman down four flights of stairs."

Luc shrugged. Peachy had seen him offer the same dismissive response to a reporter who'd tried to interview him at the scene of the fire. It was obvious he was discomfited by the notion that there'd been anything exceptional about his behavior.

"Better unconscious than hysterical," he said, thrusting a hand through his dark, disordered hair. There was a smudge of soot on his temple.

The elevator car ground past the second floor.

Peachy sighed and toyed with her locket, wondering for the dozenth time whether any of the local TV crews who'd shown up to cover the fire had captured her and Luc on tape. She fervently hoped not. The potential repercussions if so much as a single shot of the two of them, together, outside a hotel, turned up on the eleven o'clock news were unnerving to contemplate.

Bestselling author, Lucien Devereaux, and yet another unidentified companion, the little voice in the back of her skull summed up snidely.

Peachy went rigid, an emotion she couldn't identify twisting in the pit of her stomach like a snake.

Do you think anyone would believe the two of you haven't *done it?* her internal inquisitor persisted.

Forget the "anyone" else! she thought, her temper fraying to the snapping point. *She* didn't believe it! She'd been trying to lose her virginity to Lucien Devereaux for thirteen days, and she still hadn't succeeded! Oh, sure, she'd come close. Painfully close. Passionately close. Closer than she'd come to losing it to Jake Pearman, with whom she'd foolishly believed she was in love, on prom night. But since close only counted when it came to horseshoes and hand grenades, so what?

Maybe it's not meant to be, Pamela Gayle.

"Damn!" Luc suddenly exclaimed, pressing his finger against a button on the control panel.

"Wh-what?" Peachy asked, thoroughly startled.

"We just missed your floor, *cher.*"

She stared at her companion as though she'd never seen him before. The phrase *not meant to be* was reverberating through her brain like a demented mantra.

No, she denied with a ferocity that seemed to surge up from the very center of her soul.

Yes. The contradiction was immediate and implacable. *And all things considered, it's probably for the best.*

What things? she demanded of the voice. Of herself.

If you'd done it the first night you asked him, maybe you would have been able to keep that no-strings pledge you offered, came the steady reply. *But now? After all the time you've spent with him? After all the things you've learned about him? Do you honestly believe you could still make love with Luc once and walk away? That you could have him and hold him for a single night and then let him go forever?*

"Peachy?"

Something perilously close to a sob forced its way up her throat. Peachy converted it to a shattered little laugh a split second before it broke from her lips, then said, "We seem to be missing a lot of things, Luc."

His brow furrowed. He took a step toward her, obliterating most of the physical distance between them. For a moment it seemed he would reach out for her. She steeled herself against the contact only to see him control the urge to touch by a palpable act of will.

"I don't understand," he told her. His voice was gentle. Almost tender. And the expression in his dark eyes matched his tone.

The elevator lurched to a stop. Jolted, Peachy staggered and nearly fell.

Luc caught her.

Steadied her.

Then, after an interval of time that was both far too long and far too short, he opened his hands and released her to stand on her own.

"I'm . . . sorry," she said.

"No need," he replied.

The elevator door wheezed open. Luc used his foot to prevent it from reclosing.

"Would you like to come in for a few minutes?" he asked, nodding toward his apartment.

Peachy hesitated, still feeling the imprint of his fingers against her upper arms. "I . . . don't think I'd better."

"Why not?"

"After everything that's happened?"

"Tonight, you mean."

"And before."

He cocked his head, his brows drawing together. "Are we back to the plot to keep you pure?"

Peachy gestured helplessly, her sense of confusion acute. "Maybe."

There was a pause. Then, carefully, "I won't hurt you, Peachy."

Her throat constricted. Her chest tightened as well. Her heart started beating in an erratic rhythm, and she had to struggle to draw breath. "I know," she finally said, dropping her gaze.

"What about . . . tomorrow?" The question was very quiet.

"That—" Peachy forced herself to meet his eyes once again "—I don't know."

Luc blinked once. His face went blank. "I see."

She would have welcomed a contribution from her know-it-all little voice at that moment, but it remained stubbornly silent.

"I need some time," she finally declared.

"Oh, I'm sure you do."

"It's nothing *personal*, Luc," Peachy insisted, her inflection rising. Then she almost groaned aloud as she realized she'd unwittingly used the same words he'd employed nearly two weeks ago when he'd tried to explain his initial refusal of her request that he deflower her. "I mean—"

"I understand what you mean," her companion calmly said. "And I'm sure that it's not." Then, with great deliberation, he lifted his hand and laid it against the side of her face for the space of a single heartbeat. "Good night, *cher*."

He was out of the elevator and halfway down the fourth-floor hallway before Peachy found her voice.

"Luc!" she called, shoving back the elevator door as it started to shut.

He pivoted to face her, his expression wary, his posture taut. "Yes?"

"Do you trust me?"

He waited a long time to answer. And when he did, his response left her more confused than ever.

"More than I trust myself."

So he trusts you more than he trusts himself, Pamela Gayle, the ubiquitous voice mused, a little more than a day and a half later. *Now what?*

"Now...nothing," Peachy muttered, rearranging a double row of moonstones and black seed pearls on an egg-shaped pendant of sterling silver that had been inlaid with twenty-four-karat gold and niello.

She hadn't seen nor spoken to Luc since their ambiguous parting on Wednesday night. Whether this was the result of him avoiding her or her avoiding him or simply the way things happened to turn out, she honestly didn't know. And if truth be told, she wasn't certain she wanted to find out.

You mean you're giving up—?

"Uh-huh." Peachy used a pair of tweezers to maneuver one of the moonstones a millimeter to the left then narrowed her eyes, scrutinizing the effect. It was either extremely elegant in an avant-garde kind of way or a total botch, she decided with dismal humor after a few seconds. And maybe once she got her head screwed on straight again, she'd be able to determine which.

Oh, geez.

Peachy grimaced, nudging one of the pearls two millimeters to the right of where she'd previously positioned it. "You're the one who said it wasn't meant to be."

Well, yes, the voice concurred with a hint of exasperation. *But since I'm just you talking to yourself and you're head-over-heels in love with the man, there's no way you're going to end up—*

The tweezers dropped from slackened fingers. They hit the edge of the pendant, flipping it sideways.

"No," she gasped.

"Problem?" the colleague who sat in the cubicle to the left of hers called out.

Peachy swallowed convulsively. "Nothing I can't handle, thanks," she called back, trying to pick up the rice-shaped pearls and luminous cabochon-cut stones that had scattered across her worktable. Her hands were shaking so badly she had to stop, fearing she'd knock something onto the floor and damage it.

"Head-over-heels in love?" she whispered, aghast. She sought the sleek silver comfort of her Wedding Belle locket with violently trembling fingers.

She was prepared to admit to a lot of things, Peachy told herself. Including to being a twenty-three-year-old virgin with a ridiculous nickname, who carried on conversations with herself, and who no longer gave a rat's rear end whether the entire world was conspiring to keep her maidenhead intact until it was time for the tomb. But she was not—absolutely, positively was *not!*—ready to admit to being in love with Lucien Devereaux.

She was attracted to him, yes. Intensely. Extremely. Maybe even a little irrationally after what had—or should that be hadn't?— happened between them during the last two weeks. *But she was not in love with him!*

She had the hots for the guy. She was warm for his form. She had the urge to merge, two into one.

She, and heaven only knew how many other women. Most of whom Luc had probably slept with already. Or would get around to sleeping with once he stopped being celibate and reverted to his usual studly style of life.

It was lust she felt for the man she'd wanted as her first lover, nothing more.

Lust. Pure and simple.

Pure and simple?

All right! Fine! Peachy backpedaled furiously. Forget the pure. Forget the simple. Call it unconsummated lust and concede that it was as complicated as anything she'd ever experienced. It was still a physical itch, not an emotional attachment. It was a matter of howling hormones, not a commitment of the heart.

And yet . . .

And yet, when the phone in her work cubicle rang a moment later, Peachy snatched the receiver up, praying to hear the voice of the man she'd told herself she didn't love on the other end of the line.

Some prayers get answered.

Some prayers don't.

Nine

It was 10:45 p.m. and Lucien Devereaux was beyond thinking the worst. As he paced around his darkened apartment like a caged animal, he was beginning to contemplate the unthinkable.

He had no idea where Peachy was.

He had no idea what Peachy was doing.

He had no idea who Peachy was with.

He had no idea whether he was ever going to see her again.

His ignorance was killing him by inches.

Luc knew Peachy had been all right when she'd left for work that morning. He'd monitored her departure from one of the windows of his living room, tracking the sway of her slender hips beneath the apricot-and-cream dress she had on. She'd been wearing a straw hat. It had been wide-brimmed and blooming with a flirtatious band of pinky-gold flowers. He'd hated the thing because it had blocked his view of her face.

That had been fifteen hours ago.

Nine hundred minutes.

Fifty-four thousand seconds and counting.

"I need some time," she'd told him Wednesday night in the wake of their thwarted lovemaking at the hotel.

"I'm sure you do," he'd replied, neglecting to add that he knew he needed some time, too.

He'd deliberately steered clear of Peachy the following day, struggling to regain a modicum of the detachment that had always been his strongest source of defense against the vicissitudes of life. He'd also forgone his customary run this morning, deeming himself too raw to risk an encounter with her in the lobby. This evening, he'd told himself. He'd be ready to see her this evening.

Well, this evening had arrived and he probably was less ready to see Peachy than he had been that morning. He was still raw. Rawer than he'd ever been, if truth be told. What's more, the waiting and watching and worrying of the past few hours had forced him to face the fact that nothing short of the psychological equivalent of an amputation would allow him to distance himself from Pamela Gayle Keene.

He'd fallen in love with her.

At least . . . he thought that was what he'd done. He couldn't be sure.

Not yet.

Maybe never.

Luc recognized that he had no standards for defining the rush of feelings that was threatening to engulf him. As he was bitterly aware, his understanding of what supposedly was the most elemental of human emotions was limited to the point of nonexistence by lack of experience. It probably was tainted by premature exposure to some of the more twisted aspects of human behavior as well.

But if what he felt for Peachy *wasn't* love—

Luc checked himself in midstride as he registered what sounded like a car pulling up in front of the apartment building. He swiftly crossed to one of the windows that overlooked Prytania Street and eased back the curtain that covered it. Standing at an angle to avoid being spotted, he peered out into the night. His throat was dry and aching. His chest felt as though it had been encircled with bands of steel.

A man got out of the driver's side of the car. Despite the silvery spill of illumination from a nearby streetlight, Luc couldn't make out the features of his face. But there was something vaguely familiar about the shape of his head. Well, no. Not the shape of his head, exactly. It was more the almost helmetlike solidity of his—

His lungs emptied in a great *whoosh* of breath as recognition bludgeoned him. His fingers clenched involuntarily against the fabric of the drapes. It was the MayWinnies' grandnephew!

A moment later the door on the front passenger's side opened. A pair of long, sleekly feminine legs swung into view.

Oh, God.

"Peachy," Luc whispered painfully, closing his eyes.

Relentlessly, remorselessly, his mind began to replay the peculiar exchange he and his erstwhile lover had had the evening after their first "nondate."

"The MayWinnies think I should go out with their grandnephew," she'd suddenly declared, breaking what had been an increasingly tense silence. She'd seemed almost surprised. Not so much that her next-door neighbors were attempting to fix her up with their relative, but rather that she'd decided to announce their matchmaking efforts to him.

"Do they?" he'd countered, already alerted to the Misses Barnes's intentions by Laila Martigny.

"Trent Barnes. The TV reporter."

"The one with the concrete coiffure."

She'd turned defensive. "He doesn't spray his hair in real life. Only when he's on camera."

There'd been an awkward pause, almost as uncomfortable as the one that had preceded her revelation about Trent Barnes. Although Luc had willed himself to stay silent, in the end he'd had to ask. He'd had to know.

"Are you?" he'd finally demanded, wondering what he'd do if she answered in the affirmative.

"Am I what?"

"Going to go out with the MayWinnies' grandnephew?"

Peachy had thought about lying to him at this point. He'd seen it in her face and had almost cried out in protest. The possibility that she would stoop to some deceptive male-female mind game had sickened him. That she might turn out to be a cheat like so many others . . .

And then her expression had changed. Calculation had given way to astonishingly fierce conviction. Her long-lashed green-gold eyes had gazed up at him with unwavering directness. He'd known she'd come to some kind of decision but he'd had no idea what it was. He'd spoken her name with a questioning inflection, his pulse beating very fast.

"I told them he could call," had been her candid response.

Obviously the MayWinnies had passed this message along and their grandnephew had acted accordingly.

Luc opened his eyes again. Peachy and her companion had walked from the car to the entrance of the apartment building. They were now standing by the front door, engaged in what seemed to be a very amiable conversation.

Because of the way the couple was positioned, he could only see the newsman's face. It was plain the guy was preparing to make his big move.

Luc suddenly remembered a piece of gossip he'd picked up a few months back. Something about some congressman punching Trent Barnes out during a live TV broadcast. There'd been a woman involved.

He felt his mouth twist, understanding the impulse to which the politician must have succumbed with gut-wrenching clarity. The idea of decking the MayWinnies' grandnephew was becoming more tempting with each passing moment.

Luc watched as Peachy gestured toward the door with the hand that wasn't clutching her flower-trimmed hat.

She was asking her escort in. Obviously.

Luc watched as Barnes smiled and said something.

He was accepting her invitation. Inevitably. What man wouldn't?

And then . . .

Oh, dear Lord.

And then Peachy took a small step forward, went up on her toes and *kissed* Trent Barnes!

Whether it was a butterfly brush to the side of the face or a flat-out smacker on the center of lips, Luc couldn't tell and didn't really care. He knew what the caress implied. He also knew there was no way he could endure it.

Peachy Keene was his, dammit! From the tips of her pedicured toenails to the top of her flame-haired head, she was *his!*

And he was hers.

For better or worse. Whether she still wanted him or not. He was hers. And one way or another, he was going to make sure she understood that.

Luc bolted for the door of his apartment.

The pain Peachy had been fighting off all evening attacked her like a mugger the moment she stepped into her apartment building elevator and pressed the third-floor button. Her soul seemed to crumple under the assault.

"Oh, God," she whispered, leaning against the wall of the car, her broad-brimmed straw hat falling from her grasp. Her right hand stole up to lift her Wedding Belle locket from beneath the bodice of her dress. She rubbed her fingertips against the skin-warmed silver.

The elevator door groaned shut.

Metal teeth bit noisily into the links of the pulley chain.

The car lurched up in a herky-jerky motion, then settled into a reasonably smooth pattern of ascent.

Accepting Trent Barnes's invitation to meet him after she finished work had been a mistake, Peachy reflected wearily as she tilted her head back and closed her eyes. Not that she hadn't enjoyed his company. She had. Oh, sure, the MayWinnies had fibbed about him not using hairspray in real life. They'd also neglected to mention that he'd taken to shading the left side of his broken nose with brown contouring powder in an apparent effort to create the illusion of straightness. Nonetheless, they'd been right on the money about him being more to her taste than their previous candidate, the oh-so-nice Daniel.

Grooming gaffes aside, she had found her neighbors' grand-nephew acerbically funny and extremely well informed. He'd even turned out to be acquainted with her fellow Wedding Belle, Annie Martin—the recently wed Mrs. Matthew Powell.

But he hadn't been Luc. And in the end, that was the only thing that had counted with her. It wasn't even a matter of her making comparisons between the two. Trenton Barnes simply wasn't Lucien Devereaux.

And Lucien Devereaux was the man she wanted with every fiber of her being.

Even if she could have him only once.

Although armored by a well-developed ego, Trent had obviously grasped the fact that he was a stand-in for someone else in fairly short order. Yet he'd had the grace to propose that they go on to dinner once they'd finished their get-acquainted drink at Napoleon House. He'd also had the tact to keep the conversation on an even keel when her increasingly stormy emotions had threatened to overwhelm her. No matter that his favorite topic of discussion was himself. The man had kept talking through moments when silence would have been insupportable to her, and for this she would always be grateful.

"So...I guess one of us should warn my great-aunts not to start planning an engagement party just yet, hmm?" he'd asked at the end of the evening as they stood at the entrance to her Prytania Street residence.

She'd gestured vaguely, conscious of a prickling sensation skittering up and down her spine. The possibility that they were being watched had flitted through her mind but she'd swiftly dismissed it. The windows in the front of the apartment building—including the ones on the fourth floor—were dark. She'd checked them when she'd gotten out of Trent's car.

"I'm sorry," she said after a few seconds, meaning it.

"No problem," Trent had responded with an ironic grin.

Peachy hadn't been quite sure what to do at that point. She'd felt that she definitely owed the man *something* for the kindness he'd shown her during the last few hours. But how much of a "something" had been a rather dicey deal.

After a brief hesitation, she'd closed the distance between them and given Trent a platonic peck on the cheek. "I hope you get that job in Washington you said you've applied for," she'd told him as she'd stepped back.

"Yeah," he'd replied feelingly. "Me, too."

The elevator came to a jolting stop. Still slumped against the wall, Peachy didn't move until she heard the door slide open. Then, sighing heavily, she reluctantly lifted her lids and focused her eyes.

Luc.

He was standing directly in front of the elevator, his body seeming to fill the doorframe. His only garment was a pair of wash-faded jeans that hugged his thighs and pelvis like a second skin and rode low on his narrow hips. He looked furious.

A distinctly feminine thrill of trepidation ran through Peachy. She darted a glance at the elevator control panel. It indicated that she was on the fourth floor.

Not the third. The fourth.

Not her floor. His.

"I didn't mean—" she started.

"Where the hell have you been?" Luc asked. His voice, like his expression, was dark and dangerous.

Peachy's mouth went dry. She licked her lips in unthinking reaction then fervently wished she hadn't when she saw what looked like a streak of summer lightning flash deep in her landlord's compelling eyes.

"O-out," she finally answered, mustering both breath and nerve as she told herself she had nothing to be ashamed of. And even if she had, it was no business of his!

"Do you have any idea what time it is?"

"Not—"

"How long I've been waiting for you?"

"—really."

There was a volatile silence. Seconds ticked by, primed for an explosion.

One wrong word . . .

One ill-considered gesture . . .

The elevator door started to close. Luc blocked it with an almost savage sweep of his arm. Muscles rippled and released beneath the hair-whorled skin of his chest.

"I saw you with Barnes, Peachy," he said.

Something inside her bridled at his accusatory tone. She stiffened, her chin lifting. What right did this man think he had to interrogate her about what she did or with whom she did it?

"Oh, really?" she countered, emphasizing each syllable.

"I saw you kiss him!"

"So?" She flashed back to the image of the darkened fourth-floor windows, her anger at his attitude escalating, her chin going up another notch. "What's wrong, Luc? Nothing better to do with your time than lurk around with the lights out spying on people?"

He took a step forward, his eyes glittering like irradiated obsidian with barely controlled temper. Peachy quailed inwardly but refused to back away. She wasn't going to let him intimidate her. She wasn't!

"What kind of game are you playing at, *cher?*" he demanded through visibly gritted teeth.

"Game?" Her voice rose and shredded on the word.

"You were thinking about making love with him, weren't you?"

"Why not?" She glared at him, goaded far beyond the limits of good sense. Fifteen days' worth of frustration coalesced, crested, then crashed down over her like a wave. "I sure haven't had much luck making it with you!"

There was one blazing, breathless moment when neither one of them moved. At the end of that brief increment of time, Luc seized Peachy by the shoulders and pulled her into his arms.

"Luck changes," he rasped in a voice she'd never heard before.

Then he bent his dark head and took her lips.

The first instant of contact was bruising—nearly brutal in its possessiveness. Peachy resisted the onslaught with every bit of strength she had. And she would have gone on resisting had the punishing caress not suddenly been transmuted into a kiss of achingly exquisite gentleness. An act of claiming became something close to an act of contrition. Selfishness gave way to supplication. She was stunned into stillness, her defenses shattering.

"Peachy," Luc murmured, his warm breath misting her skin like a soothing benediction. "Oh . . . Peachy."

He feathered his mouth back and forth over hers then languorously charted its shape with the tip of his tongue. Finally, he licked along the trembling line between her lips, coaxing her to open to him. She yielded with a sigh, a shiver of pleasure coursing through her as he increased the intimacy of the kiss.

Her senses reeled in response to his tender besiegement.

Peachy shifted her hips instinctively, conscious of the rising thrust of passion-gorged masculinity. The feel of him was intoxicating. Her body began to throb with a need so potent she wondered whether the pulsating force of it might not be visible to the naked eye.

She whimpered, bereft beyond belief, when Luc finally ended the kiss. She grasped at his tautly muscled shoulders as she forced herself to open her heavy-lidded eyes.

"Do you want this, *cher?*" His angular features were stark with restraint, his breath was coming in hard, shallow shudders.

She nodded, tightening her hold on him, trying to communicate the urgency of what she was experiencing. She felt a flush suffuse her entire body. Desire sparked along her nerve endings in a series of tiny, incendiary explosions.

"You have to say it out loud, Peachy," Luc insisted, his voice harsh. "I need to be sure."

"Yes," she managed to whisper.

"Yes . . . what?" His dark, deep-set eyes spoke of a hunger that matched and probably surpassed her own. But they also communicated an implacable degree of self-discipline.

"Yes, Luc," Peachy repeated huskily, sliding her right hand inward from his shoulder and up the side of his neck. She cupped the side of his rigidly set jaw, stroking gently. "I want us to make love."

* * *

"Are you still certain, *cher?*" Luc asked again some thirty minutes later. They were lying together on his bed. Save for the bell-shaped locket at her throat and a sheen of perspiration, Peachy was naked as a newborn. He was stripped to the skin except for a protective latex sheath. His flesh, too, was slick with sweat.

"Yes," his would-be lover assured him, underscoring the affirmative with a shaky-fingered but flagrantly effective caress. His pulse leapt in vaulting reaction to her provocative touch. "Oh, yes."

He kissed her then, long and deep. Their tongues twined. Their breaths blended. Luc savored the sweetness of Peachy's mouth until a lack of oxygen finally forced him to lift his head. Dizzy with emotion, he gazed down into her face, struggling for control.

She stared up at him, her cheeks pinkened by passion, her lips parted and moist. Her eyes locked with his in a long moment of wordless communion. Their emerald-gold depths were liquid with longing. They also shone with the gift of unconditional trust.

Luc uttered Peachy's name on a heated sigh, then used his right hand to chart the arch of her brow, the lushness of her lashes and the gamine elegance of her nose. He followed the outline of her mouth with his fingertips, a sensual thrill arrowing through him when her tongue stole out to lick at him with feline delicacy.

They kissed again, the mating of their lips more avid than it had been earlier. Luc felt Peachy's arms encircle his neck. Her hands moved upward, her fingers spasming in the dark disorder of his hair. He slanted his head, devouring her responses like a starving man.

Shifting his position slightly, he caressed downward from her face. He lingered for a few seconds at the pulse point at the base of her throat. The pounding of her blood was intensely, nearly unbearably, exciting to him.

Peachy's small but beautifully shaped breasts soon beckoned. He fondled their satin-smooth curves with slow, voluptuous strokes, savoring the soft gasps he elicited as he came closer and closer to touching the taut, petal pink nipples. She shuddered when he finally raked the budded peaks with the edges of his nails. He smiled, a fierce sense of satisfaction scorching through his veins.

It was at that point she tried to reciprocate, her intention clearly to pleasure him as he was pleasuring her. Although he found her untutored touches arousing in the extreme, Luc gently captured her hands and firmly eased them down, anchoring them at her sides.

"Don't," he said huskily, his tone balanced between imploring and imperative.

"But—"

"This night is for you, Peachy. Let me make it what it should be. This one—" he dipped his head and brushed her lips "—time. Let me."

She stared up at him for several seconds, her eyes wide and searching. "Yes," she finally assented, her inflection strangely solemn. "This ... one ... time."

Reining in the desire that was thundering from the soles of his feet to the top of his skull, Luc resumed his slow exploration of his lover-to-be's body. He wanted to rouse Peachy to rapture. To introduce her to ecstasy. To give her the sweetest of sensations before that inevitable instant when he took ... and probably caused her pain.

He caressed the red-gold triangle of hair at the apex of her trembling thighs, winnowing through the springy curls to test her readiness for the rite of passage he had pledged to perform. Gently, gently, he eased a finger into the luscious warmth of her womanhood.

"*Luc ...*"

"Shhh," he soothed. "It's all right."

He sought and found the nerve-rich nubbin hidden amid the humid petals of feminine flesh. He teased it with a feather-light touch. Peachy gasped his name again, arching convulsively into the contact.

"Yes," he said, rewarding her responsiveness with another caress. "Enjoy it, *cher.*"

Drawing on every sensual skill he'd acquired, every libidinous instinct with which he'd been endowed, Luc led his bed partner up to the peak of sensation. He held her there, trembling, for several fevered moments, then tenderly urged her over the brink.

She came apart against his hand, a startled cry escaping from her lips.

"I d-didn't ... oh ..." Peachy twisted, her head moving back and forth amid the silken tumble of her bright hair, her hips undulating in a rhythm that was as old as Eve. "Oh ... *Oh.* Oh, L-Luc."

He repeated the pattern a second time and then a third until she clutched at him with wild, wanton hands, confessing her need in shattered syllables. Then and only then did he shift himself, parting her thighs as he moved up and over her, positioning his rampant male flesh against the gateway to her secret core.

Luc hesitated, the prospect of hurting her threatening to unman him.

"Please," she pleaded urgently. "Please, Luc. *Now.*"

He inhaled a short, sharp breath, then fused his mouth to hers in the same instant he joined them with a single, gliding stroke. The brief jerk of her body as he broke through the fragile proof of her physical innocence tore at him. He groaned deep in his throat, protesting the pain, wishing desperately he could make it his.

"No," he whispered harshly, scarcely knowing he spoke aloud.

"Yes," Peachy countered, the pressure of her palms compelling against the small of his back. She rocked her pelvis up in a languid movement, sheathing him even deeper within her sweet, intoxicating heat. "Oh...yes...yes..."

Their lips met again in a kiss that both soothed and seared. "Only once," Luc promised, referring to the hurt. "Never... again."

He clasped her hips, holding her still for a few seconds as he tried to stem the tidal wave of passion building within him. Every nerve in his body was clamoring for release, but he refused to give in to it. Peachy's gratification was infinitely more important than his own.

He began to thrust. Cautiously at first, then with increasing vigor as he discovered the rhythm of arousal that was uniquely theirs.

Closer...

Closer...

Luc felt the ineffable clench of Peachy's body around his as she found fulfillment. He moved one last time, driving her to a keening, ecstatic cry that dissolved the final shred of his self-discipline.

He gave himself over to the woman in his arms and the act of love that had brought them together. He received in return the most extravagantly perfect pleasure he'd ever experienced.

It was more than sexual climax.

It was utter and absolute completion.

Afterward, when his heartbeat had slowed and his breathing pattern smoothed, Luc gathered Peachy's sated, seemingly boneless body into his arms and held her close to his heart. She curved into his embrace with a languid sigh, her breath fanning his flesh. He heard her murmur his name, then sigh again.

Exhausted by physical bliss, in thrall to a sense of peace that was unprecedented in his turbulent life, he turned his face into her fragrant hair and surrendered to the lure of sleep.

When Lucien Devereaux awoke many hours later, he was alone.

Ten

"**C**ome *on*," Peachy pleaded as she botched yet another attempt to open the door to her apartment. Her fingers were trembling so badly she couldn't insert the key into the lock. She sucked in a breath, trying to steady them.

Her brain suddenly flooded with images of the dark-haired man she'd left sleeping one floor above. She groaned inwardly, assailed by a terrible sense of loss.

Oh, Lord. If only she and Luc could find a way—

No regrets, Peachy reminded herself fiercely, invoking the pledge she'd made what now seemed a lifetime ago. *And no recriminations.*

And no requests for a return engagement, no matter what.

Her vision blurred. She blinked hard, her eyes stinging, the bridge of her nose congesting with the pressure of unshed tears.

An act of sexual initiation, with no strings attached. That's what she'd asked of Lucien Devereaux and that's what he'd given her. Even in the heat of passion, he'd stressed the singularity of what was happening between them. And she—heaven help her—had assented to every limit he'd imposed.

"This night is for you, Peachy," he'd said as he'd gently but firmly rebuffed her untutored efforts to give back at least a little of the pleasure she was receiving. "Let me make it what it should be. This one time. Let me."

"Yes," she'd responded, fully conscious that she was setting the final seal on their carnal bargain. "This . . . one . . . time."

And then, after he'd sheathed his body deep within hers, he'd made the point again. "Only once," he'd told her, his voice husky, his features taut. "Never . . . again."

As for what had happened next . . .

There were no words to describe the ecstasy she'd experienced. Even the adjective *overwhelming* was pallidly inadequate.

Had Luc wanted to talk in the immediate aftermath of their lovemaking, Peachy would have been more than willing. But he hadn't. He'd dozed off, instead.

Her first reaction had been to feel hurt. Rejected, even. One minute she'd seemed to be the center of her partner's universe. A few minutes later he'd been treating her like a pillow and practically snoring in her ear!

It had taken some time, but she'd eventually realized that Luc's apparently insensitive behavior was really for the best. It allowed her to make a clean, uncomplicated exit. It gave her an opportunity to prepare herself for their first post-consummation conversation as well. That encounter, she'd told herself, would be a lot easier conducted on the perpendicular than prone. It would also be infinitely less awkward if both of them were fully clothed.

Peachy had waited until she was certain that her one-time-only lover was completely asleep before she'd started to ease out of his embrace. Luc had tightened his hold on her as she'd pulled away, muttering something that might have been her name. His touch had felt possessive. His tone had sounded passionate.

His unwitting reaction to her withdrawal had nearly undone her conviction that it was vital for her to leave and leave quickly. The urge to remain nestled within the circle of Luc's arms had flared so strongly that every fiber of her being had seemed aflame with it. And for one breathless, burning moment, she'd almost succumbed to the temptation and stayed.

Almost, but not quite. Because staying would have required betraying the trust that had been placed in her by a man she knew had precious little reason to believe in women's promises. And that was something Pamela Gayle Keene could not—*would not!*—do. No matter what the cost to her, she would not break the covenant she'd entered into three weeks ago.

Somehow, someway, she'd managed to get up and out of bed. She'd collected her things, stuffing her underwear and stockings into her purse then hurriedly pulling on her apricot-and-cream dress over bare skin. She'd felt very exposed. It had seemed as though a protective membrane had been stripped away, leaving her vulnerable in ways she'd never dreamed possible. Her awareness of her body—of the aching tautness of her nipples, of the throbbing tenderness between her thighs—had been unsettlingly keen.

She'd resolutely kept her gaze averted from the bed as she'd donned her clothes. Only at the very end had she allowed herself to look at Luc once more. And as she'd imprinted the sight of his peacefully slumbering face on her heart and soul, she'd finally admitted to the truth.

She loved him.

But she would never, ever tell him so.

"Oh, Luc," Peachy whispered rawly, momentarily abandoning her efforts to open her front door. She lifted her free hand to the base of her throat.

Gone, she realized after a moment.

Her Wedding Belle locket was gone!

But how could that be? she wondered, her fingers closing convulsively on the thin fabric of her bodice. She was positive she'd had the necklace on earlier. She clearly remembered fiddling with it during her "date" with the MayWinnies' grandnephew, Trent Barnes. And afterward, when she'd been with Luc—

"Good evenin', Peachy dear," a pair of sweetly familiar feminine voices suddenly trilled from behind her. "Just gettin' home?"

She'd had a good reason, Luc asserted to himself as he trekked down the carpeted flight of stairs that connected the third and fourth floors of his Prytania Street apartment building. Although what in heaven's name this "good reason" might be, he had no idea. As vivid as his imagination was, he couldn't conjure up an acceptable explanation for Peachy's sneaking away from him while he was sound asleep.

Still, he was positive there had to be one. Because when all was said and done, he refused to believe that the woman he now knew he loved with all his heart and trusted with all his soul—the woman with whom he'd shared the most transcendent experience of his life—would have abandoned him without a word unless she'd been compelled to do so.

The passion they'd created the night before still astounded him. That their joining had begun in anger was something he would regret until the end of his days. As for what had come after the anger...

"Oh, Peachy," Luc murmured, his senses stirring with the heat of recollected pleasures.

Surfacing from slumber to find himself alone in his room had been a singularly unwelcome shock, of course. But not once during the first few minutes of wakefulness had he considered the possibility that his no-longer virginal lover might be gone—really, truly gone. How could he have? Her presence in his room had been palpable. The scented warmth of her body had lingered in the tangled linens of the bed. A quick lick of his lips had summoned up the sweet flavor of her kisses. And as he'd listened through the anticipatory pounding of his pulse, he would have sworn he could make out the sound of her bustling around in another part of the apartment.

He'd sat up, casting the sheets aside as he did so. His gaze had fallen on a small, reddish-brown mark. It took him a moment to realize that the mark was dried blood. *Peachy's* blood.

The significance of the stain had temporarily deprived Luc of the ability to breath. Once his lungs had resumed functioning, he'd called out for his lover in a voice that was less than steady.

There'd been no answer. What's more, the sounds he'd thought he'd heard just moments before had stopped.

Uneasy but not yet alarmed, he'd swung his legs over the side of the bed and stood up. He'd gasped in pained surprise as something small and sharp had jabbed into the bottom of his foot.

That "something" had turned out to be Peachy's Wedding Belle locket.

The precious silver pendant was now safely tucked in the front right pocket of Luc's jeans. He planned to return it at the appropriate moment.

He came to a halt in front of Peachy's door. A rush of adrenaline kicked his pulse into overdrive. His stomach knotted. His palms started to sweat.

What if he was wrong about last night? he asked himself. What if what had been a life-altering experience for him had been less— much less—for Peachy? What if *disappointment* had driven her out of his bed and away from him?

Dear Lord, what if she hadn't really—

Stop it!

Luc shook his head in vehement rejection of these insidious doubts. There was no way he could have misjudged what had happened. No way! Peachy's response to him had been genuine. Unlike so many other women of his acquaintance—unlike he, himself—she didn't know how to fake feelings.

Pray God, she'd never learn.

Luc inhaled a slow, steadying breath and squared his shoulders. He raised his right hand, fisting it, intending to knock. But he never got a chance. A split second before his knuckles touched wood, Peachy opened the door.

There was a silence. Vaguely startled on her part it seemed, utterly shocked on his.

"Luc," Peachy finally greeted him. Her voice, like the color in her cheeks, was slightly higher than normal. But only slightly. "Hi."

His brain played back the two-syllable salutation over and over again as he dissected every nuance of her appearance from the top of her well-brushed head to the tips of her neatly sandaled toes.

"May I come in?" he requested.

His Titian-haired tenant hesitated, a disturbing expression flickering through the green depths of her eyes. The doubts Luc had experienced in the moments before he'd lifted his hand to knock on her door reasserted themselves with vicious, virulent force. He opened his mouth to speak again.

"Please do," she forestalled him, beckoning him inside.

Luc stepped across the threshold, catching a whiff of freshly scrubbed feminine skin as he did so. She'd obviously bathed since leaving him. He couldn't help but wonder whether she'd done so out of habit or because she'd wanted to cleanse away the evidence of what had happened.

"Is this a bad time for you?" he asked as Peachy shut the door.

"Well, actually—" lightly glossed lips twisted "—yes. I was on my way out."

"Out?" The questions came out more sharply than he intended. "Why?"

"I'm flying back to Ohio Friday morning for my parents' anniversary party and I still need to buy them a present. I thought I could find something in the Quarter."

There was another silence. Luc thrust his hands into the pockets of his jeans. The fingertips of his right hand brushed against the sleek curves of the silver Wedding Belle locket. The feel of the talisman sent an odd jolt of energy through him.

"I woke up alone this morning," he declared without preamble. "I need to know why, Peachy."

She took a step backward. The retreat seemed instinctive, unthinking. "Why . . . what?"

"Why you left me."

"I didn't *leave* you, Luc." Her tone suggested she saw no reason for his upset.

He fought down an urge to close the physical gap she'd opened between them, sensing that any attempt to do so would drive her farther away. "What would you call sneaking out of my bed when I was asleep?"

Her chin went up. "I'd call it the best thing for both of us."

"The best thing?"

She flushed. "It seemed preferable to an uncomfortable morning-after-the-night-before scene."

"Meaning?"

"Meaning, there was no point in dragging the situation out." Her gaze was steady, her tone matter-of-fact. "I asked you to deflower me, Luc, and you did. Very skillfully. Not that I'm setting myself up as a judge of such things. But I've read and heard enough to realize that you made my first time a lot better than the 'unawful' experience I told you I'd settle for when you accepted my proposal. Still, once we were done doing it . . ." She shrugged. "It was over. You fell asleep. I left because I didn't want to impose on you any more than I already had. I thought that was what you'd want."

Something deep within Luc went cold as he absorbed the essence of Peachy's comments.

The woman to whom he'd given his heart not only didn't reciprocate his feelings, she had no inkling what those feelings were. She had no idea what their coming together the night before had meant to him. Yes, she'd found their lovemaking pleasurable—or, at least, better than "unawful." But what he'd taken to be a transcendent event in his life, she'd classified as a transitory imposition!

And yet . . .

The failure of understanding wasn't hers, was it? No, indeed. It was not. Because oblivious to his emotions though she seemed to be, Pamela Gayle Keene had been honest with him from start to finish. She'd been unfailingly frank about what she wanted, how she wanted it and why she'd sought it from him.

He, on the other hand, had lied to her from the get-go about almost everything. He'd lied and lied and lied and then he'd compounded his sins by falling in love.

There was no way she'd forgive him for going beyond the parameters of her proposal, Luc told himself bitterly. More to the point, there was no way she'd accept the idea that the past three weeks had transformed him from a man who evaded emotional intimacy as though it were a contagious disease to a man who coveted the opportunity of forging a lifetime commitment with one very special woman.

Which made the bottom line brutally simple, really.

Peachy must never, ever find out how he felt.

"Luc?"

He stiffened, schooling his expression into blandness. "What?"

"Is there something else?"

There was a hint of impatience lurking beneath the question. It was obvious to him that she wanted to be rid of him. And why shouldn't she? He'd served his purpose.

"Yeah," he replied, withdrawing his hand from the right front pocket of his jeans. "As a matter of fact, there is." He extended his hand toward her, the Wedding Belle locket swinging from his fingertips. "You were in such a rush to stop imposing on me, *cher*, you forgot this."

Peachy's reaction to the restoration of her property was...well, Luc didn't know how to interpret it. She inhaled sharply when he first brought the locket out. A wild rush of color stained her face for a moment or two then faded, leaving her fair skin more translucently pale than normal.

And then, to his utter consternation, she took a step forward, went up on tiptoe and brushed her lips lightly against his right cheek. "Thank you, Luc," she said softly.

"No big deal," he responded.

Once back in his apartment, he spent a long time wondering how a gentle kiss could feel so much like a slap across the face.

To say that Pamela Gayle Keene's morning-after encounter with Lucien Devereaux left her less than enthusiastic about going shopping for a wedding anniversary gift was to understate the case. She went out, anyway. A variety of factors—including the fear that if she stayed home she'd wind up weeping or worse—prodded her to do so.

She spent many hours trudging in and out of the antique emporiums and art galleries that lined Royal and Chartres Streets. She gave up the effort shortly after four in the afternoon and returned to her apartment. Her hands were empty, her heart was aching and her feet were very, very sore.

While there wasn't a great deal Peachy could do to ease the first two conditions, a long soak in hot water and Epsom salts helped mitigate the third. She'd just finished rubbing her soles with a peppermint-scented balm Laila Martigny had given her months before when someone knocked on her front door.

She went rigid at the sound, riven by a host of contradictory emotions.

What if it was Luc?

What if it wasn't?

She didn't know which eventuality would be more difficult with which to cope.

Peachy still had no idea where she'd found the strength—if strength was the right word—that had sustained her through her first postcoital encounter with Luc. She'd surprised herself, frankly. And not in an altogether pleasant way.

She'd always believed herself to be an open and honest person. It was disturbing to discover how great a capacity for dishonesty lurked within her nature. That she could gaze into the eyes of the man she loved and behave as though her feelings for him ran no deeper than mild affection troubled her at a very visceral level.

There was a certain cruel irony in her situation, she acknowledged. She intended to lie to Luc in hopes of persuading him that there *were* women in the world who told the truth. She was trying to purchase his trust, but the only currency at her disposal was counterfeit emotional coin.

There was another knock. At the same time, an instantly identifiable male voice called out Peachy's name. She uncorked a breath she hadn't realized she'd had bottled up inside her.

"I know you're in there," Terry Bellehurst declared through the door. "Open up. I've got something that belongs to you."

Peachy lifted her right hand in unthinking reaction to this last statement, her fingertips brushing against the surface of the Wedding Belle locket that once again dangled at the base of her throat. "Just a minute," she finally called, getting to her feet.

The "something" to which Terry had referred was a broadbrimmed straw hat banded with silk flowers which he presented with a flourish as soon as she opened the front door. Although

Peachy immediately recognized the *chapeau* as hers, she blanked when it came to answering the question of how her downstairs neighbor had gotten hold of it.

"I found it in the elevator last night," Terry explained as he stepped regally into the foyer of her apartment. He was wearing a flowing, purple paisley caftan and gold-trimmed slippers.

"The eleva—?" Peachy began confusedly, then broke off abruptly as memory came rushing back. She felt her cheeks suffuse with heat. "Oh," she murmured tightly, closing the door. "Yes. Of course."

There was a pause.

"I was visiting with the MayWinnies earlier," Terry eventually volunteered. "That's how I knew you were home."

Peachy tensed at the mention of her next-door neighbors. "Oh?"

"I happened to be looking out one of their windows and I spotted you coming up the sidewalk."

"I see."

"They, uh, mentioned you didn't get in till the wee hours of this morning."

"Really?" Peachy cocked her chin, remembering the predawn encounter in the hallway outside her door. She decided her best defense in this situation would be a strong offense. "Did they mention that the wee hours of the morning is when *they* got in, too?"

A wince. "Ah—"

"Did they mention anything about their both being plastered?"

A grimace. "Well—"

"One of them—Miss May, I think—was lugging around an open bottle of champagne. She offered me a snort, Terry. Not a ladylike sip. A *snort*. And I swear to heaven the other one had a hickey on her neck! Did they mention any of those tidbits?"

"They *did* make a passing reference to having been out reminiscing about old times with old friends."

"Nothing else?" Peachy pressed.

Terry rolled his eyes and spread his hands. "What can I say, sweetie? They were very coy about their activities last night."

"But they were plenty forthcoming with speculation about mine, right?"

"They're *concerned* about you," Terry insisted, evading the question. He let a few moments tick by, appearing to weigh what he wanted to say next. Then he expelled his breath in a frustrated-sounding sigh. "Oh, heck," he said, his voice husky with emotion. "Let's be honest. *I'm* concerned about you, too."

The plainly heartfelt admission caught Peachy unprepared. Her throat closed up. Tears pricked at the inner corners of her eyes. She pivoted away, desperately afraid she was going to break down. After a few moments a pair of ham-sized hands descended on her shoulders and carefully eased her back around.

"That bad?" Terry's voice was shorn of all camp affectation.

Peachy shrugged, keeping her eyes down. She didn't know what to say. Or whether she would have been able to say it if she had.

"Do you want to talk about it?"

She shook her head.

"It might help." A gently encouraging squeeze underscored the assertion.

Slowly, she looked up into her flamboyant friend's face. His expression was deeply compassionate. The urge to confide was very strong, but she resisted it. "I . . . can't."

"You're not holding back because of some misguided fear you'll lacerate my delicate sensibilities, are you?" he asked with self-deprecating irony. "Because I had them surgically excised sometime back. I don't think you could shock me with a cattle prod!"

Peachy smiled a little, knowing it was expected of her. "I appreciate that, Terry. But even so . . ."

Terry opened his hands, releasing her shoulders. "You're not a kiss-and-tell kind of girl."

Her dutiful smile of amusement gave way to a skin-scorching blush. "No," she managed. "I'm not."

While Luc didn't completely lose track of time in the aftermath of his confrontation with Peachy, the divisions between the five days and four nights that followed it did become rather blurred. He remained in his apartment throughout the period, working on his new book. No one came to his door. Anybody who phoned got the answering machine.

Exactly when he typed what turned out to be the opening paragraph of the final chapter of *Dark Horse*, he was never sure. Sometime Tuesday, he guessed. As for when he pecked out the last line, the line in which his ambivalent hero finally committed to his destiny . . .

He came awake very suddenly around noon on Thursday, his mind fixating on two very different facts. The first was that a typewriter was a lousy substitute for a pillow. The second was that someone was pounding on his front door.

He stumbled to his feet, stubbing the big toe of his left foot as he did so. He cursed, nearly losing his balance. Grabbing for something to steady himself, he knocked over a pile of manuscript pages. Crisp white sheets of typing paper fluttered to the floor like dried leaves.

Whoever was at his door kept on knocking.

"All right!" Luc shouted, his voice raspy from disuse. He knuckled his eyes, his stomach roiling. He couldn't remember when he'd last eaten. There was a slice of pizza sitting on his desk. With its shriveled toppings and scummily congealed cheese, it looked as though it had been there for a long time.

Knock. Knock. Knock.

"I'm coming, dammit!"

He staggered out of his small office, his gaze straying briefly into his bedroom as he passed it. His bed was unmade. He hadn't been near it since he'd gotten up Saturday morning. What sleeping he'd done since then had been on his living room couch or at his desk.

He reached the front door.

He undid its locks.

He yanked it open.

Standing on the other side of the threshold was Francis Sebastian Gilmore Smythe. He was dressed in his usual dapper fashion. His expression went from faintly anxious to flat-out appalled in about ten seconds.

"Yeah, yeah," Luc growled, gesturing the older man inside as he sought to preempt the attack he was sure was coming. "I look awful and my personal hygiene leaves a hell of a lot to be desired." He shut the door. "I tend to get careless when I'm working."

"I'm . . . sure."

There was a pause.

"You wanted something?" Luc finally prompted.

"Not me, exactly," Mr. Smythe responded, plucking a speck of dust off his sleeve. "It's the Misses Barnes again, I'm afraid."

"They sent you up here to have another man-to-man talk with me?"

"I gather they have reason to believe the situation has gone beyond that."

Luc forced himself to meet the old man's blue-gray gaze steadily. While he wasn't going to deny what he'd done, he'd be damned before he'd provide any details.

"Reason?" he echoed without inflection after a few seconds.

"It seems the ladies had a rather unsettling encounter with Peachy outside her apartment early Saturday morning. I'm not entirely clear on the details. But I understand there was some discussion about her—Peachy—having gone out with their grandnephew. That TV journalist chap. Miss Winona-Jolene and Miss Mayrielle were initially worried that he was somehow responsible for Peachy's...condition."

Luc's heart started to thud in an erratic rhythm. "And what condition was that?"

"Again, I'm not entirely sure of the details." Mr. Smythe twisted the gold signet ring he wore on his right hand. "I gather she was in something of a state of...well, dishabille."

"What did the MayWinnies do?" Luc asked roughly, shoving his hands into the pockets of his jeans. They were the same jeans he'd donned five—or was it six?—days before when he'd gone downstairs seeking the woman he loved. "Deliver a lecture about the importance of ladylike attire?"

The older man cleared his throat, plainly embarrassed. "I received the distinct impression that the Misses Barnes did not feel themselves in a position to preach propriety at the time they saw Peachy."

It took Luc a moment to translate this oh-so-gentlemanly observation into everyday English. "Are you saying you think the twins had been out carousing?"

"I'm afraid so, m'boy," Mr. Smythe affirmed, then sighed. "I'm inclined to believe that's why they waited several days before broaching their renewed anxieties with me. In addition to the hesitation engendered by their speculation about my career as a master jewel thief, of course. But, in any case, they *did* eventually come to me."

Luc thrust a hand back through his hair. "And now you've come to me."

"Yes."

"To accuse me of breaking my word?"

"Well, I wouldn't—"

"I promised I wouldn't hurt Peachy," Luc said, struggling to block the memory of the spot of dried blood that still stained his bed. Without warning, his mind darted off in another direction, flashing up snippets of his last meeting with his one-time-only lover. "I don't think I have."

Mr. Smythe furrowed his brow but said nothing.

Luc endured the silence as long as he could, then asked in a husky voice, "Have you seen her?"

"Peachy, you mean?"

"Yes."

"I had a chat with her just yesterday, as a matter of fact. She wanted some suggestions for an anniversary gift."

"Is she all right?"

The older man eyed Luc with an assessing frown. "You want the truth?"

"What else?"

"Well, then . . . I'd say Peachy seemed rather closer to being all right than you do."

Luc recoiled instinctively from the sympathy—or was it *pity?*—he thought he heard in the older man's voice. "Don't waste your time worrying about me, Mr. Smythe," he advised harshly.

"I seem to remember your agreeing to call me Francis."

"Whatever. The point is, I'm impervious."

"No." A calm shake of the head. "I think not."

"Think again, Francis." Luc gave a humorless laugh. "Better yet, ask Laila."

"I have, lad."

The quiet statement rocked Luc to the core, but he refused to let it show. "And?"

Francis Sebastian Gilmore Smythe sighed. "She says it's usually the self-inflicted wounds that cause the most pain."

By the time Friday morning rolled around, Peachy's nerves were strained to the snapping point. The last thing she needed was to bump into Luc as she was heading outside to wait for the taxi she'd phoned to convey her to the airport.

He'd obviously just come in from a long, hard run. He was standing in the middle of the lobby clad in nothing but track shoes and a skimpy pair of shorts. His lean, suavely muscled body was slick with sweat.

"L-Luc," she stammered, nearly losing her hold on her suitcase. The sudden slackening of her grip was accompanied by a weakening of her knees.

He paused in the act of blotting his perspiration-sheened arms with a wash-faded khaki T-shirt. He was breathing heavily, his hair-whorled chest expanding with the force of each deep inhalation. "Peachy," he responded.

She studied him silently for several seconds. He'd lost weight. And there were gray-violet smudges beneath his eyes. "Are you all right?"

He raked a hand through his hair, clearly annoyed by the question. "I'm fine."

"You look . . . tired." She knew she looked tired, too, underneath the concealer cream and blush she had on.

"I lost a few nights sleep finishing my book."

"Oh. Well." She summoned up a smile. "Congratulations."

"Thanks." His gaze held hers for a few moments, then slid downward to her suitcase. "Traveling?"

The question surprised her. Hadn't she said something to him—?

"Uh, yes," she answered. "I'm going home."

"Home?" He made the word sound like an alien concept. His eyes lifted to meet hers again, an expression she couldn't interpret flickering in their brown depths.

"To Ohio," she elaborated. "For my parents' wedding anniversary. I told you about it the other morning. Don't you . . . remember?"

"Oh, yes." Luc's sensually shaped lips twisted. "You were going shopping for a present."

"That's right."

"And did you find one?"

"I'm still looking."

"Mmm." He stretched, the waistband of his running shorts dipping to reveal the shallow indentation of his navel. "Are you coming back?"

Peachy had to drag her gaze away from his body. "Coming . . . back?"

"From Ohio."

"Why wouldn't I?"

Luc shrugged, seemingly indifferent.

"Are you suggesting I shouldn't?"

"Not at all."

"Then why would you ask—"

"*Why does anyone do anything, Peachy?*"

She stared at him, stunned by the sudden anger in his tone. After a moment she decided that this was neither the time nor place to thrash out what was bothering him.

"I have no idea, Luc," she said quietly. "Now, if you'll excuse me..."

She was about to push open the lobby door when Luc said her name. She hesitated then slowly turned back to face him.

"Would you like to know why I did it?" he asked her.

"Did...what?"

"What do you think?"

She flushed but didn't look away. "Accepted my proposal, you mean?"

"Exactly."

"All right." She moistened her lips. "Tell me."

"I was afraid of what would happen if I didn't."

"I...I don't understand."

"I thought if I stalled you long enough—"

"Are you saying you *never intended*—"

"No," he denied sharply, shaking his head. "That is, when I agreed—I mean, I didn't—oh, dammit. All right. *Yes.* That's what I'm saying. But it was only at first. Once I realized how I felt—"

Peachy backed away. "You *lied* to me?"

Luc obliterated the distance between them in two swift strides, catching her by the shoulders much as he'd done nearly a week before in the elevator. "If you'll just give me a chance—"

"To what?" she demanded, jerking free of his hands. Her heart was hammering. Her breath was coming in short, shallow pants. "Lie to me again?"

"I wouldn't!"

"But you did!"

There was a disastrous silence. It was punctuated by the honk of a taxi horn.

"Peachy," Luc said in a voice she'd never heard him use. His face was pale. "Please."

"I'm going," she responded numbly. "And as for my coming back here..."

Luc flinched as though he'd taken a body blow. An instant later, his expression went absolutely blank. "It's up to you."

A ragged laugh broke from Peachy's lips. "Of course it is, *cher,*" she said scathingly. "Isn't everything that happens between us supposed to be my choice?"

* * *

How long he stood in the lobby after Peachy made her exit, Luc never knew. It didn't really matter.

When he finally turned to go upstairs, he saw Laila Martigny standing by the elevator. Her topaz eyes were shuttered. Her elegant features unyielding.

"How much—?" he began

"More than enough," she answered.

Eleven

Lucien Devereaux peered blearily into the nearly emptied glass sitting on the small wooden table in front of him and tried to remember whether it had contained his fifth or sixth bourbon on the rocks.

He couldn't.

What he *could* remember was his last meeting with Pamela Gayle Keene. No matter that it had taken place more than fifteen hours ago. He could recall every gut-wrenching detail of it. And as long as he could do that, he was going to keep on drinking.

That seeking oblivion from a bottle was a dangerously stupid thing to do, he understood. He'd seen what liquor had done to his father. But just this once . . .

"Is this a private party?" a sardonic male voice drawled. "Or can anybody wallow in the general air of self-pitying gloom?"

Luc's lungs emptied in a rush. He looked up. Standing on the other side of the table was the ruggedly charismatic man he counted as his closest friend.

"Flynn?" he said, not quite believing his eyes.

"Got it in one," former Special Forces officer Gabriel Flynn said. "Mind if I sit down?"

"No." Luc shook his head for emphasis, then regretted the movement as his vision blurred. "Please."

"Thanks." Flynn settled himself with fluid economy then signaled a passing waiter. The man responded to the wordless summons with alacrity. Luc wasn't surprised. Flynn had an uncanny knack for getting people to do what he wanted, when he wanted, how he wanted. It had served him well in the military, even better in his current work as a roving troubleshooter for an international relief organization.

"It's good to see you," Luc said after the waiter double-timed away to fill Flynn's order.

Flynn raked a tanned, work-hardened hand through his shaggy, sun-streaked brown hair and leaned back in his seat. His gray-green gaze was sledgehammer direct. "How many of me are you seeing?"

Luc conceded the validity of the implied assessment of his condition with a grimace. "Just one. Although I'll admit I had a second or two when I thought you might have acquired an identical twin."

"God forbid."

The waiter hustled back at that point, delivering the draft beer for which Flynn had asked plus a complementary bowl of salted peanuts. After determining that no further service was required, he moved off to another table.

"The last I heard, you were in Africa," Luc observed after a few moments, studying the hard-featured man sitting opposite him. Gabriel Flynn was pushing forty and it showed. While there was no middle-aged sag—indeed, he had a lean, mean physique that would send a twenty-year-old gym rat running to the weight room—any boyishness he'd ever possessed had long since been boiled off. He exuded self-sufficiency and then some. "What brings you to New Orleans?"

Flynn munched on a handful of peanuts and chased them down with a swallow of beer. "Haven't bothered listening to the messages on your answering machine, huh?"

Luc shifted in his seat. "You called?"

"Three times."

"Sorry." The apology was genuine. "I've been . . . preoccupied . . . the last few days."

"So I understand."

Luc didn't have to guess about the source of this understanding. He was well aware that while Flynn had only visited the Prytania Street apartment building a few times, he was held in extremely high regard by the tenants.

"How did you know where to find me?"

"I didn't. I cabbed to your place from the airport. I ran into Francis Smythe in the lobby. He told me you'd gone out a couple of hours before and hadn't come back."

"Was that all he told you?"

Flynn took another drink of his beer. "Not exactly," he answered blandly. "While he and I were talking, May and Winnie Barnes came down in the elevator. One of them mentioned something about having seen you drive off. Given what Mr. Smythe had said, I didn't think you'd gone for a scenic tour. So I headed over here to the Quarter and did some recon. It was pure luck I spotted your 'Vette. But once I did, it was just a matter of going in and out of all the nearby bars until I found you."

"Wallowing in a general air of, uh—" Luc's alcohol-lubricated brain blocked the rest of the quote "—whatever you said before."

"Self-pitying gloom."

"Yeah. Right."

Flynn scooped up another handful of peanuts. "Do you want to talk about it?"

"Not particularly."

"I'd like to hear your version of what happened."

"It's not very edifying."

"I think I can take it."

Luc ran a finger around the rim of his glass then angled his gaze away from his friend's. After a few seconds he slowly began to recount the story of his involvement with a self-styled Wedding Belle named Peachy Keene.

"You're in love with her," Flynn summarized about twenty minutes later. The expression on his face was neutral, his tone of voice even more so.

Luc gave a weary nod.

"But you're not going to tell her."

"I *tried.*"

"The fiasco in the lobby, you mean?"

"Yeah." Luc winced inwardly, remembering the scene. He still wasn't certain why he'd behaved the way he had. All he could say was that he'd been seized by the conviction that he had to come clean with Peachy right there and right then. The sight of her turning and walking away from him, suitcase in hand, had made him a little crazy.

No. Scratch that. It had made him a *lot* crazy.

"Why did you wait so long?" Flynn pressed. "Why didn't you say something right after you'd made love with her? Or even before? If you knew how you felt—"

"I *didn't*, dammit!" Luc countered angrily, then tried to moderate his tone. "At least, not for sure. And then, when I finally was certain . . ." He paused, sucking in an unsteady breath as a surge of recollection threatened to overwhelm him. "It hurt, Flynn. Waking up to find Peachy had walked out while I was asleep, I mean. It hurt like hell. Still, I kept reassuring myself she must have had a good reason. But then when I went down to her apartment and tried to talk to her about what had happened between us, she brushed me off!"

"Banged up your ego pretty badly in the process, I'll bet."

Luc's temper flared anew. He opened his mouth to reject Flynn's barbed assertion in no uncertain terms, but shut it without uttering a word as he abruptly realized that wounded male pride *had* played a factor in his retreat from Peachy. Revealing his feelings to her would have been difficult enough had her morning-after welcome been all warmth and open arms. But baring his heart to a woman who'd been behaving as though she could barely care less—?

God. That had been impossible!

"Yeah," he conceded finally, his voice tight. "I guess she did. But it was more than that, Flynn. The way she acted that first morning, as though what we'd done really was no big deal—"

"Convincing, was she?"

It took Luc a few moments to understand what the other man was implying. Once he finally did—

"No," he denied unequivocally, shaking his head. "No *way*. Peachy isn't like that."

"Everybody's 'like that' if the stakes are high enough."

"But *why*—?"

"I think that's something you have to ask the lady."

Luc snorted. "Easier said than done."

"No guts, no glory," Flynn returned trenchantly. He paused, mouth twisting, then added, "And no guarantees, either."

There was a long pause.

"I don't know," Luc finally admitted, massaging the nape of his neck. His temples were throbbing. There was a bitter taste in his mouth. "Maybe I'm deluding myself. That first morning, I was thinking commitment. Commitment, as in marriage. Commitment, as in making a home and having a family." He gave a humorless laugh that hurt his throat. "You know my history. Can you honestly see me—*me!*—playing the loving husband and adoring daddy?"

"'Playing?'" Flynn echoed. "No. *Being?* Yeah. Sure. No problem."

Luc blinked several times, taken aback by the conviction he heard in his friend's last few words. How could Flynn possibly believe—?

"You haven't figured it out, have you."

"Figured out . . . what?"

"That if you really were the alienated son of a bitch you seem to think you are, you would have slept with your little virgin without a second thought and moved on. That you would've spent every dime of the money you've earned from your books on yourself instead of using a big chunk of it to bankroll the dreams of people like that high school buddy of yours who always wanted his own restaurant. And that you'd be holed up in solitary splendor in some Manhattan bachelor pad instead of landlording over an eccentric old apartment building that's stocked with folks you've made into the family you never had."

"I—"

"Think about it." The tone was commanding officer to raw recruit. "You've got a surrogate mother in Laila Martigny. A surrogate father in Francis Smythe. A pair of doting great-aunts in May and Winnie Barnes. So what if the dynamics are a little kinky? You *care* about the people back at Prytania Street. Deep down in that place you seem to think is so incapable of making a connection, you care about them. And they sure as hell care about you."

Luc stared at his friend, stunned by this outpouring. But once the initial sense of shock started to wear off, he did as he'd been ordered. He thought about it. He thought about it hard.

"What about Terry Bellehurst?" he finally asked.

Flynn grinned crookedly. "He's a two-fer. A big brother *and* a big sister."

"And . . . Peachy?"

Lucien Devereaux's former comrade-in-arms leaned forward and looked him squarely in the eye. "I think you've known the answer to that since the day she walked into your life."

* * *

"I don't want to talk about it," Peachy repeated for what seemed like the millionth time. It was late Saturday night. Her parents' anniversary bash was finally over. The last of the scores of friends and family who'd come to celebrate had departed for their own homes. Freed from the burden of pretending to be having a wonderful time, she'd sought refuge in her girlhood bedroom. Unfortunately, her sanctuary had been invaded by her older sister.

Eden settled herself on the edge of the quilt-covered bed. "It's either me or Mom."

Peachy had been pacing around the room. Her sibling's assertion brought an abrupt halt to her restless perambulations. She moistened her lips, anxiety lancing through her. "Mom knows something's wrong?"

"Let's just say she strongly suspects."

"And here I thought I'd done such a great job of being the life of the party."

"You were a little *too* animated, honey," Eden returned, pressing her palms gently against the rounded mound of her pregnant belly. "There were moments when it was like watching Saturday morning cartoons on fast forward."

"Oh." Peachy twiddled with her Wedding Belle locket. "How many—I mean, do you think everybody at the party—?"

"Heavens, no!" The reassurance was swift. "Why, Dad didn't notice a thing."

Peachy gulped, trying to imagine explaining the events of the last few weeks to her father. It boggled the mind.

"Come on, Peachy," her sister coaxed. "Whatever it is you've got bottled up, it will help to let it out."

Peachy hesitated a few seconds, then crossed to the bed and sat down.

"It's pretty awful," she muttered, her posture slumped, her chin resting against her chest.

"I doubt that."

"There's . . . a man."

"There usually is."

Peachy raised her head and looked at her sister. "It's Luc Devereaux."

Eden's mouth dropped open. "*Luc Devereaux?* Your landlord? The bestselling author? The tall, dark and swoon-worthy hunk Rick and I met when we were down in New Orleans? *That* Luc Devereaux?"

"That Luc Devereaux," Peachy affirmed. "I . . . asked him to deflower me."

"My God," Eden said when the tale of what her younger sister had been up to since Annie Martin's wedding had finally been told. "And to think I've spent all these years believing you'd lost your virginity to Jack Pearman the night of your senior prom."

"Jake." Peachy made the correction as she wiped her nose with a sodden piece of tissue. While she'd managed to stay dry-eyed throughout most of her recitation, her self-control had dissolved when she'd begun to describe her last encounter with Luc. A trickle of tears had turned into a torrent. "His name was *Jake* Pearman. And I almost did."

"Well, almost doesn't count in sex as long as you're careful." Eden paused for a moment, wrinkling her brow. "You and Luc did—uh—"

"Yes," Peachy snapped, flushing. "We used protection."

"That's a relief."

"Something to cling to in the middle of an otherwise unmitigated mess, huh?"

"I wouldn't go *that* far." Eden plucked at the front of the loose-fitting dress she was wearing, apparently weighing her next conversational gambit very carefully. Finally she asked, "What are you going to do?"

"I don't know," Peachy answered frankly, dabbing at her eyes. She'd been considering her options since her stormy departure from Prytania Street on Friday morning. "Move out, I guess."

"Move out?"

"You can't think I should stay there!"

"Well, I certainly don't think running away is going to help your situation."

Peachy gaped at her older sister. "Running away?"

"What would you call it?"

"Didn't you understand anything I told you?"

"I understood everything. Except the part about how you love Luc Devereaux but aren't going to tell him because of some idiotic notion that it's up to you to prove to him that women are trustworthy."

"It's *not* an idiotic notion!"

"You're lying to him, Peachy."

"So? He lied to me first!"

"Yes, but you didn't know that until after you'd started lying to him."

"What does that have to do with anything?" Peachy demanded furiously.

"How should I know?" her older sister flung back.

The emotional balance Peachy had tenuously reestablished tilted back toward tears. A shattered sob broke from her throat. She pressed shaking fingers to trembling lips, struggling not to break down again.

"Oh, honey." Eden's expression turned remorseful. Scooting sideways, she gathered Peachy in a sympathetic hug. "I'm sorry. I'm so...so...sorry."

"It's all so m-mixed up," Peachy choked out. "I thought I c-could handle it, Eden. I really did. N-no regrets. No recriminations. No requests for a return engagement, no matter what. But then...then..."

"Shh." The gentle admonition was accompanied by a soothing pat. "I know."

"I *want* to t-tell Luc how I feel. That f-first morning, it almost k-killed me to leave him. And th-then, later, when he c-came to my apartment—" Peachy broke off, the memory of her feigned indifference burning like acid. Finally she concluded, "But I *can't* say what's in my heart. I...can't...go back on the arrangement we made."

Eden heaved a weighty sigh. "What if you found out Luc didn't want that arrangement anymore?"

"He didn't want it in the beginning, you know."

"Yes, you told me. But even so, he went through with it. Didn't he."

Peachy drew back a little, gazing at her sister through tear-spangled lashes. "Y-yes," she acknowledged wetly. "He did."

Eden arched her brows. "Why do you suppose that was?"

"I don't know." Peachy snuffled several times and wiped at her nostrils. "Yesterday in the lobby, Luc said the only reason he'd accepted my proposal was that he was afraid of what would happen if he didn't. Then he started to say something about trying to stall me until—until—" She let her voice trail off, gnawing on her lower lip. Eventually she concluded in a shame-tinged voice, "I didn't let him finish. I was too angry."

"Maybe the 'stalling' was his way of giving you time to be certain about what you were doing," Eden suggested slowly, opening a little distance between them. "Or even to change your mind."

Peachy considered this for several seconds. "May—" she hiccuped "—be."

"I don't want to sound like I'm bashing the opposite sex," her sister went on. "But I don't know many guys who would have behaved the way Luc did. Frankly, I think most of them would have jumped your bones as soon as you made your, uh, proposal."

Peachy's memory flashed back to the night she and Luc had made love. Once again, she heard his voice as he'd stilled her clumsy caresses.

"This night is for you, Peachy," he'd said. "Let me make it what it should be. This one time. Let me."

Dear Lord, she thought, her heart lurching. Was it possible that she'd misunderstood what he'd been telling her?

No, she quickly denied. No! As tenderly as Luc had introduced her to the realm of physical love, he'd given her no sign he sought to follow up with any kind of emotional commitment.

Peachy met her sister's lambently searching gaze. "I know what you're trying to say, Eden. And I can't deny that Luc did everything he could to ensure that my first time was a good one. But that doesn't change anything! We made a deal. One time. No strings. And unless he says the deal's off . . ."

"You're going to keep mum, move out and end up an old maid." Eden sounded utterly disgusted by the prospect.

Peachy blinked against another buildup of tears. "Well, at least I won't have to worry about going to my grave a virgin."

"Let me get this straight," Luc said, his gaze roving slowly across the faces of the people he now realized were closer to him than his biological family had ever been. "You all came to the conclusion that I intended to have my wicked way with Peachy and took it upon yourselves to keep her out of my clutches?"

"Not *all* of us," Mr. Smythe amended uncomfortably, slanting a glance at Laila Martigny who was standing to his right. She responded with a serene smile.

"And we never thought your way was goin' to be *wicked*," one of the MayWinnies protested.

"Not that there's anythin' wrong with wicked," her twin chimed in. "Why, I can remember more than a few times when wicked was downright wonder—"

"Winona-Jolene!"

Blue eyes clashed with blue.

"Oh, don't be such a priss, Mayrielle!" Miss Winnie snapped. "You know perfectly well that both of us can recall some occasions when bein' bad felt mighty good. And if you didn't make a habit of gulpin' French champagne like it was lemonade you'd probably remember—"

"Why, I never—"

"Ladies, please," Terry interrupted, making a time-out gesture with his large hands.

Luc gave the former football star a cautious nod of gratitude. Although his head felt considerably better than it had about sixty minutes ago, his tolerance for sibling squabbling—even amusing sibling squabbling—was very low.

The last hour had been one of the oddest, yet most enlightening, of his life. He'd woken up on his living room couch with only a vague memory of having been deposited there sometime around dawn by Gabriel Flynn. He also dimly recalled himself repeatedly declaring that he was going to marry Miss Peachy Keene and that his best friend would be his best man when he did. Although he had no recollection of Flynn agreeing to this arrangement, he felt certain he had.

Flynn had been gone by the time he'd fought his way up from the depths of semistuperous slumber. The only other person in the living room had been Laila Martigny. After plying him with a glass of the vilest hangover remedy he'd ever tasted, she'd calmly informed him that there were some people waiting to see him. After allowing him a few much-needed minutes to tend to his personal hygiene, she'd ushered those people in.

"We thought we were doin' the best thing for both of you, Luc," Miss May explained tremulously after several seconds of silence. "Preventin' you from . . . you know."

"We never *dreamed* we were thwartin' the course of true love," Miss Winnie added, withdrawing a lace-trimmed hankie from the pocket of the flouncy floral dress she was wearing and sniffing into it.

"I take it the sudden rash of drop-in visits Peachy and I had a few weeks back was part of your 'prevention' plan?" Luc asked, sidestepping the volatile reference to "true love."

"There wasn't a formal plan, dear boy," Mr. Smythe asserted hurriedly. "It was rather . . . ad hoc."

What had been an inexplicable episode to Luc suddenly made a great deal of sense. "Like the power failure?"

The older man looked extremely embarrassed. He cleared his throat several times, twisting his gold signet ring. "Well...ah..."

"You did that?" the MayWinnies exclaimed in stereo.

"Well ... er..."

"Why, how *clever* of you!" Miss Winnie gushed.

"You probably know *all* about short-circuitin' wires, don't you?" Miss May declared admiringly. "What with havin' to circumvent security systems and such."

Terry looked bewildered. "Why would an antiques dealer have to circumvent security systems?"

"That's just his cover-up, dear," Miss May blithely explained.

"Exactly," Miss Winnie affirmed. "In real life, he's actually—"

"A retired member of the British intelligence service," Mr. Smythe abruptly announced, hurling himself into the conversational breach.

There was a stunned silence.

"You were a spy?" the MayWinnies squealed, nearly swooning.

"British Intelligence?" Terry went rigid. "Are you saying you worked for the people who've been bugging Buckingham Palace?"

"Oh, for heaven's sake!" Mr. Smythe reddened. "MI5 has the utmost respect for the privacy of the royal family! These allegations that the service put listening devices in the Queen's loo are tabloid slander! And before someone brings up the absurd notion that some of us in Her Majesty's service were given licenses to—"

"Do you suppose we could leave this until later, *cher?*" Laila Martigny interposed gently, taking his hand. "I think Luc still has some unanswered questions."

"Oh." Mr. Smythe cleared his throat and restiffened his upper lip. "Yes. Quite." He cast an apologetic glance in Luc's direction. "Sorry, m'boy."

Luc met the older man's gaze steadily for several seconds, then widened his focus to the others. Affection welled up within him. Flynn's assessment that the dynamics of this group were a "little kinky" had been understated to the point of being ridiculous, he thought ruefully. But in all other respects...

"Whose ad hoc idea was calling the cops about there being someone who looked just like an alleged serial killer holed up inside Peachy's apartment?" he finally asked.

Terry lifted his right hand, his expression a bit defiant. "Guilty."

"We did it," the MayWinnies confessed simultaneously.

"We realized things must be gettin' serious when darlin' Peachy asked to borrow some of our silver and china for a very special dinner," Miss Winnie said.

"Of course, she wouldn't say who she was havin' over," Miss May went on. "But we could pretty well guess."

"The problem was, we were committed to a sacred social obligation that very evenin' in Baton Rouge."

"So we went to Terry, thinkin' he might have a suggestion. And of course, he did."

"What can I say?" Terry asked rhetorically. "I'm a fan of reality-based TV crime shows."

"I was the one who phoned in the tip," Miss May noted, clearly anxious to claim her share of the responsibility—or was it the credit?—for what had happened.

"She did it from a pay booth in Baton Rouge," her sister elaborated. "So nobody could trace the call. I stood guard the whole time. *And* I reminded her to wipe down the receiver for fingerprints."

"Which was totally unnecessary, considerin' I was wearin' white gloves."

"Well, it was a very effective ploy," Luc said wryly. "What about the hotel fire?"

"Hotel . . . fire?" Francis Smythe echoed blankly. "What hotel fire?"

Luc told him.

"Oh, my Lord," Miss Winnie gasped. "You were there?"

"We heard about the fire, of course," Miss May said. "Even saw the smokin' ruins on the TV news."

"And we were perfectly devastated because—"

"—that establishment used to be a particular favorite of ours. Bein' so discreetly located and all. Why, it was just ideal for late-afternoon—"

"Mayrielle!" Miss Winnie sounded as prissy as she'd accused her twin of being a short time before.

"—tea," Miss May finished with butter-wouldn't-melt-in-her-mouth aplomb.

"I take it you and Peachy went to this hotel for . . . tea . . . on the day of the fire?" Terry inquired after a fractional pause.

Luc shifted, discomforted by the tenor of this question. "It was *my* idea," he stated. "Peachy wasn't—isn't—I mean, she's not—" He stopped, looking from face to face as he had earlier.

Finally, fiercely, he said, "I don't want *anyone* getting the wrong idea about anything she's done."

"No need to fear, lad." Mr. Smythe's solemn tone would have been suitable for the taking of a religious vow. "We know the girl, remember?"

Luc glanced at Laila Martigny, recalling the night she'd come to his apartment, asking to be told the truth about what was going on. He'd been tempted to evade—even outright lie—but he hadn't. His debt to her was too profound.

Her reaction to his confession about Peachy's proposal and his acceptance of it had been odd. That she'd been concerned had been obvious. She'd stressed several times that he was embarking on a very risky course. Yet lurking beneath the anxiety there'd been something else. A hint of . . . well, satisfaction wasn't precisely the word but it was close. He'd had the impression that for all her articulated misgivings, she genuinely approved of what he intended to do.

"So what were you doing while all this was going on?" he asked curiously.

Laila's full lips curved into a tranquil smile. "Waiting for the boy I helped raise to realize what kind of man he'd grown into."

Luc's breath clotted in his chest. His throat started to ache. He didn't know how to respond.

"We want to help," Terry said after a few moments.

"You and Peachy should be together," Miss Winnie declared.

"We know that now," Miss May averred.

Luc swallowed. "How?"

"We've seen what happens when you aren't," Mr. Smythe replied with devastating simplicity.

Luc swallowed again, still struggling with the demons of self-doubt. "But why? Why do any of you care—"

"Because we're like family, Luc."

It didn't matter which one of them had actually uttered the words. The sentiment was affirmed, unconditionally, by the expressions Lucien Devereaux saw as he looked from Laila Martigny to Francis Smythe, from Francis Smythe to the MayWinnies and from the MayWinnies to Terry Bellehurst.

"No," he contradicted, his voice husky, his heart full. "We *are* family."

Twelve

"**H**ere," Terry Bellehurst said cheerily as he held open the front door to their apartment building shortly after six on Sunday evening. "Let me help you with that."

Peachy began to demur as he reached for her suitcase, then realized there probably wasn't much point. She surrendered her bag with a smile of thanks.

"Good to be home?"

"Uh . . . yes." Peachy glanced around as they crossed the lobby. Although she knew another encounter with Luc was inevitable, she would prefer it didn't take place in front of a witness.

"How was your parents' anniversary party?" Terry inquired as they reached the elevator. He pressed the Up button.

"Fine."

"How long is it they've been married?"

"Thirty-eight years."

"Gives you faith, doesn't it? Knowing that there's people in the world who don't just promise to have and to hold, but actually do it."

Peachy slanted a sharp look at her neighbor, her stomach tightening. "Yes," she conceded after a few seconds. "I suppose it does."

The elevator arrived at this point, its door opening with the usual assortment of creaks and groans.

"Of course, it isn't easy," Terry commented, following Peachy into the car. "Sustaining a relationship, I mean. It's a lot like walking in stiletto heels, don't you think?"

"Stiletto... heels?"

"It's all a matter of balance. Why, when I think of the trouble I had—"

"Hold the elevator!" a resonant male voice suddenly called.

Terry responded instantly, thrusting his beefy forearm against the edge of the elevator door, preventing it from closing.

Oh, no, Peachy thought, going hot then cold then hot again. *Please, God. No.*

A moment later, Luc boarded the elevator. "Thanks," he said.

Peachy wanted to bolt. Had it been just she and Luc, she probably would have. But with Terry present...

The elevator closed. Gears ground. The car began to ascend.

Peachy reached instinctively for her Wedding Belle locket then realized what she was doing and lowered her hand. She kept her eyes fixed firmly on the floor. She knew Luc was watching her. She could feel the weight of his gaze.

Snatches of the conversation she'd had with her older sister the day before began caroming through her brain.

We made a deal! she heard herself declaring. *One time. No strings. And unless he says the deal's off...*

But Luc didn't seemed inclined to say anything to her, she reflected miserably. Not even hello.

The elevator lurched to a stop at the second floor.

"This is me," Terry airily announced as the door opened. "Good to have you back, Peachy. Luc, flex those pecs of yours and help her with her suitcase."

The door closed. The car resumed its upward path with audible reluctance.

Peachy shifted, feeling as though the interior of the elevator had shrunk by several square feet. Unable to help herself, she stole a glance at Luc. He appeared to be studying the toes of the battered running shoes he had on. A lock of his dark hair had fallen forward, curling down over his faintly furrowed brow. The urge to brush it back into place throbbed through her.

She tore her gaze away, focusing emotion-blurred eyes on the elevator control panel. The car was almost to the third floor, she saw. Just a few... more... seconds...

"No!" Peachy gasped as the 3 on the panel lit up but the car kept on rising. She started pressing buttons. Any buttons. All buttons. Even the red one marked Emergency. "Stop! Oh, please—*stop!*"

The elevator jerked to a halt midway between the third and fourth floors.

She kept on hitting buttons.

And then, without warning, Luc's hands closed over hers, restraining the frantic movements.

"Peachy—" he said, his voice low and gentle, his mouth so close to her ear she felt his warm breath stir her hair.

"Don't touch me!" she cried, her senses singing in response to his proximity.

Luc could have held on to her, of course. His physical strength was far superior to hers. Yet he opened his fingers within a heartbeat of her demand and let her go.

"I'm sorry," he told her, taking a step back.

She stared at her one-time lover. "For... wh-what?"

"Whatever you want."

"I don't want anything." Every fiber of Peachy's body protested the lie. She wanted Luc Devereaux. Right here. Right now. She wanted to touch him. To taste him. To take him deep within her body once again. And she was going to go on wanting him for the rest of her life. "Except to get out of this elevator."

"There's something I need to say to you first."

"You've already said plenty!"

"Most of which came out totally wrong."

Her heart skipped a beat. "Totally... wrong?"

"Just let me speak my piece, all right? I won't try to touch you, *cher.* And if you want to tell me to go to hell when I'm finished— well, I've already got the directions." Luc paused, gazing deeply into her eyes. "Please?"

The last time Pamela Gayle Keene had heard Lucien Devereaux plead for a hearing, she'd rejected him. This time she did not. "I'm listening," she said quietly.

Luc took a deep breath, obviously seeking to compose himself. A vein jumped in his temple, starkly revealing the pounding of his pulse.

"You've been special to me from the first time we met," he finally began. "The day you walked into my life, I felt this... this... *click* of connection with you. And it scared me. It scared me because I didn't know what it was. I'd never felt anything like it before. I'd never known I could! So... I pretended I didn't. Feel it, I mean." He grimaced. "I couldn't shut it off completely, but I could damned well deny it existed."

Peachy stared at him, genuinely stunned. "I...I never knew..."

"You weren't supposed to, *cher*. Nobody was. I had everything under control—or, at least, I thought I did—until the night you came to me with your...proposal. I had a lot of reasons for saying no. But the main one was that I realized there was no way I'd be able to let you go once I'd touched you as a lover."

His words triggered a wild fluttering deep in Peachy's belly. "Then why—?"

"Why did I change my mind?" Luc gestured. "Because I was genuinely afraid of what might happen if I didn't. I could see how bound and determined you were to get rid of your virginity. And when you mentioned going into a hotel bar—"

"I told you I never really intended to do that!"

"I know. I know. But that you even *considered* such a thing terrified me. There are a lot of predatory bastards in the world, Peachy, and the notion that you might innocently hand yourself over to one of them was...was—" Luc broke off, his eyes grim. "That was the main reason I changed my mind. The fear that you'd get hurt. The other reason was that I realized I couldn't endure the thought of another man touching you."

"What...what about the stalling part? Friday morning, you s-said—"

"I remember what I said." Luc thrust a hand back through his hair. "Look, I'll admit I was surprised when you told me you'd never made love. But once I got over that, I realized that you must have *chosen* to remain a virgin. I didn't want you to reject that choice because of the shock of some almost-accident. I thought if I gave you time to regain your balance—to think things through—you'd come to the conclusion that you didn't really want to toss your virginity away like a piece of outgrown clothing."

Peachy cocked her chin. "And what would you have done if I had?"

"I'd have gone back to the way things were. But I would've prayed that when you finally did decide to give yourself it would be for love and that the man would deserve you." Sensually shaped lips curved into a heartbreaking smile. "I also would have prayed that I wouldn't be around to see it."

"Oh, Luc..."

"I love you, Peachy," he said thickly. "I know that wasn't part of our arrangement. I accepted your proposal under false pretenses—"

"Forget my stupid proposal!" Peachy cried passionately, practically flinging herself into his arms. "Don't you understand? I love you, too!"

And then they kissed. Wildly. Wantonly. Wonderfully.

"Peachy," Luc groaned, pleasuring her with teeth and tongue as his hands roused her body with erotic expertise. "Oh, you don't *know* . . . "

"Y-yes," she whispered, licking his earlobe. His shudder of response thrilled her to the marrow. "Oh, yes, Luc. I do."

Finally, they eased apart. Peachy was breathing in short, shallow gasps. Her head was spinning. She knew her cheeks were wet with tears of joy.

"The morning after," Luc said huskily, cupping her face between his palms, stroking her skin tenderly with the pads of his thumbs. "When I woke up and you weren't there—"

"If I hadn't left when I did, I wouldn't have been able to go at all."

"And would that have been so awful?"

"It would have meant breaking my word to you, Luc."

"Your . . . word?"

"One time. No strings. I *promised* you."

He stared at her for several seconds, his eyes flicking back and forth, back and forth. Peachy knew, to the instant, when he understood why she'd done what she'd done—and behaved as she had. "Oh, *cher* . . . " he whispered.

"I love you," she whispered back. "I love you so much."

They kissed again, the joining of their lips much less frantic than before. The fever of reconciliation gave way to a sweet, slow-burning heat. Eventually Luc lifted his mouth from hers and murmured, "Now that we have *your* proposal out of the way, I think it's time to move on to mine."

"Your—" a shaky inhalation "—proposal?"

"It's a permanent deal with plenty of strings attached."

Her heart was beating so hard she was surprised it didn't slam through her chest. "Wh-what—?"

"Will you marry me, Peachy?"

"Yes!"

A moment later the elevator groaned to life and started to descend.

* * *

Peachy subsequently maintained that she'd been less than surprised to discover that all the other occupants of her Prytania Street residence just *happened* to be standing in the lobby when she and Luc stepped out of the elevator car. She did, however, admit to having been taken aback by the reaction she'd provoked when she'd jokingly said that she and her husband-to-be were contemplating an elopement.

First, there'd been a stunned silence. Then, a hurried exchange of deeply distressed looks. Finally, Terry Bellehurst had stepped forward.

"Peachy, honey," he'd drawled, planting his hands on his hips. "If you think we went to the trouble of trapping you two in an elevator so you could finally work things out only to have you end up deciding to get married in some tacky, hole-in-the-wall ceremony with plastic flowers and prerecorded music, you are *sadly* mistaken."

Pamela Gayle Keene and Lucien Devereaux were joined in holy matrimony on the first Saturday in August in a blossom-bedecked chapel in the Garden District. The nuptial event was coordinated by one-time Super Bowl champion Terrence Bellehurst, who was able to offer some excellent advice about trousseau necessities.

Peachy was given in marriage by her father and attended by her older sister, Eden, and the Misses Mayrielle and Winona-Jolene Barnes. Her guest list included the former Annie Martin—now Mrs. Matthew Powell—and Zoe Armitage.

Although the groom invited no blood relatives, it was noted by those present that there seemed to be a deep bond of affection between him and Dr. Laila Martigny and Mr. Francis Sebastian Gilmore Smythe. It was also noted that the alleged descendent of New Orleans's famous voodoo queen was wearing an exquisite diamond engagement ring.

The only "flaw" in the ceremony was a slight delay in its start caused by the late arrival of the best man, Gabriel Flynn. Those privy to what he'd gone through to fulfill the promise he'd given a drunken friend nearly twelve weeks before were of the opinion that it was remarkable he'd been able to get there at all.

The reception was held in the restaurant where the happy couple had had their first "date." The stunning, five-tiered wedding cake was supplied by Remy Sinclair, who reluctantly acquiesced to

his wife's command that he refrain from partnering the bride on
the top of his pastry masterpiece with an Elvis Presley figurine
rather than a traditional-style groom.

It was a grand and glorious celebration. But long before *les bon
temps* rolled to a close, Mr. and Mrs. Lucien Devereaux departed
for the Honeymoon Suite of one of New Orleans's finest hotels to
create some good times of their own....

Peachy stood in the circle of her new husband's arms, gazing up
at his angularly handsome face. "You're nervous," she said won-
deringly. "You're actually... *nervous.*"

"I've never done this before," Luc replied huskily.

"'This' being—?"

"Made love with my wife."

"Maybe if you'd availed yourself of the opportunity to make
love with your fiancée once or twice during the last twelve
weeks..." Peachy let her voice trail off, feigning a pout. To her
utter astonishment, Luc had steadfastly refused to anticipate their
vows a second time once they'd gotten engaged. Her feelings about
this turn of events had been—still were—decidedly mixed.

There was no denying she'd been deeply touched by his decision. Nor that she'd taken a deliciously wicked degree of pleasure
in trying to seduce him into changing his mind. Yet there'd also
been moments when she'd been so frustrated by his self-imposed
celibacy that she'd wanted to scream!

"I told you," Luc said, his lips curving in a smile that played
havoc with her pulse. "I wanted our wedding night to be—" he
dipped his head and brushed his lips over hers "—perfect."

She flushed at the tender determination of his tone, her bones
starting to liquify. "How could it be anything but?"

"How, indeed," he murmured, drawing her tight against the
hard proof of his masculine desire.

They kissed and caressed for several minutes. It was a heady,
heated interlude. But when Peachy felt Luc start to pluck at the row
of tiny buttons that ran down the back of her wedding gown, she
called a halt.

"No," she said, pulling away. She remembered the bold course
of action she'd been planning for several weeks. It centered on a
very intimate kind of quid pro quo.

Luc's hands stilled instantly. He gazed down at her, his brow
furrowed. "No?"

"I want you to let *me* do it," she declared, lifting her chin. "This one time. This . . . this *first* time. Please. Let me."

It was a paraphrase of what Luc had said to her the night she'd surrendered her virginity, of course. A sudden flare of excitement in the depths of his dark eyes told Peachy he'd recognized it as such.

"I'm all yours, *cher,*" he answered after a few seconds, his voice dropping into a velvet-lined register as he lowered his hands.

Smiling, her body suffusing with a lush feeling of feminine power, Peachy took her new husband at his word.

Luc had loosened the black bow tie of his wedding apparel when they'd entered their suite. She finished undoing it, then slowly withdrew it from around his neck and tossed it aside.

"There," she said softly, giving him an up-from-under-her-lashes look as she toyed with the collar of his crisp, white shirt. "Isn't that better?"

"Oh . . . much," he agreed.

She divested Luc of his black tuxedo jacket next, then unbuttoned and slid off the richly brocaded waistcoat beneath. She kept her movements unhurried, savoring every second of the procedure.

Her fingers trembled a bit when she started on the studs in his shirt, but she managed. At one point her fingertips brushed naked chest. Luc stiffened, invoking her name on a sharp inhalation of breath.

"Ah-ah-ah," Peachy reproved, catching his hands and easing them back down to his sides. "You're all mine, remember?"

"Meaning, you can do anything you want with me." There was a mixture of arousal and affronted male pride in the statement.

"Pretty much," she sweetly agreed, tugging his shirttail free from his trousers. "Of course, my definition of *anything* may not be *quite* as broad as yours . . ."

"I'm sure it will be more than sufficient."

She finished undoing the front of his shirt and eased the garment off his broad shoulders. Then she unfastened the enameled gold cuff links that had been her special gift to the groom. After a moment, she pulled his sleeves down, freeing his arms and hands.

The shirt joined the tie, jacket and waistcoat.

"Mmm . . ." she breathed, stroking his newly bared flesh with voluptuous fingers. She winnowed delicately through the rough silk of his chest hair and teased the tightly furled nubbins of his male nipples.

Luc tried to touch her again. She rebuffed the effort, lifting his captured hands to her lips one at a time to kiss his palms and lick at the tips of his fingers. He groaned deep in his throat as she took his right thumb into her mouth and sucked on it.

Peachy explored her new husband for many erotically charged minutes before softly instructing him to move to the bed and sit down. By the time she issued the command, her pulse was thrumming like a finely tuned engine. She could feel her nipples peaking against her lacy bridal lingerie.

"Now what?" Luc asked when he'd done as she'd bidden.

"Now—" she pivoted away, then glanced back over her shoulder "—you watch."

"You're sure you don't need some help? Those buttons look awfully small."

"Those buttons," she said, lifting her left arm and reaching for the zipper cleverly hidden in the side of the petal-hemmed garment, "are just for show."

A few seconds later, Peachy's wedding dress—a vaguely flapperesque garment of creamy white chiffon she'd discovered in a funky French Quarter boutique—slid to the floor.

Her audience's reaction was inarticulate but unmistakably appreciative.

Peachy glanced over her shoulder again as she reached up to unpin her upswept hair. "The garter belt was the MayWinnies' idea," she said demurely.

"Remind me to thank them," Luc managed. "Several times."

She turned back, shaking her head, enjoying the feel of her red-gold curls tumbling over her shoulders. She also enjoyed Luc's expression when he got his first look at the front of her designed-to-entice underwear.

"They let me in on a secret, you know," she confided, approaching the bed.

"How to drive a man out of his mind?" The question was hoarse. The look that accompanied it incendiary.

"Not exactly. They told me to put the garter belt on *before* my panties. That way I don't have to take it off when we . . ."

"Then you *are* intending to get around to, uh—"

"Eventually," Peachy promised, dropping to her knees. She smiled, remembering the confessions she'd heard from her neighbors following her engagement. It seemed the little voice in her head had been correct. There *had* been a conspiracy to keep her from losing her virginity! "Barring drop-in guests, police raids and electronic interference from one of Mr. Smythe's spy gadgets, of course.''

She took off Luc's socks and shoes, tracing the shape of his feet and counting his toes. She refrained from tickling, although the idea tempted her.

She finally rose and gestured for him to do the same. Once he did, she opened his trousers and slid them down his long, lean legs. Then she began to caress him, front and back, touching everywhere except the area covered by his white knit briefs. The evidence of his arousal was blatant beneath the stretchy fabric.

"Do you think you could get used to this?'' she whispered, tracing the path of his spine from his nape to the beginning of his firmly muscled buttocks.

"I think—'' Luc shuddered but accepted her fondling attentions without attempting to reciprocate ''—I could get *addicted* to it.''

As intoxicating as it was to exercise her feminine power over Luc, there came a point when Peachy wanted more. Her husband of a few hours—and lover of a single night—seemed to sense the instant her desires changed. Enforced passivity gave way to passionate adoration.

Suddenly they were on the bed together. He, naked. She, still wearing her blue-trimmed garter belt and the filmy white stockings it was holding up.

"Luc,'' she breathed as he stroked her with lavish intimacy. "Oh, Luc...''

"Peachy,'' he responded ardently, kissing one corner of her mouth and then the other. "Oh, *cher.*''

His touch was, in some ways, less deft than it had been the first time he'd made love to her. Yet Peachy gloried in the hint of clumsiness because she understood the depth of emotion it signified. Luc had managed to remain detached at some level the night he'd relieved her of her virginity. He was not detached now.

"I c-can't wait,'' he finally groaned, ravishing the portal of her feminine secrets with trembling fingers.

"Neither—'' she arched up, her body straining ''—can I.''

There was no need for Luc to take. Peachy gave, unstintingly, unconditionally. And she received back in equal measure, swept toward ecstasy by flagrant, fevered generosity.

Soon, she thought.

Oh, yes. Very, very soon.

Luc gasped out her name as he thrust home one last time.

Their release was simultaneous and utterly sensational.

* * *

Later.

Much, much later.

"I love you, Luc."

"And I love you, Peachy."

"Are you sleepy?"

"Not at all. Why?"

"Well, I was wondering whether you'd be up to considering a modest proposal...."

* * * * *

Be sure to attend the marriage of the next
WEDDING BELLE. *Don't miss*
ZOE AND THE BEST MAN,
coming in March—
only from Silhouette Desire!

SILHOUETTE® Desire®

COMING NEXT MONTH

Take 4 bestselling love stories FREE

Plus get a FREE surprise gift!

Special Limited-time Offer

Mail to Silhouette Reader Service™

> 3010 Walden Avenue
> P.O. Box 1867
> Buffalo, N.Y. 14269-1867

YES! Please send me 4 free Silhouette Desire® novels and my free surprise gift. Then send me 6 brand-new novels every month, which I will receive months before they appear in bookstores. Bill me at the low price of $2.66 each plus 25¢ delivery and applicable sales tax, if any.* That's the complete price and a savings of over 10% off the cover prices—quite a bargain! I understand that accepting the books and gift places me under no obligation ever to buy any books. I can always return a shipment and cancel at any time. Even if I never buy another book from Silhouette, the 4 free books and the surprise gift are mine to keep forever.

225 BPA AWPN

Name	(PLEASE PRINT)	
Address	Apt. No.	
City	State	Zip

This offer is limited to one order per household and not valid to present Silhouette Desire® subscribers. *Terms and prices are subject to change without notice.
Sales tax applicable in N.Y.

UDES-995

Are your lips succulent, impetuous, delicious or racy?

Find out in a very special Valentine's Day promotion—THAT SPECIAL KISS!

Inside four special Harlequin and Silhouette February books are details for THAT SPECIAL KISS! explaining how you can have your lip prints read by a romance expert.

Look for details in the following series books, written by four of Harlequin and Silhouette readers' favorite authors:

Silhouette Intimate Moments #691
Mackenzie's Pleasure by *New York Times* bestselling author Linda Howard

Harlequin Romance #3395
Because of the Baby by Debbie Macomber

Silhouette Desire #979
Megan's Marriage by Annette Broadrick

Harlequin Presents #1793
The One and Only by Carole Mortimer

Fun, romance, four top-selling authors, plus a **FREE** gift! This is a very special Valentine's Day you won't want to miss! Only from Harlequin and Silhouette.

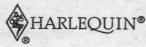 

VAL96

You're About to Become a

Privileged Woman

Reap the rewards of fabulous free gifts and benefits with proofs-of-purchase from Silhouette and Harlequin books

Pages & Privileges™

It's our way of thanking you for buying our books at your favorite retail stores.

PROOF OF PURCHASE

SD-PP91

Offer expires October 31, 1996

Harlequin and Silhouette— the most privileged readers in the world!

For more information about Harlequin and Silhouette's PAGES & PRIVILEGES program call the Pages & Privileges Benefits Desk: 1-503-794-2499

Silhouette®

SD-PP91